DATE DUE

A WANT SO WICKED

SUZANNE YOUNG

BALZER + BRAY

An Imprint of HarperCollins*Publishers*

Balzer + Bray is an imprint of HarperCollins Publishers.

A Want So Wicked
Copyright © 2012 by Suzanne Young

Library of Congress Cataloging-in-Publication Data is available.
ISBN 978-0-06-200826-8

Typography by Sarah Hoy
12 13 14 15 16   LP/RRDH   10 9 8 7 6 5 4 3 2 1
❖
First Edition

For my husband, Jesse,
who is wicked *awesome*

And in loving memory of
my grandmother Josephine Parzych

AFTER

I hear an echo as sound hums its way into my ears. It's a heavy noise, reverberating as it gets louder. Louder. Louder—I'm afraid my head will burst from the vibration, and finally my eyes flutter open and it stops.

I see sky above me—blue and cloudless. Blinking quickly, I try to get my bearings. Sensation returns to my fingers and I feel the grit of rock and sand beneath them. The air is thin and dry.

I sit up and rest my elbows on my knees, looking around. I'm in a park of some sort: Sandy hills with cacti surround me; a fountain in the center flows. It's quiet and peaceful, but at the same time, my heart starts to thump a little harder.

Where am I?

I try to think back to the last thing I remember, but nothing comes to me. It's like I just . . . appeared, alone in the desert.

I stand, stumbling when I take a step as if adjusting to my height, to my body—both unfamiliar. I'm disoriented as I walk toward the street, crossing the hot sand on my way to an empty block lined with parked cars.

The sun settles in my bones, and I lift my face, letting it warm my cheeks. The heat feels like home. Like love.

Just then a glint of light from a car's side mirror catches my eye. I stop, fear seizing me as I stare at my reflection in the passenger window, ignoring the hot pavement that's burning the soles of my feet.

Because I realize: I have no idea who I am.

CHAPTER 1

I don't recognize the face staring back at me. The girl in the reflection has blond hair and wears a plaid schoolgirl outfit, nothing like the white tank top and cutoffs I have on now. I hold up a handful of my hair, studying the deep brown waves as the reflection mimics my movement with her blond hair. I meet her eyes once again, trying not to panic. But as I watch, the girl slowly changes—her skin beginning to glisten, shine. Brighten.

I take an unsteady step back.

And suddenly my reflection explodes in golden light. When she's gone, there is only me—long dark hair with pale blue eyes and olive skin. Images fill my head and I can see my entire life being written. The universe creates me: my childhood in a sleepy Colorado town, my father teaching me how to ride a bike. I hear my sister's whispers late at night after our mother died when I was eight.

My name is Elise Landon. And I'm about to wake up.

I notice something in the back pocket of my shorts and reach for it. When I take it out and open my palm, I nearly choke on the heavy feeling that weighs in my chest. It's like a longing for another place. Another time.

In my hand I hold a small guardian angel figurine set in a smooth, clear stone. It's beautiful, a promise of love. Of forever.

For a brief second I remember everything about who and what I used to be. But most of all, I remember Harlin. And I wonder how he'll find me if I'm someone else.

The dream sticks to my skin as I turn, my legs tangling in the pink cotton blankets. The memory of it is fading fast, even as I fight to hold on to it.

"Elise," my sister says again, pushing my shoulder. I groan in response but otherwise ignore her. The edges of the dream fray, and when it's gone completely, I roll over and yawn.

"No," I say before hearing what Lucy wants. Chances are, if my sister is waking me up in the middle of the night, it's because she needs help escaping.

"Please?"

I finally open my eyes and find her standing in the dim light of my bedside lamp. I laugh, taking in her appearance. She looks like a hipster ninja—black knit cap over her short pixie cut, black tank top, leggings, and heavy lace-up boots.

Her eyeliner and lipstick are dark, her nails are blood-red, and her jangling bracelets are noisy enough to make her getup not matter. She'll never sneak up on anyone, but she looks sort of cool, so I almost appreciate it.

"Dad will hold me personally responsible," I say, gathering my brown hair on top of my head and fastening it there with an elastic band from my dresser. "What exactly will you be doing, and who will you be doing it with?"

Lucy grins wickedly. "It's not like that. He's just a friend."

"I don't slip out to see my friends at three a.m."

"You don't have any friends."

"Mean!" But I laugh and hit her with a pillow. She's not wrong, although it sounds harsher than the reality. We just moved to Thistle, Arizona (aka Middle of Nowhere), a month ago, when our dad took over as the pastor of a small church in town. Seriously, this place makes Tombstone look like a metropolis. Back in Colorado I'd had plenty of friends. I just haven't gotten around to it here yet because people are outnumbered by cacti by about a thousand to one.

"I'm sorry," Lucy says halfheartedly. "I promise you'll be popular once school starts again. Junior year is when all the fun happens, believe me. But for now, help me cultivate *my* social life and get me out of here before Dad wakes up."

"I'm borrowing your car to drive to work this afternoon."

"Fine, whatever." She waves her hands to hurry me along. "Let's go."

Victorious, I climb out of bed and open my bedroom door,

poking my head into the hallway. Moving boxes still rest on the tiled floor, and I suspect they'll stay there until my father gets around to unpacking them. But with his schedule, that's not likely to happen anytime soon.

I point my sister toward the garage as I go in the opposite direction, tiptoeing past my father's partially open bedroom door. There's no snoring or other obvious signs that he's asleep, so I say a prayer to not get caught. Which I immediately realize is kind of wrong, but it's too late to take it back.

When my older—and much less responsible—eighteen-year-old sister gets into trouble, my father usually groups me in with her punishment. Sure, I'm an accomplice, but I don't think it's entirely fair. *I'm* not the one sneaking out. Besides, Lucy is going to be a senior. She should be able to go out after dark. The restrictions of being a pastor's daughter, I guess.

I get to the keypad at our front door and type in the disarm code, wincing when it beeps. I listen, and when the house stays quiet, I give Lucy the thumbs-up and she slips into the dark garage. I count to ten, about as long as it will take her to get out the side door, and then key in the code again. It beeps, reassuring us that the house is secure—albeit less one member—and then I make the careful walk back to my room.

My sister has been sneaking out since middle school, but it wasn't until last year that my father got hip to her activities—which was hard to avoid when she was brought home by a police cruiser at two in the morning. It's part of why my father wanted to move us here—to give us a fresh start. Since that night, it has been overparenting at its best. Even though I know my father has good intentions.

The street outside is silent. Lucy knows better than to use her beat-up old Honda this late. My father has an extra sense, like a dog, that can tell the sound of her engine coming or going. So I assume her *friend* must have the wheels and is waiting at the end of the block. Lucy will text me to let her back in just before breakfast, sharing with me her secrets—both the exciting and the dangerous ones. I never really know which it'll be.

Truthfully, I'm a little jealous of her extracurriculars. She seems so . . . alive. But I'm hopeful that the new job I'm starting today at Santo's Restaurant will not only get me paid, but will also help me meet some quality people. Or I'll just eat a lot of chimichangas. I'll be all right either way.

As I get to my room, I'm struck with the oddest sensation, a déjà vu of sorts. I stop, reaching for the doorframe to steady myself. In my head I hear a whisper, or rather the memory of a whisper. The familiar voice is soft, and it warms me from the inside out as it murmurs a name: *Charlotte.*

Like a dream I can't quite remember, this déjà vu is more a feeling than something I can describe coherently. It's sweet and painful at the same time—an emotion that doesn't make sense. And when it finally fades, leaving behind little more than a dull ache, I climb into bed. My fingers touch something cool under my pillow. Surprised, I slowly slide it out.

It's an angel, set in a clear stone.

CHAPTER 2

In the morning, I decide that Lucy had to be the one who left the angel figurine under my pillow. She always does that—gives me gifts with no expectation of thanks. After losing our mother, she picked up the slack in the "leaving notes in my lunch bag" department. Although now that we're older, she spares me the smiley faces.

It's certainly odd that she picked an angel, since Lucy tries to avoid religion as much as one can in the house of a pastor. But I swear I've seen this before, and half wonder if it's a throwaway from one of her exes.

Well, wherever it's from, the gift is comforting, as if I now have someone watching out for me. So I slip it into the drawer of my bedside table and leave to shower.

* * *

I stand in the parking lot of Santo's Restaurant, ready for my first day of work—ever. I've never had a job; have never even volunteered before. I'm like fresh meat being thrown to the wolves, but my father thought it would build character. Yeah, we'll see.

A loud rumble cuts through the air, and I turn to see a hot guy ride by on his Harley, passing me on his way down Main Street. He's wearing a brown leather jacket and dark sunglasses. For a second I hope he'll look over at me, but instead he disappears around the corner at the end of the block.

My mouth twitches with a smile, as I consider any hot-guy sighting a sign of good things to come—or at least that's what Lucy would say. With my fate on the upswing, I cross the gravel parking lot.

The hostess is on the other side of the glass door of Santo's, wearing a checkered black-and-white dress with lace trim, wiping down and stacking menus.

I've eaten here a few times with my dad. Their enchiladas are tasty, their tacos not so much. When my father suggested I get a job for the summer, this was the only place I applied. I mean, the town's not very big. It was either here or the hot-dog truck on Mission Boulevard.

I take one last look around the parking lot and see a tumbleweed, an actual *tumbleweed*, roll across the road. I laugh—proof that we live in the middle of nowhere.

A bell jingles when I push the door open. The white

Formica counter is crowded with men in tan Carthartt overalls eating burritos and enchiladas. The temperature drops nearly twenty degrees as I step inside, the air-conditioning on full blast. The booths throughout the dining room are mostly empty.

The hostess snatches a menu and walks up hurriedly. "One for dinner?" she asks.

"Um . . . no. I'm Elise. I'm supposed to start today?"

The girl stares at me, her blond hair tied in a messy knot at her neck. "Oh." She shuffles through the papers on the hostess stand, seeming confused. "I'll have to grab someone." She points toward a booth. "You can wait there. I'll be right back."

I thank her, and she zigzags around the tables of the dining room toward the swinging door that leads to the kitchen. My stomach turns with anxiety as I go to sit down, smiling politely at several customers when I do. The place is small but comfortable—as if everyone who comes in has known one another forever. I feel like such an outsider.

Suddenly there's a prickle of cold air across my cheeks, over my arms. A wind that seems to brush my hair aside, although I'm sure it hasn't moved at all. I glance up and see him—a server in a white button-down shirt, black pants, and black apron. He's staring at me, his lips curved into a smile.

He murmurs something to the tattooed man behind the counter and grabs a glass of water, tucking a small pad of paper into his apron pocket. Nervousness creeps inside my chest as he walks my way. His grin is lopsided and confident against his tan skin, his black hair cropped short with the front brushed up. He's stunning.

"Stop my heart," he says, setting the glass in front of me. "You're the prettiest thing I've seen all summer. I had to give Mario twenty bucks to pick up this table. Hope you tip well."

"What?" I ask. Did he have me confused with someone else?

"And I swear I'm not just saying that because you're the only customer in here under fifty." He gestures toward the other tables.

I look around, making sure his words are meant for me. When it's clear that they are, I shake my head. "Oh, I'm not actually a—"

"By the way," he interrupts, holding out his hand. "I'm Abe. Your future love interest." I wait for him to laugh it off, but instead he sits down across from me. I lower my eyes, unable to meet his dark gaze.

Unlike my sister, I don't date. Or at least I never have. My father likes to think it's all of his "wait for the right guy" speeches, but really I just haven't found anyone who I click with as more than a friend. And Abe doesn't really seem the friend type, not with an approach like that.

"What's your name?" Abe asks, putting his elbows on the table and leaning forward.

"Elise."

His smile fades, and he tips his head back to laugh. "Aw,

man. You're the new server, aren't you?"

"I think so . . ."

"Damn. I just lost twenty bucks."

"I'm sorry."

Abe runs his hand over his face and then grins sheepishly. "For the record," he says, "the love-interest line usually works."

"I'm sure."

Abe takes his notepad from his apron and taps it on the table as if thinking. I watch him, flattered that he approached me at all. I can't remember the last time someone did.

A sunburn crosses the bridge of his nose, both charming and boyish. His dark brown eyes seem to go on forever. "I'm an idiot," Abe says.

"No. It was a perfect line. Promise."

"Thanks. And just to make this even more awkward, I'm the one who's supposed to train you."

"We can start over. Would that help?"

"No, no, I think that would just make it worse, but I appreciate the suggestion." Abe studies me. "Do you go to Mission High, Elise?" he asks.

"Yep. I'll be a junior."

"Ah, then we're rivals," he says. "I just graduated from Yuma."

"That's probably why your lines usually work so well—fresh audience. I bet you're a legend around here."

"You have no idea." He winks and then pulls out his phone, peeking at the time. "Don't want to cut this short, but I have some actual training to do," he says. "Are you a fast learner?"

"Sort of."

"Your confidence is encouraging." Abe takes a menu from behind the hot sauce and hands it to me. "Let's start with our specialties."

He takes a menu of his own, flipping it open. "There is the *pollo especial*, but don't ever order it. It's gross," Abe says, running his finger down the page. "Or the *asada*."

I try to follow along, but he's going so fast I can't keep up. And I'm sure I'll never remember the names of the food—or be able to repeat them.

"The *albondigas* soup is delicious. And the number eight *es muy bueno*," Abe sings in a perfect accent. "It's my favorite. Now, the *espinaca* is one of . . ."

Listening to Abe, I don't notice when the tingling first starts in my fingers. But as it climbs over my hand I begin to tremble. The vibration spreads up my arm, and I set my menu flat on the table to reach for the glass of water. Maybe if I have something to drink I'll feel better.

The bell above the door jingles as a guy walks in, his overalls clotted with plaster and paint. He nods to the man behind the counter and then absently looks over the restaurant. His eyes widen when he sees me.

I go still as I'm struck with an overwhelming sense of compassion, love. Suddenly the man's life unfolds within my head, my reality filled with his journey. I begin to panic, but then I'm blanketed in a sense of calm. A sense of purpose.

The guy walks slowly, almost trancelike, toward me. *"Mi angel,"* he whispers when he gets to the table. He reaches to take my hand, startling me. But I don't pull away. Instead I sway with the emotions coursing through me. Emotions that aren't mine.

"Hey," Abe says, glaring at him. "Back off, Diego."

But Diego Encina doesn't respond. Instead his eyes are glassy with tears. A sudden brightness explodes around us, blotting out the rest of the world, silencing everything beyond.

"I'm so lost," Diego murmurs to me. "Please, *angel.*"

I can't stop myself from leaning closer, squeezing his hand to comfort him. "I'm still with you," I whisper softly. But I'm not speaking for myself—I'm repeating the words running through my head. An all-knowing consciousness. Something Diego has seen before and still craves.

Six months ago Diego had been in a terrible accident with his truck, the very accident that killed his brother. Diego's internal injuries were so severe that he went into cardiac arrest three times. They'd just called the time of death when he suddenly started breathing again, his pulse strong.

Before his accident, Diego had been spending his nights drinking, driving around, and being reckless. His brother had been trying to help him when he got into the truck, attempting to wrestle away the keys. In the end he let Diego drive. It cost him his life.

After surviving, Diego vowed to change. And he has. He's working, taking care of his family—of his brother's children, too. He's become everything his older brother wanted him to be. He should be proud.

But he's not. Diego doesn't feel like he deserves this second chance. He closes his eyes and brings my hand to his mouth to kiss it, holding back a cry.

I refuse to leave him so desperate. And even though I don't understand what's happening, I find myself unable to send him away without granting him some sort of peace. I brush his damp hair from his forehead.

"Second chances aren't given lightly, Diego," I whisper in a voice only he can hear. "The children need you, especially Tomás. Don't abandon him—you have to be strong now."

Diego blinks heavily as if absorbing my words, and then he slowly regains his focus. The light around us fades away. Diego drops my hand and staggers back a step, as if just realizing where he is.

"I'm sorry, *señorita*," he says quickly, glancing once at Abe. "I didn't mean to interrupt."

I'm speechless, staring back at him, unable to process what just happened. Diego excuses himself, walking to the counter without ever looking back.

The warm, calming sensation begins to fade from my skin. Instead, energy surges through my body and I tremble with it. When I turn to my right, the room around me is frozen. No movement. No sound. And then all at once, a new scene slips into focus—a memory.

I'm on the front steps of a church, waiting for someone. My

15

blond hair blows in the wind, light droplets of rain starting above me. I glance impatiently at my phone before turning to go inside. Classes are starting, and I'm late. I knew I shouldn't have expected Sarah to be on time.

I gasp, pulled back into now. The restaurant around me suddenly comes alive again, filling my ears with the echoes of scraping forks and clinking plates. I'm disoriented—as if waking up from a really intense dream. One you think could be real.

"Why did deadbeat Diego just call you his angel?" Abe asks from across the table, sounding bewildered. "Do you know each other?"

I'm not sure how to answer, what to think. Did I know him? For a second I knew his innermost thoughts, his past. But then that memory, it wasn't mine. I've never been to Catholic school. I've never had blond hair. And who's Sarah?

I reach up to rub my forehead, squeezing my eyes shut. Fear begins to rise in my throat. I think I just had an out-of-body experience.

"Elise?" Abe says, lowering his voice. "Are you okay?" I feel his fingers brush across my hand and I jump, looking over at him.

"Yeah," I lie. I'm not sure how to explain what just happened. I'm completely overwhelmed. "He must have thought I was someone else," I say quickly. But for a second, I *was* someone else.

"He . . ." Abe stops. "Okay, that was really weird. I'm tripping out right now."

"I'm sorry," I say, trying to keep some semblance of normal. "I'm just a little light-headed. I forgot to eat lunch and I—"

I reach for my water again, but my hands are shaking so badly that the glass slips from my fingers and hits the table, splashing me in cold liquid. I yelp, brushing my lap.

Abe stands, pulling a white rag from his apron. He swipes the cubes from the table back into the glass. "God, Elise," he says with mock disappointment. "I can't take you anywhere."

I let him finish cleaning the ice off the table before sliding out. I grab a napkin and try to sop up the water on my seat, my body still uncoordinated from adrenaline.

Abe touches my shoulder. "Please don't," he says. "You're making it worse. Let me grab a dry towel." He tosses the wet one on the table. "And try not to trash the place while I'm gone, okay, *querida*?"

He strolls toward the back, leaving me standing there scared, alone, and wet. *"Querida?"* I repeat, wondering what he just called me.

"It means beloved," a middle-aged woman with a smoky voice says from the table next to mine. She's poking her refried beans with a fork, and when she looks up, she smiles. *"Querida* means wanted."

CHAPTER 3

I'm standing in the back room as Santo lectures me for (a) spilling my drink everywhere and causing a scene, and (b) not knowing the menu already. He's a big guy with a shaved head and grease burns up and down his arms, and I try to tell myself he's probably a teddy bear on the inside. But I'm pretty sure that's not true.

Santo says that he doubts I'll make a capable server, especially since I have what he calls "butterfingers," but he's willing to give me a shot since he's understaffed. I'm grateful. Humiliated, but grateful.

Even as he talks, I glance toward the dining room, thinking about Diego. About the girl on the church steps. I run through a list of possibilities: low-blood-sugar-induced hallucinations, narcolepsy, schizophrenia. Obviously there is no way that stuff *really* happened to me just now, so it has to all be in my head. There's an explanation, and I'll figure out what it is. I just can't panic in the meantime.

Noticing my distraction, Santo dismisses me to the food line to help load trays, saying that he doesn't trust me on the floor without an escort. And since the water incident, Abe has been too busy to train me.

It's nearly two hours—and countless plates of food—later when Abe comes up to me at the line, reaching past me for a tray. "Hey," he says. "Do you think you could help me out for a second?"

"Sure!" At this point I'll do anything to get out of the sweltering kitchen.

"Thanks," he says, sounding relieved. "They just sat tables seven and eight. Would you mind getting their drink orders for me? I'm slammed right now." I agree, and he rushes back onto the floor.

I follow after him, grabbing a green pad of paper from the register as I pass. I feel like a real server, and it's kind of exciting. Abe heads to the counter and I make my way over to his section.

At table seven is an older woman whose overabundance of perfume tickles my nose. She tries to give me her food order twice, but I honestly don't know what she's talking about. So I tell her I'll send Abe right over and promise to be back with her iced tea.

As I'm passing by table eight, the person there reaches to gently touch my arm, startling me. I gasp and swing around, dropping my notepad on the floor. Nice. Maybe I do have butterfingers. I bend quickly to gather the pages that have scattered.

"I'm so sorry," a soft voice says. "I didn't mean to scare you."

At the sound, my heart kicks up its pace and I slowly lift my eyes. The guy—the hot one from the motorcycle—is looking down at me, apologetic. The frazzled feeling I just had immediately evaporates as I stare at him, struck by how incredibly handsome he is up close. His eyes are an amazing shade of hazel, more green than brown. His dark hair is long, curling under his unshaven chin, evening out the prettiness of his features. He's certainly rough around the edges, but I like it. He looks kind of dangerous.

"It's okay," I say, grabbing the last of the papers and standing. I'm suddenly self-conscious and want to smooth back my hair, but decide that would be trying too hard. "Did you want something?" I ask him instead.

He chuckles. "I was hoping for food, but if that's too much . . ."

"Oh," I say, embarrassed. "I didn't mean to be rude. It's just that it's my first day and, well"—I lower my voice, confiding in him—"I have no idea what I'm doing."

He leans toward me. "I won't tell on you." He whispers as if we're in a conspiracy together.

I smile, looking down at the crumples of paper in my hand.

"I appreciate that. And I can't help with the food, but maybe a drink?"

"A Dr Pepper if you have it," he says, sitting back against the seat. He opens his menu, and I take the opportunity to run my eyes over him one more time. His brown leather jacket is worn and his dark sunglasses are tucked into the collar of his T-shirt. As he turns the pages, his every movement is tender.

When he looks in my direction again, a small smile tugging at his lips, I realize I've been staring at him long enough to be obvious.

"Sorry," I say quickly. "You're . . . really distracting."

"Thank you," he says in an amused voice. "You're a bit distracting yourself." He closes his menu and leans his elbows on the table, giving me his full attention. When his gaze locks on mine, pinning me in place, I take a deep breath. And then I remember that I'm still at work.

"I should go," I say, motioning to the tables around us. "Otherwise I'll never win employee of the month."

He smiles. "I'll be rooting for you."

And when he turns back to his menu, I walk away—pulse racing, face flushed—and hurry toward the drink station.

Abe asks for my help on another table, and I never make it back to the guy from the motorcycle. I'm seriously disappointed, but far too busy to focus on it.

I follow Abe to the table of a guy with a buzz cut and a sleeveless T-shirt that says AMERICAN MADE on it. The customer mumbles that it's about time, and by Abe's cool expression, I half wonder if he's going to dump the sizzling fajitas in the guy's lap.

"This is Elise," Abe tells him, setting the skillet down with a clack. "She's new, so tip her well."

"It took close to a half hour to get my—"

Abe leans in, his hands on either side of the table. "I said tip her well, Carl. We wouldn't want to scare her away."

My mouth opens as I'm about to tell them that it's fine, I really don't deserve a tip, but Carl reaches into his pocket. He pulls out a five-dollar bill and tosses it onto the tabletop. He glares at Abe, but says nothing else before taking a spoonful of guacamole and slopping it onto his chicken.

Abe grabs the money off the table. "Thanks," he responds brightly, turning to hand it to me. I take it awkwardly, shooting a cautious glance at Carl, who seems to have already forgotten that we exist as he shoves food into his mouth.

"Now," Abe says, putting his hand on my arm to lead me away, "I'm taking a fifteen-minute break. Come with?"

"Won't we get in trouble?" I ask.

"I never get in trouble." He grins. "Meet me out back in five?"

I nod, and then Abe strolls across the dining room. Several women lift their gazes to watch him, and by his nonreaction I guess that Abe is probably used to it. Following his cue, I leave the room, stopping to grab my phone from my purse.

I see that I've missed two calls from the "old man" already

and roll my eyes. I find my way to the back door, slipping through into the parking lot. It's quiet, the air humid with the promise of rain as I lean against the outer wall of the building. Since Abe's not here yet, I decide to check in with my dad and ask if he knows what could have possibly caused my hallucinations.

"Technically," my father says as a way of answering the phone, "I called before your shift started, so you can't yell at me for bothering you during work."

I'm immediately comforted by the sound of his voice. "What could possibly be on your mind that you had to call twice?" I ask. "I'm a mile and a half away."

"I was wondering if you've seen your sister," he says. "I know you're partners in crime, but I'm worried. You have her car, right?"

My heartbeat quickens, sure that he knows about last night. "I did borrow it, but she was home when I left. Have you called *her* twice?" I ask.

"Three times."

"Huh. I don't know, then. I'm sure she just forgot her phone somewhere." I'm surprised that Lucy isn't answering. It's unlike her to purposely worry our father. She prefers to commit her acts of rebellion in secret when possible. But my sister is the least of my concerns right now.

"Actually," I say. "I wanted to ask you—"

Abe pokes his head out of the back door then, looking around until he sees me. He smiles and walks out, holding two cups. I don't want Abe to hear about my brush with the unexplained, so I turn away to talk into the phone.

"I have to go," I say quickly to my father. "I'll call you as soon as I'm done."

"Home by eleven—"

I hang up and shove the phone into the pocket of my black pants. Abe comes to stand next to me, passing a soda in my direction. "Sorry about that," I say.

"Boyfriend?" he asks, taking a sip from his drink.

"No. Father."

His mouth quirks up. "What a sweet girl you are."

"I try."

We're quiet for a few minutes as the darkened parking lot of Santo's continues to empty. My shift is nearly over, and I'm glad. I'm exhausted from being on my feet all night.

"So," Abe says, turning to me. "Do you want to hang out after work? I'm going to a party."

I smile. The idea of going out with him is more than a little tempting. "Thanks," I say. "But I can't. My dad's on high alert right now because my sister is a rebel without a cause. He wants me home by eleven."

"Eleven? Reminds me of when I was in kindergarten," Abe says, pretending to be nostalgic.

"Shut up," I say. "It's not that bad."

"It's pretty bad. Straight home from work? Is he a police officer? Are you under house arrest?"

"Nope. He's a pastor."

Abe snorts back a laugh. "Of course he is."

"Hey!" I push his shoulder playfully. "My dad is cool."

"As are most overprotective pastor fathers," he says, like it's an obvious fact. "I bet you have to bring home all of your dates to meet him first, right?"

"No," I say, not mentioning the fact that I've never been on a date.

"Really?" he asks. "With a beautiful creature like you under his roof I'd think he'd bar the doors and windows."

"Nope, just a curfew," I say, a small catch in my voice at being called beautiful. I feel Abe's dark gaze studying me, and when I turn to him, he bumps his shoulder into mine.

"Come out anyway," he whispers. "Be bad with me, Elise."

I laugh, thinking he's all kinds of adorable. But it doesn't change the fact that I have to talk to my father about what happened to me. So my workplace romance will have to wait. "Another time, maybe," I say instead.

Abe sighs dramatically and reaches to take the cup from my hand. "Another time," he repeats, backing toward the door. "I'll hold you to that." And then he walks inside.

CHAPTER 4

By the time I finish vacuuming the dining room, Abe has already left for the night. Santo and Margie—his wife and head server—are at the door, packed up and ready to leave. And even though he doesn't come out and say it, Santo must think I did a decent enough job, because he asks me to come back tomorrow at four. Hopefully next time I'll make more than five dollars in tips.

The sky is starless as I walk out, the clouds turning the black night a dark gray. At least it's not raining. I've always hated the rain. I climb into Lucy's car and take out my phone to see if my father called again. But it won't power on. It's dead.

"Perfect," I say, and toss it onto the seat. I close my eyes, my earlier conversation with Diego haunting me. The memory that wasn't mine. I'm not sure how I'll explain this to my father in a way that doesn't make me sound crazy—even if that's how it feels.

I could never know those things about another person. No one could. So how did I—

A swift knock at my window startles me and I stifle a scream. Standing there is an old woman, a knit cap pulled down over her white hair. She's motioning for me to open my window, but I hesitate. She's creepy.

I consider starting the car and pulling away, leaving her in my dust. But it seems cruel. So I lower the window—halfway.

"Hi," I say, keeping back from the glass.

The old woman tilts her head to the side. "What are you doing here, child?" she asks in a ragged, broken voice. It's a terrible sound, and I cringe from it.

"Leaving work," I respond, glancing toward my purse. I figure she's looking for a handout, maybe hasn't even eaten today. And though the woman is freaking me out, I can't leave her here with nothing. I reach inside and take out my five-dollar bill. "This is all I have," I start to say as I hand it to her, but suddenly she grabs me by the wrist, yanking my arm out the window.

I shriek, trying to pull it back, but she's strong. I'm afraid she's going to bite me. Instead she ducks down, her wrinkled face close to the glass, and puts my palm to her cheek. "You're so bright."

"Let go!" Tears are streaming down my face and then images begin to fill my head—dark pictures of skin cracking, dead and gray underneath. "Stop!" I cry out again.

Suddenly the woman is pulled from the car, her broken nails digging into my flesh as she's yanked away.

"What's going on?" It's Abe, and he has the woman by the shoulders. "I told you not to come here anymore. Do I have to call the cops?" He looks over at me. "Elise, did she hurt you?"

Next to Abe, the woman is fragile and small. I sniffle and then shake my head no. She seems harmless now, especially near Abe's imposing frame. "Get out of here," he growls at her. "And if I see you again, I won't bother calling the cops."

The old woman turns to me as she backs out of Abe's arms. "I showed you. They're coming, child," she says, pointing to me. "Watch out for the Shadows!"

"Go!" Abe yells, pushing her toward the empty street. When she's gone, he comes to stand outside my window. "I had to come back for my jacket. But—" He stops, peeking down at me.

I'm shaking as I inspect the four long scratches raked across the inside of my arm. "Ow," I murmur, my throat thick with tears.

Abe motions to my cuts. "Looks like it hurts."

"It does. Who *was* that?"

"Local psychic. Although now she's mostly just a sad old lady who wanders around town sometimes. She's never been

28

violent before—just a pain in the ass. Why did she grab you?" he asks.

"I don't know," I say, touching the raw skin around the scratches. It really does hurt and I want to go home. I've never been attacked before. I've never even been yelled at before. I can only imagine how pink and puffy my face is from crying, but it hardly matters now. Not after the day I've had.

I wrap my uninjured arm around myself just as little taps begin to hit my windshield—drops of rain. I turn the ignition and flip on the wipers. Abe lifts his eyes toward the sky, annoyance passing over his features.

"Elise," he says. "Since I just saved your life and all, do you think you can give me a ride home?"

I nod, and as Abe crosses to the passenger side, I brush the tears off my cheeks and unlock the doors. The minute Abe's inside, I lock them again. I don't need any more crazy old ladies grabbing me tonight.

The car is silent for a long moment before Abe reaches out his hand to me. "Can I see?" he asks. I slide my palm into his and he lays my arm across his thigh to inspect my wound. "It's not so bad," he says, running his finger gently over a scratch. He traces it back up again, tickling me. "I don't think it'll scar."

"Lucky me," I say.

He lets go, and I pull my arm back in front of me. My skin tingles where he touched me.

"Why were you alone, anyway?" Abe asks. "Didn't Santo and Margie walk you out?"

"They did. I stayed an extra minute to call my dad, but my phone was dead. Then the woman came up to my window and I thought she wanted money—"

"And you gave it to her?" He laughs. "Elise, didn't your mom teach you not to talk to strangers?"

"My mom is dead."

"Oh. I'm sorry, I didn't—"

"It's okay. And yes, my dad did teach me that, but I was being nice. I didn't expect her to—"

"Hey," Abe interrupts. "You don't have to dismiss the subject like that. My mother died last year."

I look sideways at Abe, struck with sudden grief. He shrugs, as if acknowledging that we're both in the dead-parent club. And it's not really an awesome place to be.

"What happened to her?" I ask. "Was she sick?"

Abe exhales, reclining the seat back and stretching his long legs in front of him like he's settling in. "No. It was an accident. Yours?"

My mother had never smoked a day in her life, but that didn't matter when she was diagnosed with lung cancer at the age of thirty-five. I'd been eight years old. I can still remember the small things, but I've spent longer with a grieving father. So it seems that my time with her will always be overshadowed by my time without her. "She had cancer," I say, checking over my scratches as a way of distraction. "I was just a kid, though."

"I see. And how long have you been here, Elise? In Thistle?"

"A month. We moved from Colorado when my dad got a job at Mission Church. He thought my sister and I could use the change of scenery."

"I bet. Too much beauty in all those mountains up there. You needed more dry air and sand in your life." He smiles. "And your sister? Is she like you?"

"What—a victim of random attacks? No, Lucy is her own sort of trouble. She's the risk-taker of our little tribe."

"I bet she's not as pretty."

My cheeks heat as I blush, but I pretend like I didn't hear his compliment. Abe makes me feel unsteady, out of my comfort zone. But at the same time, he seems to be genuinely interested in me, and that in itself is appealing.

"What about you?" I ask. "Any brothers or sisters?"

Booming thunder fills the air, followed by blue streaks of lightning across the dark desert sky. The universe seems to open up and pour rain all around us.

"Good thing you offered the ride," Abe says. "My walk home would have been treacherous."

"I didn't actually offer," I tease him, starting the car as I shift into reverse.

"Details."

Following Abe's directions, we drive slowly, the rain making visibility zero. Lucy's car is a piece of crap, so I don't push my luck with its tire treads on the slick pavement.

"It's amazing that I was here, really," Abe says. "If I hadn't shown up at that exact moment, she might have dragged you out of the window and gobbled you up."

"That's comforting. You should consider a job in law enforcement, talking people down from ledges."

"I *will* consider it. Thanks!"

I slow to a stop at a red light, worrying when I notice it's after curfew. My father is probably having a coronary right about now. But I had to give Abe a ride home. It's the least I can do.

"Do you usually walk to work?" I ask when the signal changes.

"Yeah. I like the fresh air. Well, that and the fact that I don't have a car."

"How do you get places?"

"I go around saving attractive girls," he says. "Obviously."

I park at the curb in front of Abe's house. It's a small, stucco home with bright yellow paint and rocky landscaping with a few weeds popping through. The windows are dark and I wonder why no one is waiting up for him.

"It was *fantastic* meeting you," Abe says, sounding sincere. "Thank you for the lift."

"Anytime."

Abe smiles to himself. "I hope so."

I wait as he walks to his house, unlocking the door before slipping inside. I think then about the old woman, the visions she showed me. They were nothing like what I saw with Diego, the bright light surrounding us. The woman was sharing something else entirely. And she had a warning: *Watch out for the Shadows.*

Whatever they are.

After dropping Abe off, I head home. Our neighborhood is a community of tract homes, variations of the same style all within the desert color scheme—tan. When I pull into the driveway, I let Lucy's car idle for a moment, feeling safer now that I'm here.

The front door opens, spilling light onto the porch. My father stands there, leaning against the frame with his head cocked at a "you are so late and I can't wait to hear why" angle.

"You probably won't believe it," I say when I climb out of the car. "But I have an explanation."

"I'm sure you do." As I get closer, my father snaps his gum like a football coach on the sideline of a big game. He says he used to smoke when he was younger, and the gum-chewing replaced the habit. But now he only does it when he's frustrated. Behind his glasses his blue eyes are tired, his tall frame sagging with exhaustion. I think he's lost weight since moving here, but he blames it on the stress of having two teenage daughters.

"Elise," he says. "Your curfew is in effect for a reason. That reason being my sanity. And when you break curfew without calling, it makes me think you're hurt, lying in a ditch somewhere."

"*Or* my phone could have died and I was sidetracked by a wicked old witch in the parking lot of a Mexican restaurant."

I hold up my arm and show him the scratches, which are now an angry red.

My father practically bowls me over as he takes my arm to examine the wound. "Someone did this to you?" His voice is concerned, and I don't know how to tell him that a woman trying to pull me through a car window isn't even the weirdest thing to happen to me today.

"One of the guys from work showed up and scared her off," I say, trying to reassure him. "It was random." I lower my eyes then, thinking that it wasn't just by chance that she grabbed me. She saw something in me, the same thing that Diego saw. Just then fear crawls over the back of my neck as if I'm being watched.

"Let's go inside," I tell my father, and push his elbow back toward our well-lit house. And it isn't until we're on the other side of a dead bolt with the alarm set that I begin to relax.

CHAPTER 5

I give my father the shortened version of my attack, and even make Abe sound like a superhero—one who has excellent serving skills. My father's not impressed. He says that Santo shouldn't have left me alone in a dark parking lot in the first place. I nod in agreement, trying to take the quickest route out of the lecture.

"Hey," Lucy says to me as she walks into the kitchen. "I heard the door and hoped you were my pizza."

"Sorry to disappoint you."

Lucy must have just gotten home because she's still dressed from a night out. She's wearing heavy blue eye shadow with false lashes, the edge of her liner curved up into a cat's eye. It's not my taste, but it's a good look on her.

"I forgive you," my sister says. "I made Dad a bet that Peppino's still delivered this late, and now I'm waiting to collect my winnings."

My father pulls out a kitchen chair to sit down, chuckling to himself.

"Laugh it up," Lucy says to him playfully. "But when that pie arrives, you owe me twenty bucks. And I'll take that in small, unmarked bills." Lucy shoots me a quick smile as if it's our secret sisterly pact to give him a hard time.

Since our mother died, the three of us are close. My dad calls us his little tribe. Despite the strict rules sometimes, Lucy and I admire all he does for others, what he stands for. He's inspiring.

The doorbell rings and Lucy sticks out her pierced tongue before bolting to answer it. My father exhales, rubbing his forehead. "How I hate that piercing . . ."

I drop down in the chair, reminding him that it's a perfectly normal fashion statement. Three weeks ago Lucy had brought me with her to the tattoo shop, planning on getting a tribal armband. At the last second she decided instead to poke a hole through her tongue. Seemed like a decent enough decision at the time.

I lay my injured arm on the table, tracing the slightly raised lines. For a second I'm reminded of how Abe touched them, so gently, almost like they hurt him, too.

"You're smiling," my father says. "Why are you smiling?"

"No reason." Only I say it like there are millions of devious and unacceptable reasons. He groans.

"Does that mean it's none of my business?"

"Exactly!" I hold up my finger, letting him know he's on to something.

"Fair enough. But"—his face becomes serious—"I'd like to hear more about today. About the woman. I really think we should file a report."

"No," I say quickly. "Abe told her not to come back. Let's not start lining up creepy old women for me to identify. I just want to forget the entire thing happened."

"Sounds like denial." My father reaches to put his hand over mine, and I meet his eyes. I'm suddenly eight years old again, standing outside of a funeral home, refusing to believe my mother is gone. He knows denial is my natural instinct.

"Something else happened today," I murmur, forcing myself to confront my fear. My father tenses but doesn't speak. "There was this guy," I begin. "And when he walked into Santo's, my fingers got all tingly. I started seeing images of him, his life—but it wasn't stuff I could have known before. It was like an out-of-body experience." I pause, trying to gauge my father's reaction. "Have you heard of anything like that before?"

My dad stares down at my hand before letting it go. He pulls his brows together in thought. "No, but that doesn't mean there's not a rational explanation. What happened after that? Were you dizzy? Nauseous?"

I shake my head. "Well, it only got stranger from there. I

remembered something then, only it wasn't my memory, even though it felt like it. For a second, I was somebody else." I stop, lowering my head. "I sound crazy."

"No, you sound scared," he says. "And believe me, Elise, I've heard stranger." He pats my hand reassuringly. "I don't want you working yourself up over this. I'll do some research, okay? We'll figure out what's going on with you."

Lucy walks in just then, carrying a humongous pizza box, a two-liter bottle of Diet Pepsi under her arm. "Missed it, Elise." She beams, oblivious to the seriousness of the moment. "Pizza guy was *so* hot."

My father smiles at me. "And while I'm at it, I'll find out what's wrong with your sister, too."

I thank him, feeling a hundred times better. It can't be that bad if my father isn't more worried. Then again, he's also a crisis counselor, so he knows how to handle high-stress situations well.

"Elise?" my sister says again. "Did you hear me? Hot. Super hot. He even wrote his number on this napkin." She waves it in front of me until my father casually plucks it from her hand, wiping his mouth on it before folding it in half.

"Thanks, Lucy," he responds. "I needed a place to spit out my gum."

"Dad!" My sister laughs and lightly taps my dad in the back of his head as she passes behind him to set the pizza on the counter.

I stand to grab the plates, the bright spots of my day finally seeming worth mentioning. "Yeah, well, I met *two* cute guys today," I say quietly.

Lucy spins to face me. One of my sister's favorite pastimes involves spotting good-looking men, and then making sure to mention them to me.

"More information needed," she demands, as if I've been holding out on her.

"Well, the first was just a customer—so hot. I'll probably never see him again, though." I pout my lips for dramatic effect. "But the other," I say, bringing the plates to the table, "is a guy I work with. He's not really my type, but he is an amazing specimen."

"Oh, please," Lucy says. "Like you have a type. Now who's the specimen? I must track him down and study him."

"Your sister is very picky," my father answers for me. "She doesn't need a type. She's waiting for the—"

"Gross, Dad. Spare me," Lucy interrupts. "Elise," she says. "Tell me more about this cute boy from work."

I grin. "His name is Abe and he—"

Her blue eyes widen. "You don't mean Abe Weston, do you?"

"Um, maybe. I didn't catch his last name."

"Holy hell, Elise! I *so* know him."

"Lucy, mouth," my father warns, but he sounds like he's given up on being included in this conversation.

"Really?" I ask as my sister drops a slice onto the plate I'm

39

holding. I should have figured that Lucy would have heard of Abe. She has the scoop on everyone.

"Well, not *really* really," she says. "But I know who he is. He's from Yuma, and you're downplaying. He's incredibly cute. And from what I hear, a total slut."

"Lucy," my father says more seriously.

My sister snatches the plate from my hand and sets it in front of my father, smiling sweetly. Then she comes over to take my uninjured arm, lowering her voice. "He probably thought you were adorable. Did he ask you out?"

"Well, he did try to corrupt me out in back of Santo's," I say, earning a look from my father. "He asked if I wanted to go to a party with him tonight. Probably not as a date or—"

"Why are you here?" Lucy asks incredulously. "You didn't say yes?"

I shake my head, and my sister looks offended on behalf of the entire female species. "I'm sorry to say this, Elise," she states, taking out a slice and biting off the end. "I think you need therapy."

I hand her a plate, but she pushes it away, instead using her other hand to catch any grease that might drip. I must have thoroughly bored her, because she wanders back over to where my father is sitting.

"Can I go out for a bit?" she asks, her eyes innocent. "I'll be back at a decent hour."

"It's already past a decent hour," he answers, glancing at her above his glasses. "And you just got home. Maybe tomorrow

40

would be better—when there's daylight?"

Lucy's jaw clenches and I feel my own anxiety spike. "I'm eighteen, Dad," she says in a controlled voice. "You can't keep me an infant forever."

Our father leans toward her, his expression sympathetic, but unwavering. "I'm not trying to, Lucinda. I just want to keep you safe."

"Or locked away in a tower," she retorts. She tosses her half-eaten slice back into the box before leaving for her bedroom. We wait, and when her door slams shut, my father takes off his glasses to press his fingers into the corners of his eyes.

"She has a point," I offer. "It's not like she's going to sell her soul just because it's after midnight. Not when she can do it any old time."

"Not funny," my father says. I know how much he hates cracking down on Lucy, but ever since that incident with the cops, he doesn't trust her judgment. I wish he'd bend a little more. I hate when they argue.

We're silent as we eat, and when I'm done, I kick my sneakers off under the table, sore from my shift.

"You're tired," my dad says. "Why don't you get some sleep, and tomorrow I'll start gathering some information. I'll make an appointment with the doctor, have them do a workup. Maybe have a peek at that arm."

So he *is* worried. I nod, touching his shoulder as I stand to leave the kitchen. When I get to my room, I collapse on my flowered comforter—still in uniform. I'm so drained. I want to think about my day, try to put together the pieces of what happened, but I can't keep my eyes open. And soon I find myself drifting away completely.

I'm on the rooftop of a high-rise building. The sky is dark and starless around me, the air thick with the promise of rain. I've never been here before, I'm sure of that. I take a few steps and the cement floor is cold on my bare feet.

It's then that I notice my skin, glowing softly in the city lights. I turn my hand over, studying the gold, when the rooftop door swings open and startles me. I'm about to hide, but the man who walks out doesn't see me. Instead he saunters over to the edge, putting his boot on the raised ledge as he surveys the city.

How did he not see me?

My heart thumps in my chest, and I take in my setting once more. From here, I can't even tell what city this is. I just know it's not Arizona, not with this humidity.

The man adjusts his stance, catching my attention once again. He's tall and very handsome. He's wearing tight black pants, a white shirt. His long dark hair is fastened with a band low on his neck. But as attractive as he is . . . I take a step back. It's like I'm repelled by him.

The door opens once again, a figure standing there as she's lit from the lights behind her. I can't make out her features, but I notice her long blond hair as it cascades over her black jacket. The spiked heels of her leather boots.

"Rodney," she calls, her voice holding the slightest hint of a Russian accent.

The man on the roof tilts his head toward her, a smile on his face. "My beauty," he says. "What brings you back here so soon?"

When neither of them notices me, I know that this is a dream. Only this time, it doesn't belong to me. I'm inside someone else's head.

"You said you could help," the woman whispers. "That you could stop this. How? Tell me what I have to do!"

Rodney laughs, finally turning fully to her. His dark eyes and chiseled jaw are stunning, his arms outspread as if for a hug. "Just come to me, Onika," he says simply. "I can make it all go away. All you have to do is take my hand. It's your decision."

The woman hesitates, choking as if holding back a cry. She casts one more glance behind her before moving slowly forward. Halfway across the roof, she breaks into a jog. She runs into Rodney's arms, sobbing the moment he wraps them around her.

Rodney's mouth twists into a sinister grin; his skin cracks. I want to scream for Onika to run. That something is wrong. But before I can, Rodney leans to her ear, his lips touching the skin there and turning it gray.

"Shh . . ." he whispers as she begins to struggle. "Welcome to the Shadows, my beauty."

* * *

My eyes fly open, the ceiling fan spinning slowly above me as the chain clinks against it rhythmically. For a second I don't move, only process. The Shadows . . .

"Did I wake you?"

I jump, finding Lucy standing in my doorway, holding a cup of coffee. "I thought I heard you talking," she says, "and I wanted to make sure you were all right." She takes a long sip.

I push my sweaty hair off my forehead. "I was having a nightmare."

Her blue eyes narrow. "About?"

"It was—" I pause as the dream starts to slip away. "There was a building, a man . . . no, a woman." I exhale when the rest evaporates. "I don't remember."

"I hate when that happens." Lucy fights back a yawn, then takes a big gulp of her coffee.

"Did you just get home?" I ask, glancing at the clock. It's after five. How did she get in without my help?

"Yep. Out with a friend."

"The same friend from yesterday? A guy?"

"Ew, are you Dad right now?"

"No. It's just weird that you're not telling me about it. You usually overshare."

"Weird like getting attacked in the parking lot of Santo's? That kind of weird?" She takes another drink from her cup. I wince, not used to Lucy sounding so mean-spirited. Her shoulders slump.

"Sorry," she says. "That was jerky. I heard you talking to

44

Dad last night. I'm just really tired, I guess. You know I'll hunt down any old lady who tries to mess with my sister."

I tell her I understand, although the sting from her comment still lingers.

"And yes," she adds. "It was a guy. A sometimes-boyfriend-slash-friend that Dad doesn't need to know about."

"That sounds sketchy."

"Yeah, well. We can't all be saints, Elise." Lucy yawns again, and looks longingly toward her room. "I'm going to bed. I'll see you later?"

"Sure." She starts to walk away when I'm suddenly struck with an intense worry. It's not unusual for her to sneak out two nights in a row, and yet my stomach twists with a sharp anxiety. "Lucy," I call. She glances back over her shoulder at me, raising her pierced eyebrow. "Be careful," I say.

My sister grins. "Why start now?" Then she turns and leaves my room.

CHAPTER 6

My father wakes me up early for my doctor's appointment and tells me to ask Lucy to go with me because he has morning services. And since he's the only pastor, he can't exactly reschedule.

I'm not looking forward to being poked and prodded, especially since I have a fear of needles, and of doctors in general. Side effect of watching my mother slowly die in a hospital, I guess.

I wake up my sister and wait for her to get dressed. I'm only three sips into my glass of juice when I hear Lucy's ballet flats tapping on the tile floor of the kitchen.

"Ready?" she asks, her hair spiked up in a stylish short Mohawk.

"That was fast," I say, dumping the rest of my glass down the sink. "You're leaving the house without makeup on?" I honestly can't remember the last time that happened.

"Figured I'd show off my natural beauty instead."

"Modesty is such an attractive quality," I say, and snatch my purse from the counter. It may be an overcast morning, but it's still close to eighty degrees out, and she's wearing a dark gray hoodie.

"You cold?" I ask.

"It's that damn ice water in my veins. Keeps me cool in the summer." She grins and then goes to the front door, motioning for me to walk out first.

The doctor's office is just on the outskirts of Thistle in a small adobe-style building. Lucy stays in the waiting room, flipping through an old copy of *Family Circle* when I head to the back. The doctor listens as I tell her about the hallucination, the memory. I'm not entirely sure she believes me, though. Instead she orders blood work and then checks over my arm, saying that the scratches don't look infected and should heal up quickly.

After a visit to the office lab, the doctor tells me my vitamin D is significantly low. The symptoms of that include weakness, fatigue, and tingling. That does cover a lot of what *is* wrong with me, but I think it's too simple of an explanation. Even so, the doctor says we should rule it out before ordering a brain MRI, which just sounds frightening. I leave with a large-dose prescription in hand, and make Lucy stop by the pharmacy to fill it.

As we're waiting in the chairs at Walgreens for them to call my number, my sister checks her phone. "This is taking way too long," she says, sounding impatient. I look sideways at her, unamused.

"I had to get blood drawn. I think I'm the one who should be whining."

Lucy sighs. "Sorry. I just have to be somewhere."

"Where? It's nine a.m.?"

"I'm meeting friends for coffee," she says. "And I'm—" My sister pauses, closing her eyes as if she's struck with pain. I reach out to touch her arm and she jumps. "Sorry," she says. "I should probably see the doctor about my cramping. It's been intense lately."

"I can see that. Have you told Dad? He's worried about you."

She smiles softly. "I know he is. But like you, Elise, I'm not down for being a science experiment for doctors. You saw what they did to Mom. I don't want anyone testing their theories on me."

I furrow my brow. "About cramping?"

She looks over at me. "About anything." Lucy stands up, slightly bent as if compensating for her stomach pain. "I'm going to grab some products. You'll wait here?" she asks.

I nod, concern rushing through me. I watch her leave to head down the aisle, and just then the pharmacist calls my name. As I stand at the register, the guy clicking numbers into his computer, I start to feel it. A vibration in my fingers, slowly crawling up my arms. I close my eyes, hot sensations racing over my skin.

"You'll want to take these with food," the pharmacist explains. But I'm starting to shake, unable to respond. Instead, I look behind him and catch my reflection in the mirrored cabinet.

I'm nearly struck down with fear.

The person in my image is someone else. She's wearing a Catholic school uniform, long blond hair behind her ears. My mouth parts with a gasp, but as I watch, the reflection starts to change. Her skin starts turning gold.

I cry out and stumble backward, bumping into the person in line behind me. The woman reaches to steady me, but I fall past her, nearly pulling her down with me. The back of my head hits the linoleum, and I roll onto my side. There are a few startled screams and it takes a minute for the pain to ease off enough for me to sit up. The pharmacist runs from around the counter to kneel in front of me, asking if I'm okay. I tell him that I am. But I'm not.

When he helps me to my feet, amid the stares of concerned customers, I crane my neck to peer around him—to find the girl in the mirror again. But it's just me, standing in a Walgreens, pale as the dead. The pharmacist asks if I'd like some water, but I can't answer. Instead I stare at my reflection, my dark hair, my blue eyes—and suddenly I think . . . I look wrong.

* * *

"I'm so sorry," Lucy says, holding my arm as she leads us to the parking lot. "I had to buy tampons. I didn't think you were going to have a seizure in the middle of the store."

"I didn't have a seizure," I tell her, still rubbing at the back of my head. After I'd gotten up, the staff made me drink a glass of water, asking repeatedly if I wanted an ambulance. But I was fine, other than a headache. And the fact that I'm suffering from hallucinations.

Lucy starts the car, her sleeves pulled down over her hands, her thumb poking out where she cut a hole in the cuff. She glances sideways at me, her lips pressed tightly together. "You sure you're okay?" She sounds concerned.

I lower my head. "Yeah. I saw something and it freaked me out."

My sister cranks up the air-conditioning and checks over her shoulder before pulling out into the street. "What was it?"

"A reflection. Only it wasn't mine. I looked like someone else."

Lucy's back straightens. "Seriously? Who?"

"I don't know. I can't really remember her face. But strange things keep happening," I say. "First the parking lot with that old woman, then . . . other things. There's no way this is a result of a vitamin deficiency." I notice Lucy's knuckles turning white as she grips the steering wheel.

"That sounds like a plausible enough explanation," she says.

My heart beats quickly in my chest as I hear the catch in my sister's voice. "Do you see things too?" I ask.

"What? No." She looks at me, a surprised expression on her face. "As I'm sure you've noticed, Elise, I'm very well-adjusted."

We both smile, but when she turns to the road, she gasps and slams on the brakes. I fly forward before my seat belt catches me, yanking me back. "Ouch!" I say, rubbing at where the belt has probably bruised my neck.

"I could have killed him," Lucy murmurs, reaching up to brush her hair back with her fingers. In front of us the traffic-light is still red, a rear wheel of a motorcycle only inches from our bumper. I pause when I realize it's the guy. The one I saw in Santo's. He glances back over his shoulder at us, his eyes shielded by dark glasses.

"You almost ran over the hottest guy in town," I whisper.

Lucy laughs, looking sideways. "You're feeling better."

Then she sticks her head out the window and waves to the guy. "Sorry about that!" she calls. When he doesn't immediately respond, Lucy hikes her thumb in my direction. "Also, this one here thinks you're really cute."

"Lucy!" I shove her shoulder.

The guy's mouth twitches with the start of a smile, but then the light turns green and he puts his boots back on his bike and drives away before turning at the next street.

"Can't believe you just did that," I say.

Lucy leans over to kiss my cheek dramatically as if this all falls under the sisterly code of conduct. She eases the car forward before picking up speed. "Now," she says. "Let's get home before I nearly kill anyone else."

I agree, but as we drive, I peek down the street where the motorcycle turned, hoping to catch another glimpse of the guy. But he's gone. I bury my fear from the reflection and tear open the bag from the pharmacy, swallowing a pill dry.

Monsoon season is in full effect, the announcer on the radio says. And Thistle is getting unprecedented amounts of rain—continuing today.

I groan as I pull Lucy's car into Santo's parking lot at four, clicking off the stereo. The place is packed and I have to turn up the hill to the back lot. I pull the emergency brake and take a second to check my reflection, feeling utterly exhausted. My hair is in a knot at my neck and I'm wearing Lucy's eyeliner, hoping it will help me appear less tired. It doesn't.

When I get out of the car, I notice the sky—the clouds covering any hint of blue. I'm not a meteorologist, but I'm pretty sure that the desert is supposed to be sunny—especially in the summer. It's not fair that it's so miserable out, especially when I could really use the vitamin D right now.

I head toward the glass door of Santo's, passing three men smoking cigarettes. One mumbles something perverted under his breath, and I turn, ready to tell him off. But the second I see him, I'm hit with a searing heat over my body. Oh no. Not again.

Bright light illuminates the world around us, blocking out everything else. I'm submerged again in the compassion, the love. I struggle to keep my focus, but then images fill my head—the guy's life unfolding there.

Paul Rockland is in his forties, with graying black hair and a suggestive smile. But it fades from his face as I stare back into his brown eyes. I make a small sound, unable to fight off the desire to speak to him.

"Paul," I say breathlessly.

"It's you," he murmurs, sounding both frightened and relieved.

Paul's in town to evict the single mother who complained about his property being infested with cockroaches. With filth. Paul knows his building is uninhabitable, but he doesn't want to spend the money to fix it. Instead he's going to threaten her and her children until she leaves. He'll keep her deposit, making it impossible for her to get another place. I see all of this, and the lines of his face deepen as he cowers under my stare.

"Don't do this," I whisper, sad at how he's forgotten his own childhood. The force inside of me pushes my words forward, even if I'm not entirely sure what they mean. "You won't be able to turn back," I say. "Not if you go down this path. Remember where you came from."

When Paul was a boy, he took care of his mother, a woman unable to hold a steady job. She was illiterate because of a learning disability and it left her easy prey in their seedy neighborhood. Paul worked two jobs under the table to pay rent, rent that was raised unjustly. And when they couldn't pay, the man asked for a trade. With nowhere else to go, Paul's mother agreed and walked to the back bedroom, leaving Paul in the hallway, crying and punching the wall. He couldn't bear his mother being degraded, but he felt helpless to stop it.

At fourteen years old, Paul nearly killed that man. But he didn't. A light came into his life at the right moment, with the right message. He sees that same sort of light in me now, and his shame is almost too much for him to bear.

"I'm sorry," he says, starting to cry. He thinks of his mother, how her death several years ago has turned him bitter. Angry. He has so much regret.

I put my hand on his arm, comforting him when he needs it most. Letting him know that he always has a choice. That this is his second chance. And then I tell him to go home.

When I step back from Paul, it breaks our bond—the light gone from around us. His friends are there, although their voices are barely registering in my ears. Paul wipes his face, looking purposefully toward his car, as if about to leave. But I'm the one who is stunned.

I try to move away but stumble—catching myself with my hand on the siding of Santo's. The warmth is fading from my body, replaced with anxious energy.

That definitely happened. There's no way that was only in my head. Frightened, I move past the men into the restaurant.

CHAPTER 7

When I rush into Santo's, I find the room frozen. The hostess is in her checkered dress, holding a menu. A customer has his hand raised to get a server's attention. Even a glass of soda, half over the edge and about to spill, is motionless.

I gasp, and then the scene slips away entirely as I'm flooded with a memory.

I'm lying in bed, his arms wrapped around me from behind. He's half-asleep but still murmuring in my ear, his breath tickling my skin.

"Let's run away together," he whispers. "Let's run far away and never come back."

I smile, my love for him so strong that it almost hurts. "You always say that," I say, intertwining my fingers with his as I pull him tighter around me. "And I always say yes. Yes, just so long as I'm with you."

The memory stops suddenly and reality hits me. I cry out, startled, and the frozen world snaps back to life: the hostess drops her stack of menus, the customer waves his hand, the soda spills—prompting a shout from the woman across the table. And then everyone turns to me as I stand in the doorway, trembling.

"Elise," Abe calls, jogging from behind the counter. He looks concerned, but I'm speechless, darting my gaze around the room. When Abe comes to stand in front of me, he reaches out. "Are you—"

"What's happening to me?" I murmur as tears spring to my eyes. Before he can touch me, I rush past him toward the back.

Panic, thick and suffocating, rages over me as I lock myself in the employee bathroom. I rest my hands on either side of the pedestal sink, crying softly. That memory—my memory—has left me absolutely heartbroken. I feel shattered, as if pieces of me are scattered about, no longer able to fit together.

"Elise," Abe says softly on the other side of the door. "Are you okay? Do you want me to call your dad or something?"

"No," I say automatically. The last thing I need is for my father to get a call from a stranger about his daughter losing it at work. I squeeze my eyes shut one more time, willing away the images of Paul's life. The feeling of being in love. Those aren't my thoughts; those aren't my memories.

I straighten then, looking in the mirror. My eyes are

red-rimmed, and I splash cold water on my face, pulling myself together. Something is happening to me, something unnatural. I know I can tell my father, think I should, but at the same time—the idea terrifies me. I don't know what I'd do if he didn't believe me.

I have to try to figure this out on my own. Or at least try to. But I can't do that locked in the bathroom of a Mexican restaurant.

"Not to sound insensitive," Abe says, his voice echoing off the door as if he's leaning against it, "but Santo is probably going to hassle you for the outburst. And you're sort of late for work now. Is there—"

I open the door, and Abe nearly falls in, catching himself at the last second. He's pale as if stricken with worry.

"Sorry," I say, trying to sound normal. "I'm obviously off my meds."

He laughs, looking unsure of my stability. "Yeah, well," he says. "Maybe counseling would be a good next step."

I move past him, careful not to meet his eyes, not to give away my fear. I go to the time clock, punching my card. But as I hang it back up, I feel Abe's hand slide onto my shoulder.

"If you need to freak out about something," he whispers, "I totally understand. But you should try to keep it together today. I don't want you to get fired."

I close my eyes, his smooth voice setting me at ease. His hand steady on my shoulder, holding me still. He's right. I don't want to get fired.

Abe smiles when I look at him. "Better?" he asks, studying

my expression. When I nod, he brushes the backs of his fingers gently over my jaw. "Good."

And then he turns and leaves the kitchen.

As I start my shift, I find that my panic has settled into a soft dread—something manageable. And it seems that work helps to keep my mind focused, almost as if I'm able to forget about earlier by acting normal. Acting as if it never happened.

I avoid a lecture from Santo, sneaking past his office to meet Abe out on the floor. It's nice to be able to throw myself into work, even if I'm still following Abe as part of the training. But he lets me take the orders, standing at my side like my own personal Mexican food encyclopedia. He interjects only when I really mess up my pronunciation. I've taken to just pointing at various things on the menu, but Abe is hip to my game and makes me try to sound them out.

"There is nothing difficult about the word *albondigas*. Say it with me, Elise." He squeezes my mouth and moves it in tandem with the syllables. *"Al-bon-di-gas."* I make the attempt, but then forget immediately when I'm at the next table telling them our soup of the day.

We dive into the shift, the evening passing quickly as Abe explains how to garnish a plate, how to act offended when customers order a cheeseburger. Santo's is especially busy, and Abe tells me it's never been this crowded. He says they must be here for me.

The job is fun, though. With so many customers it's all

a blur of smiles and half-filled iced tea pitchers. Between tables Abe's got me cracking up, introducing me with a different name to each patron. I was Doris, Consuela, and even Godzilla—which he told them was my nickname. I think he was taking a shot at my five-eight height, but he says he wasn't. Either way, I was a little annoyed after that one so he went back to calling me Elise.

I'm pouring myself a cup of coffee in the kitchen when Abe comes up, smirking. "How will you ever sleep tonight?"

"I still have an hour here," I say, glancing at the clock to see it's almost nine. "And besides, I haven't been sleeping all that well."

"You're the hardest-working woman in the restaurant business." He takes a packet of sugar and hands it over to me, leaning against the food counter while I stir in the sweetener. "Do you like it here?" he asks offhandedly, examining his fingernails.

"It's the best job I've ever had. It's also the only job I've ever had, so it doesn't have much to compete with. But I do like it. For the most part."

Abe looks up as if he's surprised by my answer. "No, not at Santo's. I mean—"

"Elise," Santo calls from the kitchen, his voice having its usual gruff edge. I worry that I'm in trouble as I head back there. Abe follows, and I find Santo at the grill, flipping strips of chicken and green peppers. When he notices me, he wipes his hands on the white towel he has thrown over his shoulder.

"Go ahead and take off," he says with a head nod toward the front door. My stomach drops.

"I'm fired?"

Abe laughs from behind me, and Santo shakes his head. "What? No. I just don't need you anymore tonight." He pauses, as if he doesn't want to say the next part. "Nice work out there." He pours oil on the grill, drowning out the sound of my thank-you with a sizzle.

I go to grab my purse, untying my apron as Abe snorts. "What?" I ask. I can't help but smile, a little embarrassed about my exchange with Santo.

"Nothing," Abe says. "I just think it's funny that when your boss tells you that you can take off, your first instinct is to think you're fired."

"Maybe I'm not all that confident in my server skills yet."

"I understand that. You're awful at it."

"Hey!" I laugh, slapping his shoulder. He doesn't apologize, but motions toward the kitchen.

"I'll be right back," he says. "Wait for me?"

I agree, and lean against the wall, facing the dining room. There are only two tables, and Margie's able to handle them both with ease. I think about Paul, about the terrible things he's gone through, the terrible things he planned to do. I just wish I knew *how* I could see those things.

"All right, let's go," Abe says, startling me as he walks up.

"Go? Where?"

"You have some time before you have to be home, right? Let me buy you dinner."

"Who's open this late besides us?"

He grins. "You'll see."

A Slim Jim, a Coke, and a pack of yellow cupcakes hit the spot as we sit on the bumper of Lucy's car in the 7-Eleven parking lot. Abe is eating a nasty-looking hot dog that he plucked from the heat rollers in the glass cabinet, but I passed.

"Tell me about yourself, Elise," Abe says between bites. "I must admit that I am fascinated."

I brush my hair behind my ear in a nervous movement. "And why is that?"

Abe takes another bite before answering. "You're gorgeous. Innocent. And yet"—he points his finger—"there is something very unusual about you."

"You mean strange?"

"No," Abe says seriously. "I mean fascinating." I'm not sure how to respond, but I don't have to because Abe stands, crumpling up his napkin as he finishes off his hot dog. He tosses the wrapper in the trash before wandering back over.

"I'm close with my family," I say, answering his earlier question. "My father does a lot of work for the church, so Lucy and I spent most of our childhood there. But now he lets us decide for ourselves when and if we want to go."

Abe eases down next to me. "He sounds like a very practical man."

"He's great," I say, fully aware that talking about my *dad* might be lame. "And when we left Colorado last month, I wasn't sure if I'd ever make another friend again."

"But then I came into your life. Sounds like fate to me."

I turn, but find I can't hold Abe's dark gaze. When I look away, he chuckles.

"And now that I've properly humiliated myself with my constant flirtation," he adds, "I'll say good night, and hope that tomorrow night we can have dinner again. In seats, maybe?"

"Like a date?" My heartbeat quickens.

"Like dinner." He turns to leave, sliding his hands into the pockets of his work pants as he begins to whistle. I'd offered him a ride home, but he said he preferred to walk. And once he's gone, I bite off a piece of jerky, thinking about tomorrow.

Lucy is going to be so proud.

A loud rumble cuts through the cooling night air, and I look up to see a motorcycle pull into the 7-Eleven. My heart skips a beat when I recognize the rider, and I set the beef jerky aside.

He notices me and comes to park next to my car, cutting the engine. The silence is thick around us when he does. "Hi," he says, like he's surprised to see me here. He takes off his helmet, hanging it on the handle bar. "Late-night fix?" He grins and motions to the cupcake wrapper.

"If I see another taco I just might poke my eyes out," I respond, standing and smoothing down my shirt. "So I thought this was a good alternative."

The guy nods politely, then glances back at the store. "I should, uh—" He points toward the door, as if asking my permission to leave.

"Of course," I say. "You know, you should come by the restaurant again one day. Maybe this time I'll be the one to bring your soda."

"I sure hope so," he says. "Your coworker was highly efficient, but not nearly as distracting. You might have some competition for employee of the month."

"Well, as long as you're rooting for me."

"I definitely am," he murmurs, watching me as I walk around the car to get in. I'm glad he didn't mention the fact that my sister nearly ran him down earlier.

"When do you work next?" he asks suddenly. I look over my shoulder.

"Tomorrow."

"Then I'll see you tomorrow."

He's so calm and collected—confident in a way I've never seen. It's like I could tell him anything. I decide to start with my name. "I'm Elise, by the way," I offer. "Since you never asked."

He winces as if he's shocked by his own behavior. "That was awfully rude of me," he says, his voice tender. He takes a step closer, the lights of the store showering his face in a soft glow. I'm once again stunned by how handsome he is. "It's nice to meet you, Elise," he says, a slow, sexy smile pulling at his lips. "I'm Harlin."

CHAPTER 3

When Harlin goes inside the convenience store, I leave for home—the dread returning. In just a matter of days, my life has begun to spiral out of control. Hallucinations, memories . . . visions. On top of that, my sister is disappearing all the time, my dad is overworked and worried, and I have a sort of date with Abe tomorrow.

And of course, now there's Harlin.

When I pull up to my house, the front door opens. Lucy bounds toward me as I park the car. She's dressed in all black except for the light reflecting off her eyebrow ring.

"You're late," she says, reaching out her hand for the keys. "Thought you'd be home a half hour ago, but thank God for small favors, right?" She climbs into the driver's seat, cringing as she does. She raises her eyes to meet mine. "Stupid lady parts," she says.

"Wait, what about Dad?" I ask, checking the time on my phone.

"I'll be back before then."

Our father does a midnight service on Wednesdays at his church. A lot of his parishioners can't make it in the morning or on the weekends because of their jobs, so he started this to accommodate them. It's been a big hit, but I know he worries about us when he's gone. I hope he doesn't call to ask about Lucy.

"If you hear from him, just tell him I'm in the shower. Then text me and I'll call him." She slides a CD into the stereo, cranking it up.

"Lucy—"

"Don't worry," she says over the loud music. "It's going to be fine." Her expression falters for a second, but she recovers to smile at me. "Promise."

I watch my sister back out of the driveway and then I go inside, opting to spend the next few hours researching the web for out-of-body experiences. I turn up little to explain what's happening to me. I think back on Diego, on Paul—they were surrounded in some kind of light.

There's nothing online about bright lights other than near-death experiences—and I'm pretty sure I didn't die. Or at least I hope not. I end up spending a half hour looking up past lives. It feels wrong, especially since my father is a pastor. Still, the idea is fascinating—the thought that a soul can return—sometimes with flashes of memories. The more I read, the more plausible it seems.

As I sit at the kitchen table, I rub my eyes. Seriously, Elise. Past lives?

I push back in my chair and click off the computer. I decide to get some rest, hoping it'll help clear the fog in my head, maybe help me come up with better answers. As I lie in bed, I hear my sister's car return, the engine idling a long minute before the front door opens.

I sit up, glancing toward the hall. I want to ask her what's going on—*really* going on—on these late-night rendezvous. My sister may date a lot, but she's not completely irresponsible. She doesn't drink or sleep around. At least she never used to.

My feet touch the cool floor as I stand, but just then I hear the shower turn on. I sit back on the edge of my bed, debating whether or not to knock. It's nearly twelve thirty and I know my dad will be home any second, so I decide that now might not be the best time to start an intervention. I prop myself up on the pillow, my eyelids getting heavier with each blink. And then they close altogether and I drift off.

I'm standing on a sidewalk in London, the street bustling around me. People walk past, not seeing me, and I realize I'm in a vision—but it's not my own. I see the woman from the rooftop and remember her—Onika. She's strolling past, beautiful as ever. Her wrist is looped through the arm of a handsome young guy. He's distinguished looking—blond hair, tan sports coat, and loafers. They look absolutely in love.

I wonder what happened to her since her time with Rodney, when he turned her skin gray. He welcomed her to the Shadows, but I don't understand what that means. She seems fine now, content. Just then, Onika flinches and darts a look toward the bus-stop bench.

I follow her line of sight, spotting the man sitting there, his hair a mess, his clothes wrinkled. Onika's eyes narrow on him as she passes, her teeth gritted as if she's fighting back a pain.

My heart skips a beat when I see a fine crack appear in her skin, racing over her cheek. She reaches up to touch it, shooting an alarmed glance at her boyfriend. But he doesn't notice. He's talking and holding her as if all is well.

"Give me a minute, lover," she says to him, her voice silky and warm. She untangles herself, turning quickly before he can see her face. Her hair flutters in the wind as she spins, walking back to where the man sits at the bus stop.

Her boyfriend stays where she left him, staring into a store window at the jewelry, his mouth pulled into a soft smile. Onika's boots clack on the pavement until she reaches the man on the bench. She slides in next to him, tilting her head in his direction.

"Poor, sweet Charles," she whispers, drawing his gaze. "I'm so sorry to hear about your wife."

A flash of pain crosses the man's face. "Who are you?" he asks.

"Shh . . ." She puts a gloved finger to his lips. "I am no one. But you, darling," she murmurs, fresh cracks rippling through her flesh. "You should go home, find the gun that's hidden on the upper shelf of your closet. And then, Charles, you should teach that wife of yours a lesson, yes?"

"Yes."

"That's right. You'll show her. You'll show them all."

"I'll show them all," he repeats, a sense of bravery in his voice.

Onika smiles, inhaling deeply as if relieved. And then her face is beautiful once again, flawless. And when the man on the bench gets up, rushing away, Onika stands and goes back to meet her love on the sidewalk.

I wake up with a start, the dream staying with me—or at least partly. The woman, Onika, is a haunting vision. And like my memories of a life that's not mine, she feels real. As if she's not just a figment of my imagination.

Unsettled, I wander out to the kitchen to get some juice and find my father sitting at the kitchen table, sorting through a stack of papers. When he sees me stumbling half-asleep from the hallway, he offers a weary smile. "Hey, kid. How was the doctor's?"

"Vitamin deficiency," I offer, the ridiculousness of the diagnosis clear now. I pour a glass of orange juice and sit next to my dad, peeking over at his papers. "What have you got there?" I ask, pushing one aside to see a black-and-white photo underneath. "Who's this?"

My father picks it up, studying it closely. "This girl," he says. "She disappeared a while ago, the daughter of a member of the church."

"A missing person?"

"Maybe. I've had this picture on my desk since the day I started, her mother asking me to say prayers that she'll return."

"That's so tragic," I murmur. She can't be more than fifteen. When he's quiet for a long moment, I lower my eyes. "Dad," I ask. "Do you believe in past lives?"

"No. Why do you ask?"

"Just thinking about it. If it's possible."

"That doesn't really go along with our faith, Elise." He pauses. "But I suppose there are other views out there—who's to say what's right anymore?"

Surprised by his answer, I turn to my dad to find his eyes welling up as he looks over the picture of the missing girl. His heart breaks for this family he hardly knows, always putting the problems of others above his own. I lean to put my head on his shoulder.

"I love you," I say.

"Is that a real 'I love you'?" he asks. "Or an 'I want something' 'I love you'?"

"The real one."

"Then I love you, too, kid."

When I straighten, he sets down the picture of the girl, sniffling back what was the start of tears. I decide then not to tell him about my encounter with Paul or the memory of being in bed with a boy I couldn't see. I don't even tell him about the dream of a woman with a broken face. Even though I've always been honest with my father, I'm afraid that these episodes will only worry him more—taking him away from others who need him. And I don't think I can be that selfish.

It occurs to me then to ask someone who may have a better idea of what is going on, even though I'd have to be absolutely out of my mind to follow through. But something happened the other night. I felt it. She felt it too. So I decide that in the morning, I'm going to track down the old lady from the parking lot.

And hope she doesn't really want to gobble me up.

My Thursday shift at Santo's ends at seven, long enough to take the brunt of the dinner crowd but early enough to avoid the late-night stragglers. Harlin never materializes, which sort of hurts. But then I remind myself that he's practically a stranger and I have much bigger things to worry about.

I'm distracted as I think about the old psychic. During a lull in customers, I corner Mario behind the counter and ask him if he knows of a woman who hangs out in the parking lot. He scratches his neck where his tattoos poke out from the collar of his uniform shirt and stares blankly at me.

When Margie walks by, I ask her and she says the only psychic in town is Madame Marceline. She lives on Mission Boulevard and is, as Margie puts it, "bat-shit crazy." I thank her, and plan to find the woman in the morning.

Abe's been silent through most of the shift—which is totally unlike him. He hasn't even mentioned the fact that he asked me to dinner. I think he's changed his mind.

I'm a bit deflated by the time I punch my timecard at 7:05, and take out my phone to call my house. If I'm going to be stuck there, dinnerless, I should at least bring some burritos with me.

On the third ring Lucy picks up. "What?" she says, her voice low and irritated.

"Hey," I respond, furrowing my brow. "It's me. It's Elise."

"Oh, sorry. Hi." She doesn't go on, and across the room Abe walks in, eyeing me curiously.

"I just got done with work," I tell Lucy, "and I was checking to see if you wanted me to bring home food?"

"Naw. Dad made mac 'n' cheese."

"Ew."

"Exactly." She makes a soft groan off-line.

"Are you still having pain?" I ask. "Lucy, this isn't normal. I'm going to tell Dad."

"Please don't," she says. "Just stay out of it, Elise."

"Out of what? And no, I won't stay out of anything. In case you've forgotten, ignoring medical problems doesn't exactly make them go away."

My sister is quiet, and I feel my eyes begin to tear up. It wasn't right of me to bring up our mother like that. But I'm scared and worried. I'm not sure what else will get through to her.

"I'll talk to the doctor," she says quietly. "Will that make you happy, tyrant?"

I smile. "Yes."

There's a rustling on her end like the phone is being shifted. "I'm glad," she says sarcastically, sounding like herself again. "I'll see you when you get home."

We say good-bye, and the minute I slide my phone into my pocket, Abe comes to lean against the wall in front of me. "Trying to get out of dinner?" he asks with a slight edge to his voice.

"I thought maybe you changed your mind."

"Never."

I like how seriously he says it, as if it's impossible. And right now, it just feels good to be wanted—especially with all the uncertainty around me. All the worry and fear. Abe's interest in me seems unwavering.

I wait quietly while he counts his money, checking out with the hostess. My mind swirls with all the different possibilities for dinner—not that Thistle has much to choose from. I even wonder if it'll be romantic. And I wonder if I want it to be.

Abe meets me by the exit, a devious smile on his lips. "I'm an amazing date," he says.

My stomach flips. "Thought you said this was just dinner?"

Abe opens the glass door and holds it for me. As I pass by him, he lowers his head so that his voice is close to my ear. "It's never just dinner."

And then we walk outside.

CHAPTER 9

When we get into the parking lot, the sky is brighter than it has been in weeks. I can actually see stars. I'm standing there, looking up, when Abe comes over to pluck the keys from my hand. "I'll drive," he answers.

"But—"

"This is a little out of the way, so you're just going to have to trust me, Elise." He walks around to open the passenger side first. "Sort of exciting, right?" he asks.

My heart races, nervousness churning in my stomach. This is an adventure, a new experience. I'm not one to take risks, but with Abe I almost have to. He's so tempting.

Once inside the car, Abe adjusts the seat and pulls out a CD from his backpack before inserting it into the stereo. "If it'll calm your nerves," he says offhandedly as he turns up the heavy blues music, a rumbling voice rolling out of the speakers. "I won't ruin you, Elise. I know how innocent you are."

"*Ruin?* Well, glad to hear it," I respond, smiling at his choice of words. "That would probably make for an awkward silence later."

Abe turns, his dark eyes raking slowly over me until they stare back seductively into mine. "Or maybe I'll ruin you just a little," he whispers.

I hold his gaze for a second before facing the window, the parking lot outside slowly emptying of cars. Although Abe didn't touch me, I'm covered in goose bumps—feeling vulnerable. Exposed. But I'm also drawn to him, and slowly look at him again, almost like I can't help it. He smiles and then backs out of Santo's lot.

The stores on Main Street are closed as we drive past, the town sleepy and empty ahead of us. I think about the old woman, and how I still have to find her. Abe begins to accelerate and I notice he's merged onto the freeway.

I lower the stereo. "Where exactly are you bringing me?"

"You get one hint," he says. "It involves fire."

"Fire?"

"Yep."

"Okay," I laugh. "Now I'm scared."

Abe turns the music back up, the bass vibrating in my bones. "You should be."

* * *

It's nearly thirty minutes later when we pull onto a sandy street in the middle of the desert. And I mean the middle of the freaking desert—only cactus and hills of sand surrounding us.

"Abe," I say, my voice a little strained. "Where are we going? For real."

"I need a place to bury your body, right?"

My expression falters and Abe looks at me, his eyes hidden in the shadows of the night. Then he chuckles. "Dear God, Elise. Get a sense of humor."

But it's like I suddenly realize how alone we are, as if waking from a dream only to realize I've wandered onto the ledge of a building. The only light outside of the car is from the headlights, and I'm scared. I tell him so.

"Aw, you're making me feel bad," Abe says sincerely. "I was kidding around about murdering you. We're hanging out at a campsite. See the fire over that hill?"

Sure enough, I see a flickering light just over the next mound of sand. My tension releases slightly, and as we get closer, I notice a Jeep and another car pulled to the side.

"Camping?" I ask, feeling ridiculous for being so paranoid. I watch as the glow from the fire fills the car, illuminating Abe's face in soft amber. He's so handsome, so inviting.

And yet my heart tells me that something is off—like that anxiety you get when you're not sure if you've locked the front door. Or maybe it's guilt. Although I can't think of a reason to be sorry for being out with Abe. It's not like I have a boyfriend waiting by the phone for me to call.

Abe reaches to take my hand, as if reading the hesitance in my expression. "It's not a sleepover, Elise. I just wanted to introduce you to some of my friends. Cook some burgers. It's all innocent. I swear."

My worry fades. I'm flattered that Abe wants me to meet his friends. As if he's proud to show me off. His skin is warm on mine. "I hope these burgers are better than what they have to offer at 7-Eleven," I say, trying not to sound nearly as nervous as I feel.

"Doubtful." Abe takes his hand from mine to undo his seat belt. He looks past me to where the party is. "But we should head over. I wouldn't want you to miss your curfew. Not on our first night."

He gets out, walking ahead to where the people are. When they see him, a few jump up—girls hug him, guys slap his hand. Abe has that way about him, attracting people without even seeming to try. Maybe that's what's worrying me, the idea that Abe is so much more experienced than I am.

I push back the anxiety that continues to linger, and open the passenger door to cross the sand. The night has cooled considerably, but as I get closer, the flames from the huge fire lick out toward me. The heat is divine on my skin.

"There she is," Abe announces, as if he was just talking about me.

"Hey, Elise," a cute guy with a pierced lip calls from where he's sitting on a canvas folding chair.

"Oh," I answer, surprised he knows my name. "Hi."

"That's Craig," Abe says, coming to stand next to me. He leans against my shoulder but doesn't put his arm around me. Instead he points out a stunning redhead. "This is Marissa. She's feisty, so watch out for her."

Not sure how to respond to that, I just say hi and she does the same.

"Bridget," he continues, moving down the line. "Of course, Molly." Molly has short brown hair, kind of like Lucy's, and she giggles the minute Abe says her name.

The girls are practically drooling over him. This is going to be so awkward.

I meet Fernando, Johnny, and Pete, but before the introductions go on too long, Abe finds me a seat on the far end of the half circle. I've barely sat down when Marissa calls to Abe, using her finger to invite him over. Abe touches my shoulder as he passes, saying he'll be right back.

"Drink?" Fernando asks me, motioning toward the cooler.

"No, but thank you." I'm still watching Abe. And I know it's stupid, but I'm a tiny bit jealous. This is supposed to be my date, not a visit to the Abe fan club.

Craig is readying the hibachi with charcoal when I catch Abe close to Marissa, whispering something in her ear. She closes her eyes, leaning into him, and a sinking sensation fills my chest. Just then Abe notices the insecurity on my face.

He stands, Marissa's hands falling from his shoulder. He ignores her when she calls his name and he crosses the space between us, stepping right over the fire as he heads toward me. My heart speeds up.

"Sorry," he says simply, and drops down in the sand next to my chair. "Had to tie up some loose ends." He looks sideways at me, waiting for my reaction.

"I'm sure," I mumble, surprising myself with how bitter I sound. But I'm not going to let Abe humiliate me. I don't care how cute he is.

He lets out a low whistle. "Wow. That shoulder is cold, Elise," he whispers, glancing past me. "I wasn't flirting, if that's what you think."

"I didn't—" My breath catches as Abe reaches over me, his arm across my waist as he opens the cooler to pull out a can.

"Excuse me," he murmurs.

His touch sends my pulse racing once again, and I don't feel insecure anymore. Instead, I'm smiling. "You could have asked me to get that for you," I say.

"I know." Abe pops the top on the soda and takes a drink.

When the charcoal is ready, Abe moves to help me grill my hamburger, burning the outside for what he claims is "maximum flavor." At one point he even brushes his lips over my ear when leaning in to talk to me. I'm so comfortable with him. I can't believe I haven't known him all my life.

About an hour after we arrive, his friends are a little drunk. Abe and I are roasting marshmallows, quiet and close as he sits at my feet in the sand. I listen to their stories about setting a fire in Santo's back room in an unfortunate silverware-in-the-microwave incident. Abe launches into one about an ex-server who was caught hooking up in the walk-in freezer, and soon I'm laughing so hard I can barely hold on to my marshmallow stick.

"He wasn't always so cool, you know?" Marissa calls out to me suddenly.

"What's that?" I ask, still chuckling a little bit.

Her face tightens in the orange glow of the fire. "Abe," she goes on. "He wasn't always like this. He used to be quiet." She meets his eyes. "Not nearly as sexy."

Next to me, Abe is sliding sand away from his sneaker, silent.

"Uh . . . okay," I answer. I'm not exactly sure what reaction she expects from me, but I want to defend Abe. He's been nothing but nice to me, no matter what he's done in the past.

"In fact," Marissa says, her voice beginning to drip with contempt, "Abe used to be in love with me. But I wouldn't give him the time of day."

"Give it a rest, Marissa," Craig says from next to her, taking a sip from his drink. But Marissa's watching Abe, a story obviously under the surface. I hate that he's silent in return, as if she's demeaning him somehow. I want to punch her for that.

"Things have obviously changed since then," I say seriously. "As far as I can tell, you're the one in love now."

Her eyes snap to mine, and from next to me I hear Abe snort back a laugh.

"It would seem that way," she says. "The question is, why?"

"Be quiet now," Abe murmurs. I wonder if he broke her heart and if that's why she's lashing out now.

Marissa's eyes blaze, but she falls silent, opting to watch the fire instead. Craig changes the subject, something about Margie once coming on to him when Santo was out of town.

The party goes on for another hour, the laughs slowly coming back. Abe does a dead-on impression of Santo, and it's hilarious to hear about Molly's new job at a local breakfast place. Turns out they're all servers somewhere.

Marissa doesn't participate in any of the stories, and she avoids any conversation with Abe altogether. She won't even look at him. This entire night would be uncomfortable, it should be, but I'm wrapped up in the moment. It's the first time since Colorado that I feel like I have friends.

Next to me Abe yawns, lifting his arms over his head before resting one casually across my lap. He bends his head closer. "We should go," he says. "It's late."

I nod, checking the time. If we leave now, I'll still make curfew. Abe gets up and says good-bye to his friends. Across the fire Marissa sits motionless, not acknowledging any of us.

I try not to stare at her as I say good-bye to the rest of the party, but her eyes have glazed over, the lower lids brimming with tears. Sorrow fills me, and I take a step toward her before Abe takes my hand, pulling me in the other direction.

We walk back to the car, the desert air getting crisp the

farther away from the fire we get. "Did you have fun?" Abe asks, opening the door for me.

"I really did. Maybe next time I'll actually camp?"

"Intriguing thought."

I catch something out of the corner of my eye and turn to see Marissa standing on the hill, the light from the fire illuminating her from behind. Her arms hang at her sides and her shoulders are slumped. She looks absolutely desperate.

"Elise," Abe says, smiling softly at me. "I'm gonna go say good-bye."

"Sure."

He leaves, walking toward Marissa as she moves to meet him halfway. I open the passenger door and get in, closing it quietly. My window is still down from the drive up and I can hear them talking. I feel like I'm spying.

"That wasn't very nice of you, Riss," Abe says, reaching to brush her red hair behind her ear. "I thought we were past all this."

"I'm sorry," she answers automatically, without reacting to his touch.

"I know you are." He leans forward and kisses her forehead, pausing there a long moment. When he pulls back, Marissa grabs his forearms as if trying to keep him close.

"You don't need me anymore, do you?" she asks, her voice choked off.

"You were out of control tonight," he says quietly. "It hurt my feelings."

Marissa doesn't respond. The whole conversation is surreal and I have no idea what's going on. They must have had a romance gone tragically wrong. I don't want to be in the middle of something like this.

"Be careful of the cliff beyond the tents," Abe tells Marissa. "It's a nasty fall to the bottom. Don't go wandering off by yourself, okay?"

Marissa is frozen, and at first I'm not even sure she heard him. But then she nods slowly, before leaving to walk silently up the hill back to the party.

Abe seems rejuvenated when he gets in next to me, the interior light illuminating him. "Marissa's not a fan," he says. "But she wanted me to tell you good-bye."

She didn't say that, but I don't want to admit that I was listening. "She seems pleasant," I respond. "Ex-girlfriend?"

"Sort of. But she hates me now, in case that wasn't obvious."

"Oh, it was."

Abe chuckles, doing a three-point turn to get the car turned around to head back toward town. When we're moving, he reaches to brush his fingers down my arm, over the place where my scratches are now fading. "As long as you don't hate me, Elise," he whispers. "The rest of them can go to hell."

My eyelids flutter and I'm suddenly tired, completely drained as if I've been working all night. I lean my head back against the seat, Abe's hand slowly caressing my skin. Comforting me as I drift into a light sleep. We're not far when a high-pitched howl breaks in the distance. Startled, I sit up,

Abe's hand falling from me. I try to see out the window but it's too dark.

"Coyotes," Abe says, clicking on the radio. "They come out late at night around here. Lots of vicious things do."

The car's headlights cut through the desert night, and ahead of us the world is blank. A film reel of desert playing over and over. I see Abe's fingers twitch as if he means to reach for me again, but instead he adjusts the volume and puts his hands on the steering wheel.

I lean back into the seat, staring straight ahead as a voice nags at me. Because although I'm tired, I hear words in the back of my mind—even though I'm sure I never heard them said out loud.

Jump off the cliff.

CHAPTER 10

Abe touches my shoulder to wake me up when we finally arrive at my house. We're parked in my driveway and it's only ten thirty, a half hour early for my curfew.

"Thanks for taking me out, Abraham," I say, my voice a little sleepy. "Who would have thought you were such a gentleman?"

He scowls. "Don't use my full name. And I am a gentleman. Or at least I am to you." He pauses. "Right?"

"You are indeed charming." I unbuckle my seat belt, grabbing my purse from the floor as he shuts off the engine.

"Which is impressive. I'm usually bored with girls after one day."

I laugh. "I must be special."

"You have no idea," he murmurs. "Can I walk you to your door?"

My house is dark other than the front porch light as Abe and I move toward it silently. I wonder if my dad is already asleep or if he's waiting for me on the couch. I just hope he's not peeking out the window.

When we stop, Abe puts his arms around my waist, holding me close to him as he looks down at me. As tall as I feel, he's taller and I have to tip my head back to see his face. His eyes are dark and deep.

"I should go," he says, but doesn't pull away.

"Probably." I'm suddenly hyperconscious of Abe against me, the way his fingers are intertwined behind my back. My heart thumps and I'm not sure if it's from nervousness or desire.

A slow smile spreads across Abe's face. "Can I kiss you good night?" he asks.

I swallow hard, thinking back to Marissa. The contempt in her eyes from across the fire. The pathetic way she came after him later. I don't want that to be me. "Abe," I start. "I don't think so. I don't want us to end up hating each other."

"You could never hate me."

"Crazier things have happened."

He seems to consider this, but then moves to rest his palm on my neck, a tender spot just under my jaw. "We could just try it," he whispers. "If it doesn't feel good we could stop."

My stomach flutters at the thought. "Chances are, it will feel great. That's not what I'm worried about."

"Then you worry too much."

I'm about to tell him that he sounds like a trashy-romance-novel hero when he leans down and brings his mouth right to the corner of mine, but not touching me. "Can I kiss you now?"

"I . . ." His breath is warm across my lips, his thumb gently stroking my jaw. But when I close my eyes, there is only panic and guilt. "I can't."

Abe sighs, sounding disappointed, but not angry. "You'll change your mind," he says, quickly kissing my cheek before letting me go. It takes me a minute to gather myself, my body still humming with adrenaline.

Abe backs away, holding up his hand to say good-bye. "Have a nice evening, Elise," he calls. "Told you I wouldn't ruin you yet." And with that, he turns to leave.

I watch after him, not sure why I didn't kiss him. He's certainly cute enough. Sweet. Charming. But at the same time, I couldn't bring myself to do it. Maybe everyone's right. Maybe I do need therapy.

I go inside, and my dad and Lucy are asleep, the house still as I crawl into bed. I think about Madame Marceline. I'll find her tomorrow. I'll ask her exactly what's going on with me. I just hope she has an answer.

Above me the rhythmic ticking of my ceiling fan begins to lull me to sleep. And when I close my eyes, the world slips away altogether.

* * *

I'm on the roof of a high-rise building again as rain falls all around me. My body glows in the dim light, but this time I know immediately that I'm in her vision. Onika sits on the ledge of the building, her feet dangling over. The rain doesn't touch her, but I can't see her face, can't see what's behind her curtain of blond hair. By the set of her shoulders I think that she's determined to jump. Will she?

The door opens and the man stalks out, his skin flawless, nothing like the cracked horror I'd seen last time. "Onika," he calls out, sounding like a disappointed father. "Enough with this temper tantrum."

She turns to glare at him fiercely. "You lied, Rodney. I can't keep him. I can't keep any of them."

"You'll find others."

"I don't want anyone else. You told me that if I loved him, if I loved him enough, that I could continue living. But he sees me, Rodney. He sees what you've made me become, the things I have to do now. I'm not escaping being Forgotten—not really. I'm only compelled in a different way."

"Onika," he responds as if he's tired of talking to her. "If you want your lover then whisper to him. Make him do what you want."

"No." She sounds horrified by the thought. "I want to keep him as he is," she says desperately. "You've ruined everything."

"It was *your* decision, my beauty. All I did was provide the temptation."

"You tricked me!"

"And if I did? What will you do now—jump off this building again? How many times must you do that before you realize that you're bound to the earth? There is no way out, not for us. The light doesn't want you, Onika. We made a choice."

"You *lied*!" she roars. "You said nothing would change."

"But it has. And you need to accept it." He pauses, disgust crossing his face. "Or just jump. I don't care."

Onika lets out a sad laugh, hinged with misery. Devastation. And then she leans forward and falls off the roof once again.

But as I watch, the only sound is my scream—forcing me awake.

It's morning and my head is foggy from a restless night's sleep, the image of the woman falling from the building still in my mind. When I walk into the kitchen I find my sister at the table, typing on her laptop. I swipe her hair when I pass behind, saying hello to my father as he flips through the newspaper across from her.

"Have you ever had a recurring nightmare?" I ask them, taking a spot between their chairs. My sister looks up quickly, seemingly taken aback by the question.

"Sure," my father says, folding the page in front of him. "I think I used to have one about drowning when I was a kid. And your sister used to have them after your mother died. Remember, Lucinda?"

"No, Doug," she responds, and goes back to typing. Her

curt response makes me wonder if her pain level is causing her increasingly moody behavior. And then I wonder if she's told my father about it yet.

"Don't get so upset," my father says, sounding surprised. "I was just pointing it out." He turns to me. "She used to wake me up with stories of a man with a broken face trying to push her off of a tower. You don't forget things like that when they're coming from your nine-year-old."

"Dad." My sister turns to him, closing her laptop. "I don't think my creepy childhood dreams are appropriate breakfast conversation. I'd almost rather hear about Elise's G-rated love life."

I pretend to be offended. "Actually," I say, "I had a date last night."

"What?" Lucy practically shouts. "Did you know about this?" she asks my father accusingly.

He nods, sipping from his coffee, looking proud that he knew something about a boy that she didn't.

"And would you like to know *who* I went out with last night?" I ask, taking a piece of toast off the plate in the center of the table.

"If you say Abe Weston I'm going to scream."

"It was Abe Weston."

My father covers his ears, but Lucy waves him off. "I'm just kidding," she says. "It's too early for screaming. So . . ." She turns to me. "Tell me *everything*."

"Well, he said he was taking me to dinner, but actually we

drove out to a campsite where his friends were hanging out."

"Drinking?" my father interrupts.

"No," I lie. But I wasn't drinking, so it should still count. "Anyway, it was fun. We had burgers, some marshmallows. He brought me home and even walked me to the door." I give my father a sidelong glance to emphasize the politeness of the gesture.

"And he kissed you," Lucy finishes for me.

"No, I chickened out. It was close, though."

"Wow," Lucy says. "That sounds romantic. Disappointing for Abe, I'm sure. But romantic for you. I'm going to bump your rating up to PG." She stands and winks at me. "I have to take a shower," she says. "Do you need a ride to work later?"

"Can I borrow the car instead?" I ask. "I have an errand to run first." My heart rate spikes as I think about Madame Marceline, and whether I'll be able to find her. And what I'll say when I do.

Lucy sighs. "Fine, but put gas in it this time." She pats the top of my head and then leaves. When she's gone, my father clears his throat.

"How are you feeling, kid?" he asks, taking off his glasses to set them in front of him. "The vitamins helping?"

"It's only been a day," I say. "Ask me again in a week." I look toward the bathroom, listening for the shower. When I hear it, I lean toward my dad. "Has Lucy talked to you about her cramps?"

"Cramps? Like menstrual?"

"I don't know," I say. "But she acts like they really hurt. She's having them every day, too. I don't think it's normal, but she told me to stay out of it."

My dad smiles. "Telling you to stay out of something is the same as telling you to get involved."

"Exactly. Cry for help, maybe?" I'm joking, but I am concerned. When my father says he'll make an appointment for her with the doctor, I thank him. I know Lucy might get mad that I told him, but she's going to have to deal with it. Secrets suck. Including the one I'm holding as I leave the kitchen table.

I'm going to drive down Mission Boulevard until I find Madame Marceline's house, and then I'm going to knock on her door and demand answers. And if that doesn't work—

I sway suddenly, catching myself on the wall of the hallway and banging my shin on a box. Before I can even acknowledge the pain, I'm flooded instead with a memory.

There is water rushing below as I stand on the railing of a bridge. The wind whips past me and I'm scared—so scared that I'll fall. Then he walks up, compassion in his eyes. And Monroe whispers, "Jump."

My legs give out and I fall onto the boxes, knocking some over. The crash echoes through the house and I hear my father's footsteps. "Elise?" he calls.

But the fear from the vision is still with me, making tears leak from my eyes. I've never been that afraid of anything before, and yet . . . it feels like me. It feels like I was the one standing on that railing, about to jump. And who is Monroe?

He looks like an older version of the guy Onika was with in my dreams. What's going on? The line between reality and my dreams is becoming blurred.

"Are you all right?" My father puts his hand on my elbow, helping me up. "I'm so sorry I haven't gotten these out of here. I'll move them to the garage."

"Banged my shin," I say to explain the crying. I wipe hard at my face, still shaking. I need to leave, to figure out what's happening.

"Let me—"

"I'm fine, Dad," I say quickly, backing away from him. It occurs to me how much I sound like Lucy right now. And I realize that if she's as bad off as me, she needs more help than I thought.

CHAPTER 11

I'm standing on the sidewalk facing a worn hand-painted sign that reads: MADAME MARCELINE'S FORTUNES. The house wasn't difficult to find, and the car ride had helped to clear my mind—at least to a functioning level. But as I stare ahead, anxiety twists through my stomach. Am I really going to do this? It seemed so much more rational on the way over.

I start up the walkway to the small, white block home, my heart beating fast. This is the same woman who tried to drag me out of my car two days ago. I'm not sure that I'm making the best life decision. At the same time, she acted as if she knew me, shared mental pictures of horrible things. Obviously we have some sort of connection. And although I don't believe in it—or at least I never used to—maybe she's an actual psychic.

The front door opens and I lower my head, not wanting to be noticed. What if they know my father? He'd be horrified to hear I came to a psychic and not him.

"Hey, you."

Startled, I look up, surprised to see Harlin starting down the walkway. He smiles, seeming thrilled to bump into me, but then he stops. "What—" He looks back at the building, pulling his eyebrows together. "What are you doing here?"

"I could ask you the same thing."

"Is it immature if I answer with *I asked you first*?"

I laugh. "Yes."

"I'm visiting an old friend," he says in his low voice. "How do you know Marceline?" His hazel eyes study me as if he'll be able to tell if I'm lying. So I opt not to.

"She attacked me," I say, as if it's not a big deal. "And I want to ask her why."

Harlin takes a step back, shaking his head. "What? She's like, *ninety*. She attacked you?"

I hold up my arm as proof, and I'm surprised when Harlin reaches out suddenly to take it, looking over the scratches. His hand on my skin sends a shot of electricity through my body, and he must feel it too, because he takes in a sharp breath.

Slowly he brings his gaze to mine, his lips slightly parted. As he looks at me, his expression softens. "I came to see you last night," he murmurs. "But you were already gone."

Butterflies flutter in my stomach. "You did? I thought

you forgot about me," I say.

"I'll never forget about you."

"Well, it's about time," a ragged voice cuts through the air. I jump, looking behind Harlin. On the front porch of the house is the crazy old lady, a big grin plastered across her face. "Harlin," the old woman says. "Stop harassing that poor thing and let her come inside."

"Do you know her, Marceline?" he asks, not looking back. He's watching me instead, his eyes searching my face. I can't believe he said he's friends with her. Who is this guy?

"I don't think we've been formally introduced," the woman says to him. "Now go away and let me talk to her."

I slowly take my arm from Harlin's grasp, his fingers sliding down my skin the entire way, reluctant to let me go. "I should . . ." I motion toward the house.

"Yeah," he says, sounding confused. "I'll see you around." He flexes his hand as if the electricity is still tingling. When he walks past me, his shoulder brushes mine.

"Bye," I murmur, and then slowly make my way up the path. When I get to the front step, I hear a motorcycle roar to life behind me. The old woman's eyes follow Harlin as he drives away, and then she focuses her attention on me.

Standing this close, I'm almost embarrassed that I was scared of her. She's small, fragile looking. Her white hair pokes out from under her knit cap. She smiles and her teeth are yellow and broken. But now she doesn't look so sinister.

"Let's get inside," she says, moving for the door—her silver bracelets jangling loudly. "Before your other boyfriend finds you here."

She goes in before I can tell her that I don't have any boyfriends, let alone two. Instead I just follow her into the dimly lit house.

Marceline's house is bathed in low amber lighting, pictures plastered all over the walls, covering nearly every inch. It's bizarre and comforting at the same time.

"Have a seat," she says, motioning to the tattered green sofa. "Don't worry." She sits across from me in a rocking chair. "I don't bite."

I cringe at the thought, and take a spot on the couch. The room smells slightly of peppermint as I try to keep my composure. I'm frightened, although no longer of her. I'm scared of what she has to say.

When we're silent for an uncomfortable amount of time, I clear my throat. "So," I begin. "You grabbed me the other night outside of Santo's."

She nods, sitting back in her chair, rocking slowly.

"Why?"

"I'm sorry about that," she says. "I didn't mean to hurt you. I was just overcome. I'm psychic, or at least that's what it says on the sign out front." I don't laugh, and she exhales as if I'm boring her. "I was just passing by, you see. But when I got a look at you"—she lowers her voice—"at what's inside of you, it was quite a shock to my system. As I'm sure you can imagine."

I feel the blood drain from my face. "What's inside of me?" I demand.

"You already know. You just can't remember." She leans forward, the rocking chair creaking, to grab a mint from a bowl in the center of the coffee table. The peppermints are old and nasty, and I'm thinking that's how she broke her teeth in the first place. Marceline pops one into her mouth.

"Now," she says. "What I'm going to tell you next will sound unbelievable. But you need to listen to your heart. You'll know I'm telling the truth."

"Okay . . ." My stomach is sick, my heart racing. I can't believe I'm sitting through this. The first time she asks me for money, I'm bolting. She's obviously—

"You're not human," she starts. "You're not like us. Then again, you're not like anyone, are you?"

I scoff and stand up—sure that she's just as unbalanced as I thought. "Not human?" I say. "You know, everyone was right about you. You are crazy. I don't even know why I'm here."

"Sit down," she snaps. "And let me tell you right now: You'd better stop trusting things that the people in this town are whispering to you."

At the force of her words, I rest back on the couch. I wonder what she means—if she's bitter about her station in life, or if there's something I should truly be afraid of.

"Fine," I say. "But no more riddles. I'm not here for the psychic tour. My life is coming undone. Do you know what's wrong with me or not?"

"There's nothing wrong with you," she says. "But you can't fully understand that yet. You're not whole, child. Part of you is missing. You need to remember what it is."

At the mention of remembering, I feel the first prickles of goose bumps. "And how exactly do I do that?" I ask softly. Could she really know about the memories I've been having?

"You've got to fill the Need. That's what you like to call it, right? The Need."

When she says it, I'm struck with déjà vu. I've heard this before—somewhere; I've heard all of this before. "What is the Need?" I ask her.

Marceline widens her eyes as if it's a long story, and settles back into her chair. "There are a group of beings," she begins in a low voice, "called the Forgotten. They are a type of . . . angel on earth. No wings. No heaven. No hell. They are part of the light of the universe. And their purpose is to spread hope, to change lives for the better where they can."

I smile, thinking she's telling a legend from her considerable past, and I cross my arms over my chest. This is absolutely no help at all. "They sound inspiring," I say. She gives me a sharp look.

"Listen," she hisses, showing me a glimpse of the scary woman she was in the parking lot of Santo's. My heart kicks up a beat. "The Forgotten don't have an easy path, child. Their existences are blessed, or cursed if you will. They are physically compelled to help people, to the point that their bodies begin to wear away. The skin rubbing off to reveal the pure

98

light underneath. This painful process goes on until they have one last Need, something that sets them free of their form to return to the universe."

"That sounds awful." I breathe out, fear crawling over my skin.

"No." She smiles. "It's beautiful. But there is always a price. When they're gone, the Forgotten are wiped out of time, as if they never existed at all. The universe corrects the space around them, filling in histories—adjusting memories. But everyone who's ever known or was touched by them has a renewed sense of hope, of purpose. The Forgotten are true sacrifice."

Her words are making my chest ache, and I'm starting to think that this isn't just a myth. I've heard this before, only I'm certain it wasn't in this life. Tears well up in my eyes. "Why are you telling me this?" I ask.

"Because, child," she says. "You are one."

I stare at her, a tear trickling down my cheek. "If you're just trying to scare me . . ." I say, choking back my sobs. Even though I know what she's saying is impossible, I am absolutely consumed with grief. Horror.

"It's okay to cry," she says softly, looking almost bewildered that I'd hold it in. "You've already gone through this once. I'd cry too. You've lost so much."

"I don't know what you're talking about," I say, wanting to run away. Wanting to shout that she's a liar. But I can't.

She nods as if I'm having a perfectly acceptable response to her telling me that I not only lived before, but that I'm not even human. After a minute, she pulls a tissue from her shirtsleeve and holds it out to me. I shake my head no.

"So," I begin, my voice shaky. "I'm a Forgotten?"

"Mostly," she says, slowly rocking again. "But you're so much more."

It starts. Vibrations up my arms, through my chest. Marceline smiles at me as she slips out of focus.

"You're keeping something from me," his voice says on the other end of the phone line. "How are we supposed to have a relationship when all you do is lie?"

I'm crying, cradling the phone to my ear, so afraid I'm losing him. "But I love you," I whisper. "Why can't that be enough?"

"Where were you?" he repeats.

"Please, I can't—"

"Stop lying!" he yells. He takes in a jagged breath, and then it's quiet. "Love isn't enough anymore," he says simply. "It's killing us." And then he hangs up.

"Please—" I yell out, and suddenly realize I'm in Marceline's living room again. The old woman is rocking back and forth, watching me as if she's fascinated. But I'm trembling, tears wet on my face.

"Who is he?" I ask her. "Who are these people in my head?" I cry, covering my face with my palms. I feel like I'm in a nightmare I can't wake up from. "Please make it stop," I whisper, unable to look up.

"Aw, child," she says soothingly. "No one can stop it. But I

100

think you've learned enough for one day, don't you think? I'm not sure you can handle the rest."

I look up at her. "There's more?"

She presses her lips together and nods slowly. "Have a mint. It'll calm your nerves."

"I don't want a mint," I snap. "Tell me what else there is."

She reaches to push the bowl toward me, her bracelets clinking together. "Take a mint," she repeats. "And I'm not ready to tell you more. These things must be done right. You come back another day, after I've had some rest." She motions to the lump of candies. "Now go on."

Reluctantly I break off a piece and slip it between my lips. The peppermint is overpowering at first, but then I taste something tangy underneath. I look over at her. "What kind of mint is this?"

"Just something to calm your nerves," she says.

I immediately spit it out into my hand. "You're drugging me?"

"Oh, hush," she says, as if I'm overreacting. "It's a mild sedative. My own special blend. We Seers are fond of our medications. And I can't have you breaking down on me, not when there's still so much to do."

I stand up, shocked that I let myself get so completely fooled. I toss the candy onto the table and it shatters into pieces. Marceline watches with little more than curiosity in her expression. Then she turns toward the window.

"You should go. Your boy is out there waiting for you. And

I'd prefer if he didn't come in."

I glance in the direction she's looking, but the blinds are down. I'm guessing she's talking about Abe since she already had Harlin in here today. Wait. What was Harlin doing here?

"The guy earlier," I say. "Why—"

"Don't you worry yourself about Harlin, child. He's a tortured soul. He'll find you when he's ready. Right now, you have bigger things to deal with," she says, walking to the door.

A wave of relaxation stretches over me, my eyes taking a second to adjust on her as I follow behind. It's the sedative taking effect. It must have been strong. What would have happened if I ate the whole thing?

"The Shadows can be very tricky," she says. "But as you know, you always have a choice. Well . . ." She pauses as if thinking about it. "That used to be the case. I believe things are changing now. Which, of course, is why you're here."

"What?" I ask, confused. Slightly disoriented. I hope she didn't poison me with that stupid mint. "I—"

"You'll be fine," she says, patting my arm. "Only lasts an hour or so. Now no more talking today. I'll see you soon enough."

CHAPTER 12

Marceline opens the door, and I hear her crunch down on the rest of her peppermint, the noise loud enough to make me think she cracked a few more teeth in the process. I turn to ask if she's okay when I see her looking past me. I follow her gaze, and see Abe standing on the sidewalk, facing her house with his hands casually in the pockets of his black pants. He's devilishly handsome with a crisp white T-shirt, his hair brushed to the side. When he sees me, he offers a subtle wave. I smile.

"Go on now," Marceline says, putting her hand on the small of my back to usher me out. "No one can help you, child. It's up to you. You have to follow your Need. It's the only way to remember."

I turn back to ask her again about the Need, but she closes the door, the lock snapping shut. For a moment, I stand there, facing the house—swaying a little on my feet. Her story of the Forgotten seems ridiculous outside of her small living room. I almost wonder if all of this is part of a hallucination. Just then, Abe calls my name.

"Thought maybe you'd want to hang out before work," he says as if that's a completely normal reason for him to have tracked me down at the house of the town psychic.

"How did you know I was here?" I ask, stepping off the patio to make my way toward him. The air is heating up as the afternoon quickly approaches.

"Was it a secret?" he asks.

"No." I'm embarrassed as I answer, knowing that I was hoping to hide it from him. It makes me think of the memory I had in Marceline's living room about lying to someone I loved. Fresh hurt opens in my chest.

Abe's eyes check me over when I reach him. He brushes the back of his finger over my cheek. "You were crying," he says, shooting an alarmed look behind me. "Did she hurt you again?"

"Nothing like that," I say, afraid to tell him why I'm really here. Afraid to tell him about the stories, especially since I refuse to believe them myself. "I just wanted to ask her why she attacked me."

"And?"

"It was an accident." I shrug. "Case closed, I guess."

Abe watches me, a small smile crossing his lips. "You are a

terrible liar, Elise. But if you don't want to tell me, that's fine. Just know that you can."

"Thanks." I rub my face, trying to get my bearings now that I'm outside.

"She gave you a mint?" Abe asks, sounding amused. I turn quickly to him.

"You know about that?"

He grins. "She gives everyone a mint. How else will they believe the garbage she tells them? I just hope you didn't eat the whole thing."

I shake my head. "No, I didn't. But I am a little foggy."

"Here." He offers his hand to me. I catch his gaze for a second, his expression sweet. Inviting. I let him take my palm and feel instantly better.

When we get to the car, I'm back to myself—or a slightly calmer version. Marceline's stories are pushed away, almost silly now. What was I thinking, listening to a psychic? I'm embarrassed for myself.

I turn the ignition of Lucy's car, but there is only a series of metallic clicks. "Not now," I say, and groan. I try it again. This time I get nothing.

I glance over to Abe. "You don't happen to be a skilled mechanic?" I ask.

"See this face, Elise," he says, using his finger to circle his features. "Do I look like the kind of guy who can fix cars?"

"No," I say, sounding disappointed. "You're way too pretty to get dirty."

"Exactly. You should call home."

I fish out my phone and dial the house, but it rings without anyone picking up. I try Lucy's cell, but she doesn't answer that either. It's still too early to call my father, so I'll have to wait until his services are over. Great. What am I supposed to do until then?

"No answer?" Abe asks.

"Nope."

"Huh. Well, I live close. You can come to my house, at least until your dad can pick you up." He raises his eyebrow as he looks over, and I have to smile.

"Is this just a clever ruse to get me to come home with you?"

"You think I tampered with your spark plugs and unhooked your home phone line? That's at least two steps further than I would go for a girl. So what's it gonna be, Elise? Hang out in front of Madame Marceline's house for all to see, or come check out where I live?"

"When you put it that way . . ."

I grab my purse, locking the car door before pulling my hair into a low knot to keep it out of my face. But as we start to walk, Abe reaches over to undo it, letting the strands cascade down my back.

"I like your hair better like this," he says, running his fingers over it. And then he smiles to himself and we walk toward his house.

As we tread the cracked cement pavers to Abe's front door, a sudden nervousness starts to twist in my stomach. This is the first time I've gone home with a guy—technically. But I have other worries. Lots of them. Marceline's story tries to come back into my consciousness, but I push it away. It's ridiculous.

"Welcome home," Abe says as he opens his front door. I meet his eyes, feeling a bit uncertain. His gaze is steady and intense. And after a long moment, I walk inside.

The living room is small, dark even in the afternoon light. It smells mildly of smoke, not cigarette, but campfire or wood stove. The furniture is old, the carpet is worn, but the house is tidy and well kept.

But I do notice one thing: There are no pictures—a complete contrast to Marceline's cluttered living room. Abe's walls are naked, even though there are rectangular outlines where I believe frames used to hang. Goose bumps rise on my arms as a chill runs over me. I'm about to ask Abe about the spaces when he tosses his house keys on a table next to the door, making a loud clang. "Drink?" he asks.

Abe's demeanor is different, almost angry. Bitter.

"What's wrong?" I ask, setting my purse on his couch. Abe pauses in the archway between his living room and kitchen, hanging his head.

"You don't like it," he says quietly. "You don't want to be here."

I'm a little taken aback by his statement. "What do you mean? I like it. I'm glad you asked me over."

Abe doesn't move at first, but then he straightens and leaves the room. I hate that he's suddenly insecure, and I wonder if

I've done something to cause it. The light of the refrigerator illuminates the small space in the kitchen, and then Abe comes back with two sodas.

He hands me one, and then motions to the couch. When we're next to each other, Abe lounges back, stretching his legs under the coffee table. He sips from his drink, the silence going on too long.

"I grew up in this house," he says finally. "Have been here all my life."

I look sideways at him, the darkness in the room playing across his features, shading his eyes. "Does your dad live with you?" I ask.

"No. No, *querida*. It's just me. And now you?" He turns to smile at me. "You're welcome to spend the night."

"That is very gracious."

Abe sets his drink down, pausing as if lost in thought. "Elise," he says. "You know I like you. I think you like me. Why are you dragging this out?"

I laugh nervously. "I'm not dragging anything out. We just met. I'm a cautious girl, I guess. Maybe you haven't wooed me properly."

"Interesting point." He stretches his arms over his head, letting one fall behind me on the couch. "How about I take you to a party with me tonight? As my date. I'll give you lots of reasons to be with me. I can be very convincing."

"I'm sure." Just then my phone vibrates in my purse next to me, and I grab it, happy for the distraction. It's Lucy. My

108

entire body is on pins and needles right now, the conversation making me uneasy.

"Missed your call," Lucy says the minute I click the phone on. "What's up?"

"Your car won't start," I say. "Is Dad there?"

She exhales. "That thing is such trash. Yeah, he just got back. Dad!" she yells off the line, and I wince. She could have at least covered the receiver.

When my father gets on the phone, I tell him that I'm at Abe's and give him directions. He doesn't sound entirely pleased that I'm at the house of a guy he already assumes I'm dating. But I'm relieved when he says he's on his way.

When my father arrives and beeps the horn, Abe walks me to the door. He's been silent during the entire ten-minute wait.

"Thanks for coming over," he says quietly, as if still self-conscious. "Sorry it wasn't more exciting."

Abe seems so disappointed that I impulsively hug him, wrapping my arms around his waist as I rest my head on his chest. I feel him relax, his cheek on the top of my head. Sadness fills me, as if it's spreading from Abe's body to mine. But before I say anything, the car horn beeps again, and I pull away.

When I get outside, I tell my father that I was picking up Abe for lunch when Lucy's car died. I don't mention the fact that it's in front of a psychic's house, hoping he won't notice. I'm not sure how I'll explain it if he asks, because Abe's right—I'm a terrible liar.

Oddly enough, Lucy's car purrs to life the first time my dad turns the ignition. He shoots me a pointed look, as if asking me what I've *really* been up to all morning.

But just being close to Marceline's house again has put me on edge. I remember our conversation, the fear and grief I felt. The story she told can't be real. Because if I believe her, I have to believe that I'm not human. And I just can't accept that.

After we get home, I take a nap—sleeping off the residual effects of the mint—and then shower for work. As I stand at the bathroom mirror with my hair twisted up in a towel, I notice the dark circles under my eyes. I feel like I haven't slept in weeks, as if I'm . . . The thought sticks in my head, making tears gather. It's as if I'm wearing away.

I sniffle back the start of my cry and find Lucy's makeup bag. I dab on her concealer, even a little eyeliner. Anything I can to look normal. When I'm done, I'm better. Not great— but better.

I walk out and find my dad in the kitchen making an early dinner, a red dish towel hanging over his shoulder. "And the dead have risen," he says without looking up. He's been using that same joke for years, but it's suddenly not very funny. "How was the nap?" he adds.

"Refreshing." I pull out the pitcher of lemonade and I pour myself a cup, sipping slowly. "So . . ." I start. He side-eyes me.

"What?"

"Abe asked me to a party tonight."

"I'm not sure I like it, Elise. I knew you'd date eventually, but he just seems too experienced for you."

"That's just a rumor. I mean, Lucy doesn't even know him. I want to go to a party, Dad. And Abe's a gentleman. Completely, I swear."

My father looks doubtful.

"What if I bring him to church?" I offer. "If he can sit through your sermon he has to have pure intentions. No one else would subject themselves to that sort of torture." I smile. My father takes a lot of pride in his sermons, but I can't help it—they're boring. So Lucy and I tease him about it sometimes.

"Sunday," my father says, as if it's settled. "I'll expect you and your . . . guy friend in the front row. Paying very close attention."

"Wow," I say. "What will you ever do if I get a *boy*friend?"

"Fret."

I sit down and wait for dinner, clicking through the laptop that Lucy left out. The bookmarked page is WebMD and I worry again about her cramping.

My father sets a plate of pasta in front of me before sitting. "Have you or your sister tampered with the security alarm?" he asks.

"Uh, no. Not that I know of."

"Doesn't set anymore."

I widen my eyes as if that's fascinating and take a bite of

111

food. It sounds to me like the gods of sneaking out have smiled upon Lucy.

"Have you been taking your vitamins?" my father asks.

"Yes," I mumble, knowing that the vitamins won't help. I quickly compliment my father on his ever-improving culinary skills, determined to not think about Marceline's stories.

"They say good cooking keeps teenagers home more often," my father says. He pauses, staring into his plate. "You know, Elise. I've been thinking about what's happening with you— the out-of-body feeling."

I look up. My father doesn't even know half of what's wrong with me, but he might still have answers. Better and more rational ones than an old psychic's.

"I think it could be delayed grief from your mother's passing," he continues. "Or even this move from Colorado. Maybe it was too sudden. I should have thought it through longer."

"Dad," I say, reaching for his hand. "This isn't your fault. Lucy and I could have dug in our heels and demanded to stay in Colorado, but we didn't. So if I'm emotionally scarred for life, you're not the one to blame." I smile, unable to let him beat himself up. "It's Lucy's fault too."

He chuckles, telling me to finish my dinner. It's difficult at first, but I swallow it down, along with my fear. I wish I could talk to him about the Forgotten, but I know he'll be disappointed in me for going to the old woman in the first place. My father grows silent. Thoughtful.

"Elise," he says after a long moment. "Do you remember

what your mother used to say near the end, when she was very sick?"

Pain aches in my heart, reminding me of the loss. "She said life was too short to mourn the dead."

He nods. "Your mother—she lived life to the fullest. Every second of it, even when—" He chokes up and stops talking, waiting for the grief to pass. "She loved you girls," he says after a moment. "And I know she wouldn't forgive me if I made you unhappy with all of my rules." He reaches to tug on his lip, sniffling back his cry. "Am I doing all right, kid?"

"I think you're doing a bang-up job," I say as tears gather in my eyes. "Even if the noodles are now cold because you can't stop talking."

He ruffles my hair before leaning back in his chair, seeming more content that he did a few minutes ago. As I finish dinner, we don't mention my mother again. Or my episodes. Instead we slowly ease into proper table conversation.

I think about what he said, though. How my mother thought living was the most important thing. That was all she wanted—to keep living. To be happy. So maybe that's what I need to focus on right now: finding happiness.

"So a date, huh?" my father asks, sounding defeated. "Why couldn't you stay ten forever?"

I smile. "I really tried, Dad. So can I go?"

A date with Abe sends a mixture of feelings through me. I chalk it up to my courting inexperience, because I like Abe—I really do. And although he's a bit unsettling sometimes, he also seems to understand me. Is patient with me. He can't be as bad as his reputation, not after he took my non-kiss in stride. Not after he was so kind to Marissa while she was a total wench. Abe is a sweetheart despite the rumors. And who knows, he might not even be that slutty.

"Don't break curfew," my father says. "I'm even tempted to make it earlier since I'll be at church."

"No need to go overboard, old man."

My father eyes me as if he's not sure he's making the right decision, but then he nods. "All right, kid. Have fun. And, please—"

I get up quickly and back away from the table, hoping to avoid any dating advice. I thank him and go to my room to gather clothes for later, stuffing them into my backpack as I smile. I'm going to make myself happy—despite the craziness around me. It's what my mother would have wanted.

CHAPTER 13

Every time my conversation with Marceline tries to sneak into my head, I beat it back with a fresh dose of denial and rationalization. I'm not human? Right. I'm sure my father would love to hear that one.

I hurry out of the house, glad for the work distraction— anything to keep my mind off of earlier. When I get to Santo's, the place is filled with energy, Abe especially charming. He's making me laugh, making me forget about everything. I think that he is exactly what I want in my life right now. He's loud and mischievous, and like he told me my first day, he never gets in trouble. Abe makes me feel normal.

When my shift is almost over, Abe meets me near the walk-in where I'm filling the sour-cream gun, my plastic gloves sticky. It's calm back here, the sounds of the restaurant drowned out by the hum of the freezer.

"School starts in a few weeks," Abe says. "You excited?"

"Ecstatic."

"I bet you're supersmart. Do all your homework. Teacher's pet and all that."

I wipe down the utensil and then pull off my gloves before tossing them in the trash. "I have been known to get straight As."

Abe closes his eyes, grinning as if I sound delicious. "God, Elise," he says. "I am going to have so much fun corrupting you. I'm practically giddy."

"I can tell."

He laughs. "Don't worry," he says. "I corrupt in the best way possible."

"Which is?"

He leans closer, holding my gaze. "Kiss me and find out." He pauses there, a smile pulling at his lips. He knows I'm not going to kiss him in the back room of Santo's, but he must also read that I'm tempted. He winks and straightens up before walking back to his section.

We leave thirty minutes later, Abe driving Lucy's car again. Anxiety begins to knot in my stomach as we park on a crowded residential street. I'm not nearly as excited now that he's told me whose party we're going to.

"Are you sure you're all right with this?" Abe asks as we head up the driveway to Bridget's house—one of the girls from the campsite. I'm in a summer dress, my makeup heavier

116

than I'd normally wear it. Abe looks at me nervously. "I don't want it to be weird for you," he says for the third time.

"I'm fine." I don't mention that I'm scared to see Marissa again after her display of nonaffection while we were at the camp. "Just one request," I add. "If any of your ex-girlfriends try to start a fight with me, you have to step in."

Abe chuckles. "No ex-girlfriends will be here. And I'm wooing, remember? By definition that means I keep you out of fistfights."

"Sounds like you have big plans."

Abe pauses on the front patio. "Very big." And then he opens the door of the small block home.

Music fills the living room as we step inside. There are people scattered around, talking and playing cards. I follow behind as Abe weaves through the party. The walls of the house are painted bright oranges and yellows, tapestries hanging with Native American prints. Through the sliding glass doors I can see the keg set up in the yard. And in the kitchen there's a blender and bottles of alcohol lining the counter.

"Did you want a drink?" Abe asks, eyeing the keg out back.

"No, thanks."

He turns, his eyes filled with a playfulness I haven't seen in him before. He grabs my arm and pulls me to him, smiling broadly. "I can't wait until you're mine," he whispers.

I'm silent, unsure of how to respond when he leans down to kiss my cheek. He backs up, his eyes still ablaze with whatever emotion just raged through him, and says he's going to get a drink. When he walks away, I decide to find the bathroom to check my makeup. Maybe take a few calming breaths while I'm at it.

Abe is a bit overwhelming. It's apparent how enamored he is of me, but I'm not entirely sure why. He could date most anyone here, girls that seem more his style. But it's clear that all he wants is me.

Only I'm not certain of how I feel in return.

I walk down the hallway, excusing myself around the people standing and talking. A few eye me curiously, and it reminds me that I'm out of place—or even more obvious, out of place with Abe.

When I find the right door, I rush in and quickly shut out the noise of the party. I cross to the sink and rest my palms on either side of the counter, studying my reflection. Next to me the shower curtain sways, and I start. Then I hear the soft sound of a girl crying.

"Are you okay?" I ask, taking a tentative step forward. There's no answer, and I wonder if I should give her some privacy. But I decide to first make sure she's not injured. Slowly I pull back the curtain and there, sitting in the bathtub, is a girl about my age with short brown hair, mascara streaked down her face. She turns to me fiercely as if she's about to cuss me out, but she stops short. Instead she dissolves into another crying fit, covering her face.

I should definitely find her friends. But as I start to move away, I feel it—a pull to help her. A desire to help her. I glance down at the girl and the tingling begins in the tips of my fingers, as if I'm bringing it on myself. As if I'm willing . . . the Need.

A light glows around us and the knowledge hits, flowing through me. I can see her entire life. I close my eyes, terrified that it's happening again but unable to stop the warm feelings of love coursing through me. Love that's not mine.

Sixteen-year-old Anahi Cabrone is five months pregnant. She hasn't told anyone, concealing the pregnancy by eating less to avoid weight gain, wearing baggier clothes. She hasn't even told her boyfriend, Daniel—a twenty-three-year-old cook—afraid he'd break up with her.

But tonight her father found out about the baby, about her secretly dating Daniel. Anahi's parents made an appointment at a private clinic outside of town, one that will still do a procedure so late-term. Anahi came here to find Daniel. To tell him. To make him run away with her. But instead she found him with another girl.

"Anahi," I murmur, my heart heavy with her sorrow. She feels alone and hopeless. She doesn't think she can go on. I see an image of her mother—when she was the same age as Anahi—pregnant with her.

The light had come to her mother then, helping her to face her own decision. And now it's back to help Anahi, giving her the comfort she needs. I lower my eyes, the fact that I'm understanding this nearly devastating. I don't know what this means for me. I don't know if I can keep denying these episodes anymore.

But the words run through my head, pushing me forward. "I know this isn't an easy choice," I tell Anahi. "But it is *your* choice. Go home; talk with your parents. Make the decision for yourself, but not out of desperation, or sadness. Or guilt."

Anahi is quiet for a long moment, and then she nods, wiping absently at her cheeks.

The visions in my mind flash forward to Anahi arriving home, her parents waiting at the door for her, having been terrified that she'd never come back. And this time, they'll listen to her. They'll talk.

Anahi tries to stand, and I help her out of the bathtub, steadying her. The minute I let go of her arm, the light is gone. Anahi blinks rapidly as if just realizing where she is.

"Oh," she says, furrowing her brow. "I . . . I'm sorry. I didn't know anyone else was in here."

And suddenly I'm back to myself, staring at this girl who is equally alarmed to see me. She touches her stomach protectively, but then quickly lets her arm fall to her side, as if afraid she'd given away her secret. She turns then, confused, and leaves.

I wait a minute; only silence outside the open door. My heart thuds in my chest, and I step forward to look out. The people in the hall are still, the sound on mute. Nothing moves.

The memory floods in.

I can't fight the Need. I'm lying on the floor of a car, tears streaking down my face. The pain is unbearable—unimaginable. And when I push aside the shoulder of my dress, I see it and it stops my heart. Skin—dead and gray, rotting me from the inside out.

I suck in a breath, falling against the wall, and the party snaps back into motion. The room sways with movement, music in the background, murmurs of conversation. I lean my head against the bathroom wall, squeezing my eyes shut.

This is my life—not whoever these memories belong to. Not the voice that's inside of me, pushing me forward. Forgotten or not, they can't have me. I fight my tears, wishing it all away. I want my life back now.

I straighten then, knowing that I'll have to go see Madame Marceline tomorrow. I can't wait until Sunday. I'm going to tell her to make the voices go away. Make the memories go away. I'm following my happiness now. Because whoever I used to be—if I've actually lived before—is gone. And like my mother taught me, there isn't time to mourn the dead.

I press back the panic that's bubbling up and smooth down the front of my dress. I can't freak out here. Not now. I won't tell Abe about this.

And something inside tells me I never should.

Abe is sitting by himself on the couch sipping from a red plastic cup, looking bored. When he sees me move through the crowded hallway, he lifts an eyebrow.

I join him on the couch, immediately smelling something minty. Abe brings his cup to his lips, pausing to examine me. "Where were you?" he asks before taking a sip.

"Bathroom." I meet his quizzical stare. Now that I'm back out in the party, my exchange with Anahi is an afterthought. Abe shifts next to me suddenly, and a splash of beer spills over the lip of the cup and onto my leg. It's cold, snapping me awake. I groan and slap Abe in the chest. "Abe!"

"Sorry." He sets the cup on the coffee table. "Here, let me

get that." He starts brushing the alcohol off my bare thigh just below the hem of my dress with the sleeve of his shirt. His fingers brush my skin. "You're so warm," he murmurs, taking his time.

"I think you got it all," I say.

Abe leaves his hand on my leg an extra second before going for his drink. We're quiet and he leans his shoulder against mine as we watch the party, conversations floating around us like white noise. Just as I'm starting to relax, someone calls his name.

"Abe!" the high-pitched voice yells again. Bridget's standing in the hallway wearing a red tube top and a short denim skirt. We both get up and she rushes to hug Abe, squeezing him a little longer than necessary.

"Hi, Elise," she says, turning to me. "Nice to see you."

"You too." I can tell that she'd rather I wasn't here with Abe, but she's doing her best to hide it, so I try not to hold it against her. I check the time on my phone to see how close it is to curfew.

"Did you know that Marissa took off?" Bridget asks Abe, grabbing his arm for emphasis. "Craig thinks she left with a guy, but we haven't seen her since the campsite. All of her stuff is gone from her apartment, too."

"Really?" Abe says, surprised. "She didn't tell anyone where she was going?"

"Nope."

My shoulders tense as a thought nags at the back of my mind, the idea that something horrible has happened to

Marissa. "Do you think she's okay?" I ask, butting into their conversation.

"Yes," Abe answers automatically, not looking over.

Bridget scoffs at my concern. "She's fine. She does this crap all the time. Abe, remember when she disappeared for a week last year? I had to step in and take over all of her shifts."

"It's true," Abe says. "Marissa is unpredictable at best. We don't worry about her little tantrums anymore." Abe sounds calm, collected. His dark gaze reassures me.

Bridget giggles next to us. "I bet she was pissed about your new girlfriend here. Believe me, she doesn't share. None of your girls do. We all just love to hate you."

"I can be fun to despise," he says evenly.

"Oh, I know." Bridget grins. "You're fun for *a lot* of things."

I shift uneasily, embarrassment spreading as I realize I'm at a party with the town Casanova. I was stupid not to listen to Lucy's gossip, even if she also told me to make out with him.

"It was wonderful seeing you, Elise," Bridget calls out. "And Abe, find me later, okay? I'd like to have some of that fun we were talking about."

But Abe doesn't answer immediately. Instead he stares at Bridget until her face drains of color. "You're making Elise uncomfortable," he murmurs, his tone controlled. "That makes *me* uncomfortable."

Bridget starts to apologize, but Abe raises his hand, cutting her off. "I know," he says. "But you should get back to your party now, Bridget. You wouldn't want it getting out of hand, not with the history this neighborhood has of gang violence."

Bridget nods, and I'm suddenly struck with a worry—as if that was an actual threat, even though Abe didn't necessarily say it that way. But the anxiety fades as Bridget rushes away without looking back at us.

When she's gone, Abe turns to me. "If it helps, I never slept with her."

My lips part to ask "Well, then what *did* you do with her?" but I stop myself. It was before I met him, possibly before I even moved here. It's really none of my business, even if it makes me jealous—sort of.

"I'm sorry," Abe says. "Maybe this party wasn't a fantastic date idea. 7-Eleven might be more our speed."

"You can't help that you're popular."

"Ah," he answers, as if discovering the problem. "Is this about my reputation? I assure you, the rumors are untrue."

"Really?" I ask, turning to him.

He pauses. "No, they're true. I lied. But that's the past, Elise. If I'd known you were coming—" He stops, laughing to himself. "Let's just say, you are exactly what I want. You're everything I want. And I want you . . . right now."

I'm unable to look away from him this time. Abe reaches over to brush a lock of my hair behind my ear, keeping his hand there.

"I should take you home," he whispers. "Don't you think so?"

Abe's voice is like syrup—sticky and sweet—as it winds through me, clouding my judgment. All I can think is that he's right. We should go home.

In the kitchen someone drops a bottle and when it smashes on the floor, the room erupts in cheers.

Words nag at my brain until I finally turn to Abe, putting my hand on his arm. "Do you want to come over?" I ask, feeling better the minute I say it. "My father's working late and Lucy's never there."

"Why, Elise," Abe says, grinning down at me. "I do think you have succumbed to my wooing."

"Maybe," I answer. "Or maybe I'd rather not be at the party of one of your exes."

"That's a good reason too."

Abe leads me outside, and we walk down the driveway, his arm over my shoulders. I'm not sure why, but I just invited a boy back to my house. The idea of it fills me with all sorts of unease. But then I remind myself that it's Abe—and that he is always a gentleman when it comes to me.

The house is dark when we walk in, and I practically dive for the lights. The idea of being alone with Abe is starting to intimidate me. I can't believe I invited him back to my house. It's so brazen.

"Soda?" I ask as he closes and locks the door.

Abe nods, and I walk into the kitchen, pulling open the fridge door. As I take out two cans, I also check my phone for missed calls from my dad or Lucy. Nothing.

On the couch, Abe is already clicking through the channels with the remote. I put a Coke in front of him, not sure if I should sit next to him. He seems to notice.

"Come here," he says, patting the spot next to him. "I'll be careful with you."

I wait for him to laugh off the comment, but he doesn't. I'm slightly perplexed as I ease down next to him. We're quiet at first, the television silently showing a *Project Runway* rerun. Abe's shoulder rests against mine, solid and warm. He shifts, turning toward me. "Elise," he says softly. "Do you want to be with me?"

The question is blunt and I'm completely unprepared for it. My lips part, but no words come out. And although it feels almost cruel, I can't respond. I don't know the answer.

Abe swallows hard, the noise audible in the room. "I promise I won't hurt you. Not if you stay with me."

I'm surprised by his words, what they could possibly mean. But when I look at him, I get caught up in his dark gaze and feel myself drift away slightly.

"We belong together," Abe says, drowning out my thoughts with his words, making them hard to sort out. "Why can't you see that?" I don't respond, struck silent. I can feel him—his desire. It's like I can see inside his head and know that he's been so lonely without me. He thinks I'm beautiful.

"I'm going to kiss you now," he murmurs, and draws me to him, his mouth covering mine. His fingers knot in my hair, tipping my head back as he kisses my neck, breathing heavily in my ear. "Just say yes and we'll be together. Just say yes."

I barely register what's happening as Abe's mouth is on mine again, softly whispering how much he wants me. It's then that it begins—the numbing sensation.

What starts as a soft tingling in my lips begins to spread through my face. My neck. I put my hands on Abe's chest, trying to move him back as he continues to kiss me. A shock of cold, like ice water pumped into my veins, tears at my flesh.

Finding my strength, I push Abe off and jump up from the sofa, wrapping my arms around myself.

Abe looks startled and reaches for me. "Elise?"

I don't know what's happening, but I have to get away from him. I turn and run toward my room, my body cold. Everything aching. It's not Abe's fault; it was just a kiss. A kiss can't do this. It's another sign that something is seriously wrong with me.

When I reach my room, I slam my door and lock it. Still shivering, I slide down until I'm on the floor, legs stretched out in front of me. I'm filled with absolute sadness, as if my heart is broken—no, shattered. I'm drowning in misery. And then an old memory slips in place.

He loves me. He loves me like no one else can, no one else will. He is mine forever. And with that knowledge, I know that I can let go. Because he'll never forget.

"Elise?" Abe says softly on the other side of the door.

"I can't," I try to say, covering my face with my hands. I want the memories to stop, but at the same time I miss him—the guy in my thoughts. I think I might die, I miss him so badly.

"I'm sorry," Abe says. "It wasn't supposed to happen like that. You're . . . different." He exhales. "Please come out."

I lift my head then, staring straight ahead toward my reflection in the bottom half of the closet mirror. "Who are you?" I ask myself silently, tears streaming down my cheeks. But nothing happens; the reflection doesn't change. Instead, I'm just sitting on my bedroom floor, a guy outside my door begging to talk to me. But I'm a freak. And I tell him to go home and leave me alone.

"We need to talk, *querida*," Abe says, sounding miserable. "I can't just let you go. Not now."

Headlights of a passing car illuminate the room, and when it does, I notice a glimmer under the bed. I reach for it, both comforted and saddened when I find it. It's my angel statue set in a clear stone.

On the other side of the door, Abe's feet shuffle. "Look, I'll leave. But . . ." He stops, as if uncertain of what to say next. So when he doesn't say anything at all, only closes the front door as he leaves, I start to cry harder.

I climb into bed, pulling the covers up over my head. I want to hide from the dark thoughts chasing me. I clasp the stone angel to my chest as I squeeze my eyes shut, wishing all of the creepiness away. Wishing I could live a normal life again. And when I'm done wishing—I pray.

CHAPTER 14

I'm in the middle of a road, a tumbleweed rushing past me. It's daytime, but the overcast sky sets everything in a gray light. I'm the only thing glowing—a golden light under my skin.

I'm dreaming. Dread twists in my stomach, a feeling of something not right.

"What are you, Elise?"

Startled, I turn to see Abe, handsome as ever in a black suit as he walks toward me.

"What do you mean?" I ask, but my words come out too soft, too weak. I'm afraid as a sense of foreboding, a pressure, builds around us.

"You can tell me," he adds, smiling gently. "I know you're

not like the others." He holds open his arms, coming to wrap me in a hug. I let him, trying to process what's going on as his fingers trail over the bare skin of my arm.

"I'm sorry to invade your dreams," he says, his lips against my temple. He kisses the skin there, then the high point of my cheek. "But I had to see you," he murmurs. "I want you, Elise." His lips graze mine. "I want you to stay with me."

But in this world, in this dream, I suddenly know that's not possible. "I can't be with you," I say, putting my arms between us to break away. Abe keeps me close to him, bringing his face near mine.

"Silly girl," he says, a devious twinkle in his eyes. He runs his hand down my neck, over my collarbone, before sighing longingly. "You already belong to me."

"Elise?"

I wake with a start and see my dad standing in my doorway, holding it half-open. The green numbers on my alarm clock read that it's after midnight. "Hey," I say, taking a second to get my bearings, the dream evaporating almost instantly. I sit up and touch my lips. They're cold.

"Just got home and wanted to make sure you were okay," my father says, sounding exhausted. He sits on the end of my bed, the light from the hallway casting shadows over the room. "Okay, maybe I wasn't so much making sure you were okay as I was checking to see that you were home. I hope the date went well?"

"Date?" Fear rushes through me as I remember what

happened with Abe, what happened when he kissed me. "It was fine," I say, quickly brushing back my hair. But it's not fine. It's so freaking far from fine that I'm trembling, barely able to keep myself from screaming.

"Honey," my father says, touching my arm. "You're so pale."

I'm not sure how to answer, how to explain that a psychic told me I wasn't human and now I'm starting to believe her. How can I tell my father that memories are trying to take me over—memories that aren't even mine? Instead I reach out and hug him, letting him hold me until I stop shaking.

"Elise," he says. "Has something else happened? If you're still having those episodes, we should take you back to the doctor. We'll find every specialist we can, drive up to Phoenix, even. Someone has to know what's going on with you."

It never occurred to me what it would really mean to try to find a logical solution. But now I understand—I'll be trapped in a hospital bed, undergoing surgeries and tests, blood work and X-rays. I'll be like my mother in her final days. Only my affliction won't be so easy to diagnose. What will they do to me?

"I'm just really tired," I say, straightening up. "Santo's has been way more physical than I thought, and I'm working too many hours. The low vitamin D only adds to that. . . ."

My father seems to consider this, nodding after a moment. "I think I should set you up with one of the other counselors at the church," he offers. "If this is mental somehow—"

"It's exhaustion," I say.

"If this happens again . . ."

"Hospital," I reply quickly. "I promise."

He exhales, but his worry lines don't diminish. I can tell he has another reason for talking to me tonight.

"What is it?" I ask.

"It's your sister."

My heart skips a beat. "What's wrong with Lucy?"

"It's just that . . ." He glances toward the hallway, lowering his voice. "I took her to see the doctor this morning. And after, Lucy said she had a clean bill of health. But there is something different about her. You see it, don't you?"

"Like a new piercing?"

"I don't know," my father says. "I can't quite figure out what it is." He rubs his forehead, a movement similar to one of my own.

"It's okay, Dad." I rest my cheek on his shoulder. "She's probably found a weirdo boyfriend who you'll hate and forbid her to spend time with. Then everything will be back to normal."

"Sounds awful, but I hope you're right."

I close my eyes, thinking about Lucy, about the horrible things happening to me. It's like our family is falling apart— breaking down a little each day. I'm not sure what to do anymore, but I have to fix this myself. Marceline said that no one else could help me. And I'm starting to see that she's right.

I promise my father that I'll talk to Santo about cutting down on my hours, and in return he agrees to try to do the same at the church. I feel immediately better because that means he'll be around more for me and Lucy. It gives me hope that there's a chance we can get through this. Even so, I secretly hope it doesn't resurrect his family game-night ideas.

I plan to go to Marceline's, and this time I'm not just going for her creepy mythology lessons. I want answers. I want to know how to stop what's happening to me.

I ask my dad to drop me off at the café on Mission Boulevard, telling him I'm meeting Abe for lunch. He doesn't need to know that I haven't heard from him. I'd checked my phone all morning, thinking he'd call, but there was nothing. What does Abe think happened? Did he feel the cold, or was it just me? Does he think I'm a prude who can't handle being touched? His perfect silence is killing me.

After my father drops me off, I wait for him to drive away and then start toward Marceline's. I didn't have her number to call—it wasn't even listed—but I have to talk to her. She can't turn me away.

When I get closer to her house, I notice someone just ahead. My heartbeat quickens. Harlin is sitting on his motorcycle at the curb—looking smoking hot as usual.

He glances up as I approach, a slow smile pulling at his lips. "I'd love to tell you this is a coincidence," he says.

I hike my backpack up on my shoulder. "Are you saying you're here for me and not a tarot card reading?"

"I am definitely here for you," he says in that same low voice. "I've already had my cards read this week."

I laugh. "Hope it was good news." I pause, looking him over. "How did you know I'd be here?"

He shrugs. "Just did."

I stand on the sidewalk, wondering how Harlin could have guessed something like that. I consider asking him, but I'm afraid of the answer. Does he know about the stories Marceline told me? Does he know about me?

"I have to go," I say, pointing toward the house. I start down the path to the front door when Harlin calls to me.

"She's not home," he says. "I already knocked on the door."

"Oh." I stop then, both disappointed and relieved. I want answers, but at the same time, I'm terrified of what they are. "Do you think she'll be back later?" I ask, not clear on how Harlin fits into the life of an old psychic in the first place.

"Maybe. If you want, I can keep you company while you wait."

I look around the street. "Here?"

"Or I can take you to lunch," he offers. "That is, if you're free?"

"Well," I say, starting toward him. I don't know what it is about him, but when I'm around Harlin I'm so much braver. "I guess it depends."

His mouth spreads in a slow smile. "On?"

I motion toward his bike. "Are you going to take me on that Harley?"

Harlin's hazel eyes flash wickedly. "Yeah," he says, reaching for my hand. "I am."

When he touches me it's like a current of electricity, warming me all over. He holds my gaze as he licks his bottom lip, the movement sexy. Inviting. I lean forward, planning on kissing him right here on the street. But before I get close enough, he turns away.

"Someone's looking for you," he murmurs, letting his hand slip from mine. I'm dazed, caught up in the moment, when I hear my name.

"Elise!"

My stomach drops when I see Abe jog toward us. He waves, casually glancing at Harlin, and then slows down his approach.

I take a step back, feeling like a terrible person. I was just out on a date with Abe last night, and here I am flirting with Harlin. I almost tried to kiss him. What was I thinking after what happened with Abe?

"I've been searching everywhere for you, *querida*," Abe says with a wry smile. "Off getting harassed by transients again, I see."

Harlin chuckles from next to me, folding his hands in his lap as he rests back on his bike, not looking intimidated in the least. I, on the other hand, think I might puke.

"Abe," I say, my voice a little weak. "This is Harlin." Abe sizes Harlin up with little more than a head nod before turning his dark gaze on me. Technically Abe isn't my boyfriend. And honestly, after last night, I don't really want him to be. It was a disaster.

"Elise." Abe takes my wrist, tugging me gently forward. "We need to talk. I came to meet you, and Margie said you called in. I went to your house—no answer. Then I find you on the street with some . . . *guy*."

I don't appreciate the insinuation, the accusation in his words. Any guilt I had for leading Abe on quickly evaporates. He's different somehow, his charming exterior fading into possessiveness. But I don't belong to him.

"Stop," I say, trying to twist free of his grip.

Abe's face drains of color and his eyes narrow. Fog begins to slide inside my head, whispering. Blocking out my thoughts.

Leave.

I hear Harlin shift next to me. Suddenly my confusion clears and I yank my arm from Abe, backing up. "Don't grab me like that," I say. The skin of my wrist aches, even though he didn't grip me that hard.

Abe's color returns immediately and he shakes his head, like he doesn't know what he was thinking.

"I'm sorry," he says, a half grin pulling at his lips, boyish and sweet. "I apologize. You can't blame me for getting a little jealous, can you?" He motions to Harlin.

"I'll call you when I get home," I offer, knowing that I can't avoid the discussion with him. I don't want to hurt Abe. I know he likes me, and I thought I liked him. But something's changed.

Underneath his white T-shirt, Abe's muscles tense and a pained expression crosses his features, as if he heard my thoughts. But then it fades, replaced with something cold.

"Yes, you do that," he says, backing away. "Don't forget." His eyes flick to Harlin's with some amusement, like it's an inside joke they share. And then Abe stalks down the street, turning at the next corner.

"Boyfriend?" Harlin asks, adjusting the mirror on his bike.

"Not really," I say. "I'm not sure what he is, I guess."

Harlin seems to consider this and then shrugs as if he doesn't care if I have some weird love affair going on with my coworker. "I've got a pretty good idea," he says.

"Do you have a girlfriend?" I ask him. To my dismay, Harlin is quiet long enough to make my insides knot. Then he lowers his eyes.

"No," he says softly. "No, I don't."

I'm reminded of when Marceline called him a tortured soul. It's been a long time since I've seen someone as torn up as Harlin looks right now. I reach to touch his arm, drawing his gaze.

"I don't know what's wrong," I say. "But I'm sorry for whatever's hurting you. Though if I'm honest, you're sort of bumming me out."

"Well, that is definitely not the emotion I'm working toward," he says, moving up on his bike to throw back the kickstand.

"No? Which one are you going for?"

Harlin takes his sunglasses off his collar, sliding them on before turning my way. "I think mutual attraction is a good place to start."

I laugh, setting my backpack over both shoulders as I climb onto his bike. "Oh," I say, wrapping my arms around his waist as the Harley roars to life. "I'm pretty sure we've already got that covered."

CHAPTER 15

Rosita's Hot Dogs is a silver food truck in the parking lot of an abandoned Super Saver. As unpromising as that sounds, I've heard from several customers that they actually have the best hot dogs in the Southwest. So I decide to give it a try.

As we order, Harlin and I wait under the truck's overhang, both of us quiet. Once we get our food, we head to the small white tent with three picnic tables inside. The seating area is empty, private.

"I'm scared of this," Harlin says, holding up the hot dog. When he does, ketchup drips from the end of the bun. "Is that bacon?" He looks at me helplessly. "Who puts bacon on a hot dog?"

"It's delicious," I say, taking another bite.

Harlin stares doubtfully back to his food. "If I have a heart attack right here you'd better resuscitate me."

I smile at the thought of mouth-to-mouth. "I'll try my best."

Harlin catches the insinuation and chuckles to himself before taking a big bite. "Is it wrong that I'm wishing for congestive heart failure now?" he asks through the food. When he finishes his mouthful, he nods. "You know what?" he says. "That's goddamn delicious."

"See!"

"You have excellent taste . . . Elise." He stumbles on my name, but then quickly takes another bite. I'm a little offended, but I try not to let it bother me as we finish our meal.

When we're done, I clean up the plates, Harlin watching me silently. I sit back down, and he leans his elbows on the table.

"Why were you at Marceline's yesterday?" he asks, sounding curious. "If it was just because she attacked you, I think you would have sent the police instead."

My expression falters as I'm reminded of how abnormal my life is outside of this tent. For a while I actually forgot. "Maybe I wanted my fortune read," I say, meeting his gaze.

He scratches his beard as he tries to figure me out. "What did you two talk about?"

I take a long drink and then shake the ice in the cup. "That's kind of personal, don't you think?"

Harlin stops, closing his eyes like he's embarrassed. "You're

139

right," he says. "It's none of my business. You're not one of mine."

I scoff. "Oh? Do you have several?"

He looks at me quickly. "No, that's not what I mean—"

"You sure? Because it sounded ridiculously bad."

He tilts his head, as if telling me I shouldn't even begin to think he's talking about another girl. "I promise you," he says in that smoky voice. "There is no one else. I am very much alone."

I lower my eyes, feeling the sadness roll off of him again. "You don't have to be alone," I say.

"It's easier," he says, mostly to himself. When I look up, he smiles gently. "Although it's always nice to make new friends."

"Who are mutually attracted?"

"That's a bonus."

Heat pulsates under my skin, a desire to touch him. Without thinking I reach for his hand as it rests on the table, sliding my palm into it. He stills, and then he runs his thumb over my skin.

"You remind me of someone," he murmurs.

I deflate a little, hoping he's not referring to an ex-girlfriend. When I don't reply, he slowly pulls his hand from mine to rub his face as if trying to clear his head.

"Looks like it might rain," he says, glancing at the sky outside of the tent. "I don't ride in bad weather, so I should probably get you home."

"My father will appreciate you not risking my life."

140

"Think he'll like me?" Harlin asks with a smile.

"It's possible." I pause. "Hey, what are you doing on Sunday?"

"Do you have something in mind?" he asks, brushing his long hair behind his ear.

"Church?" I'm slightly embarrassed saying it, not because I think it's a lame option, but because I'm used to people laughing. Harlin just pulls his eyebrows together.

"Church," he repeats, as if he's never heard of it before. "What time?"

Surprised, I straighten. "Oh, uh . . . eleven?"

He pauses. "You really want to go to church?"

"My dad's the pastor."

For a second I don't think Harlin will answer. But then he motions to himself. "I have to get a haircut first."

I smile broadly, elated that he'll go—which will definitely impress my father. "I don't think there's a decent barber in town," I say. "But you can maybe go to Ward—the next town over?"

Harlin rests his thumb on his bottom lip. The butterflies in my stomach are back, especially with the way he's sliding his gaze over me. "Can you cut hair?" he asks.

"No. But I'm a quick study."

"You'll be careful with me, right?"

"So careful."

He pauses, seeming to think about it. "Okay," he says. "I'll go to church if you cut my hair tomorrow. But then you have to let me paint your portrait sometime."

"You paint?" I'm honestly surprised.

"I haven't in a long time," he says. "But I find you inspiring."

"I'd be interested to see your work," I say. "Wait, you don't mean nude or anything, right?"

He laughs. "No. You'll be fully clothed."

Harlin stands and then offers his arm to help me up. When I'm in front of him, I will him to flirt back. Or at least be more obvious about it.

"You sure you're a fast learner?" he asks, starting to look a little fearful of my lack of salon experience.

I put my hand on his cheek and nod, reassuring him. Harlin closes his eyes as if comforted by my touch, and turns his face into my palm to brush his lips over my skin.

Another wave of desire crashes over me, and I move to kiss him. But Harlin steps away without another word and walks to where he's parked. With a slight sting of rejection, I follow quietly behind him.

I ask Harlin if he wants to come inside, but he says he can't. He takes my number and agrees to meet me at Santo's at two tomorrow since I have to pick up my check.

The house is empty, the lingering smell of spaghetti sauce still in the air. I click on the lamp next to the couch before crossing the room.

"Dad?" I call. When there's no answer, I check the kitchen and see the crockpot going, then notice a note stuck to the fridge with a Grand Canyon magnet.

Elise,

Lucy's car died again. Picking her up. Stir the sauce for me.
—Dad

Lucy's right. The car is a piece of trash. I tend to the sauce, still slightly wound up from riding around on a motorcycle. "Harlin," I murmur aloud to the empty room. Even his name is hot.

I walk over to the couch, collapsing on the cushion as I click on the television. I get lost in old reruns of *America's Next Top Model* and before I know it, it's gotten dark outside. Where are my father and sister? But I've barely gotten my phone out of my pocket when it begins vibrating. A quick glance at the screen sends my pulse racing with anxiety. Abe.

"Hi," I say into the receiver as I put it to my ear. I hate the way Abe and I left things, but I also don't want him treating me like I'm his property.

"I'm sorry," he says quietly. "I don't know what I was thinking."

Guilt rushes over me, and I take an objective step back. Yes, Abe was out of line, and I will definitely tell him that. But I at least owe him an explanation for last night.

"Abe—"

"No," he interrupts, sounding miserable. "I was an ass, I know that. I'll make it up to you. In fact, I brought you something."

"You didn't have to bring me anything," I say.

"I have donuts."

I smile. "Well, in that case."

"Can I come in?"

I look over my shoulder toward the closed blinds of the picture window. "Are you—"

"I'm out front. Will you hang out with me for a little while?"

I cross the room and peek through the wooden slats of the blinds. Sure enough, Abe is standing in my driveway with a white bag and a phone pressed to his ear. He sees me and walks to the door. When I swing it open, Abe leans against the frame.

"For you, *querida*," he says, holding out the bag.

"You're being nice."

"I'm always nice."

"You're nice when you want something."

"Maybe what I want is to be nice."

I hold his gaze, his dark eyes innocent. "Come inside," I say, and push the door open wider.

Abe strolls in like he never had a doubt I'd let him. He's changed clothes from what he was wearing earlier. Now he has on a yellow polo shirt, which is amazing against his tanned skin. His short hair is combed perfectly and he smells lightly of cologne.

"So," he says, turning to me. "Tell me about your new boy-friend."

I exhale and walk past him, plucking the bag of donuts

out of his hand. I take them over to the coffee table, pushing aside the remote and magazines. I should have known that Abe would be up-front. "He's not my boyfriend," I say, looking back at him. "I've seen him around town, and he asked me out to lunch."

Abe nods, although his jaw is clenched as he crosses to sit next to me. "Romantic?"

"Abe." I wince. How did my relatively inexperienced dating life suddenly become so complicated? "I'm not trying to lead you on," I tell him, my voice twinging in what sounds like pity. But it's the truth. I don't want to hurt him. "You said we wouldn't end up hating each other."

He stares into his lap. "I lied. So what is it about him?"

Now I'm uncomfortable. "I really don't know him, Abe. And I don't think—"

"Shh . . ." he murmurs, lifting his head. His eyes are dark and deep, and when he starts talking, his voice is silky. "You're too tired to argue with me tonight," he says.

The minute the words are out of his mouth, I feel a sudden heaviness, like all my exhaustion hits at once. "Oh, whoa." I sway, leaning into the couch cushion. Each time I blink, my eyelids stay closed a little longer.

"Come here," Abe says, taking my arm gently to lay me across his lap. As he brushes my hair back from my forehead, it occurs to me that this is wrong. I don't understand what's happening.

Abe takes the knit blanket from the back of the sofa and

covers me, taking care as if tucking me in. His fingers begin twisting strands of my hair. "Who is he, Elise?"

"Harlin," I breathe out, almost like I'm calling for him.

Abe's hand stops in my hair, and I begin to drift away. The peace of sleep beckoning me. "Let me help you to bed," he says. I can barely keep my eyes open as he picks me up, carrying me down the hall. Abe murmurs as he walks, the words not quite recognizable. I feel my bed underneath me, the sheets icy and the mattress soft.

Abe slides in next to me, covering us both with the blanket. "Don't," I manage to say, even as Abe curls up behind me. He shouldn't be in my bed. "My dad will be home."

"No," Abe says. "He and Lucy will be out until after midnight. Your dad's car got a flat tire, no cell reception. They're fine, don't worry. But we're alone."

Even though sleep is the only thing I consciously want, I know inside that this isn't right. I try to crawl away, but Abe reaches to pull me effortlessly to him, his chest pressed against my back, his lips on my neck.

"Don't fight," he says into the skin there. "I just want to talk. Now tell me." He traces a finger over my temple, down my cheek. "How do you really know that Seer? You're not his Forgotten. So why is he trying to take you from me?"

I'm confused that Abe knows about the Forgotten, that he uses the same words as Marceline. But I answer him anyway. "I'm not yours to keep," I respond, my eyelids fluttering closed.

He laughs as if that's a silly thing for me to say. Then he

kisses my hair, my ear, my cheek. "Do you love me, Elise?"

"No."

He pauses, his grip tightening around my waist. "Do you love him?"

I think of Harlin, how handsome he looked on his motorcycle, waiting for me. The sadness surrounding him that I want to make go away.

"Do you love him?" Abe asks again, his voice smooth and inviting.

"Yes," I say finally, a smile crawling across my lips. "I love him."

Abe's hands slide to my neck, his fingers wrapping around my throat, but not squeezing. His body shakes with the anger radiating off his body, chilling mine. But I'm not scared.

I'm too tired to fight with him tonight.

"Well then," Abe says after a moment, his hands leaving my neck to rub my shoulders. "Harlin is a dead man."

CHAPTER 16

I'm in her vision again. I see Onika as she stares down at the city—her blond hair blowing in the cool wind of the afternoon. A smile touches her lips, and it sets me at ease. I wonder if she's found a kind of peace.

The rooftop door opens, but this time it's not Rodney. It's a younger guy, about twenty or so, with short blond hair and a sharp jaw. He's handsome and distinguished looking in a tan jacket and loafers.

"Onika," he calls, his British accent twinged with concern. "What are you doing up here? It's freezing."

"Is it?" she asks, peeking over her shoulder at him. "I can't feel it anymore."

The guy stops, cutting off his walk toward her as if he's

scared. She senses it. "What, lover?" she asks. "Do I frighten you now?"

He doesn't flinch from her words, only holds her cold gaze. "Yes."

"I can't go back, Monroe. I made the choice and the light won't have me. What do you suggest?"

Monroe swallows hard, kicking at the cement with the toe of his shoe. "I told you not to," he says quietly. "I told you—"

"Well, it's too goddamn late now, isn't it?" she snaps. "Can you not bear the sight of me?" She stomps across the roof, her heels clacking with menace. "Have you stopped loving me now that I'm not your precious Forgotten?"

She stops directly in front of him, but Monroe keeps his eyes downcast.

"I'll never stop loving you," he says. "You're the only woman I've ever loved—which is why I tried to let you go. I didn't want this. I never would have wanted this for you." He lifts his head. "But I know what you are now. I know what you've done, what you will do. I saw you whisper to that woman, heard you tell her to . . . kill herself. She did, you know? I saw it in the paper today." His blue eyes fill with tears and his hand twitches as if he's about to reach for Onika, but instead he balls it into a fist at his side. "*You* did that," he says. "Can't you see that you've become a monster?"

Even just watching, I feel like I've been punched in the stomach. But Onika only smiles as the pale skin on her face cracks, revealing the gray beneath.

Monroe steps back from her, repulsed. Onika takes in a deep breath, as if she's inhaling his fear. And then she licks her dry lips and smiles.

"I could make you jump off this building with just a whisper," she murmurs sweetly as if it's a love poem. "But I won't. Instead I will take all of your Forgotten. You can't hide them from me because I'll seek them out and extinguish them one by one for all of eternity. And know, lover"—she reaches to run a finger across his cheek—"I will haunt your dreams until the day you die."

With that, she disappears, leaving Monroe alone on the roof until the sky opens up, pouring rain all around him.

I wake with a start, bolting upright in bed. The clock reads 3:00 a.m. and the temperature in my room has to be below sixty degrees. I think about the dream that's fading quickly, but something else catches my eye.

My angel stone is on my bedside table, smashed to bits.

The next morning, I clean up the shards. I'm devastated by the loss of my stone, but more importantly, I don't know how it happened. Pieces of my dream are still with me—Onika and Monroe even clearer in my head now. I want to pretend that they're parts of a reccurring nightmare, but I'm not entirely sure what's real anymore. All I know is that I have to keep going, have to get through this. So I dump the remains of the angel in the trash and push away my fear.

When I walk into the kitchen, Lucy's sitting at the table, staring into her cup of coffee.

"You okay?" I ask.

She glances up, the dark liner having run under her eyes as if she hadn't bothered to wash it off the night before. Her hair is matted, her skin pale. "Sure," she answers, her voice heavy with indifference. "Just not sleeping well."

"Me either." I pour a cup of coffee, hoping for a caffeine boost.

"Not to mention I was stuck on the side of the road with Dad for several miserable hours last night," she says. "I had to sit through a lecture about responsibility while we waited for a passerby to rescue us." She sighs. "I swear I'm going to burn my car for the insurance money. We didn't get home until after midnight."

"Yeah, well. I don't even remember going to sleep last night." I glance around. "Where is Dad?"

"Church. By the way," she says, "he wanted me to remind you that you said you were bringing Abe to services tomorrow. Is it getting that serious between you two?"

My stomach knots at the mention of Abe. I feel awful for how I've treated him. He brought me donuts, but I was so tired, I'm not even sure what I said to him. I just hope he doesn't hate me.

"Uh-oh," Lucy says, standing to cross the room toward me. "What's changed?"

I lean closer and lower my voice. "I kissed Abe the other night," I say, my anxiety spiking. Exactly how much do I tell my sister about what's going on with me?

Lucy's eyes widen. "You *what*? And you didn't wake me up and tell me?" She looks hurt.

"No," I say. "Because it didn't go all that well. In fact, I'm not even sure why I let him kiss me in the first place. And when he did . . ." I'm trying to think of the best way to describe it without letting her know I'm a freak. "I got a shock."

"Like static electricity?"

I shake my head. "No, Lucy, you know how I told you strange things keep happening to me?"

"The reflection, the creepy old woman . . ." she says, gesturing for me to elaborate.

"Well, this was another strange thing. I actually felt repelled by Abe. It was painful to kiss him."

"Did he hurt you?" She sounds like she might track him down and beat him.

"No. It was me. My body sort of freaked out—cold and shaking—and I ran to my room and locked the door. It was all fairly dramatic and traumatizing."

"Wow," she says, leaning against the counter, processing.

"And then yesterday," I continue. "I talked with that customer I told you about—the one I said I'd probably never see again? Anyway, I bumped into him, and then Abe saw us. He went a little caveman on me. I'm not sure where we stand anymore."

My sister looks scandalized. "You've certainly broken out of your shell."

"Things have definitely gotten complicated."

"Sounds like it. Is there anything I can do?"

I shrug. "Rewind time? I wish I never agreed to go out with Abe. How am I supposed to work with him when I feel so horrible about everything?"

"Elise," Lucy says, before moving toward the fridge. "Abe Weston is a big boy. I'm sure he can handle himself, even if he's not used to rejection."

"I hope so."

Lucy grabs out the entire stack of cold cuts—ham, turkey, salami—and tosses them onto the counter before getting a Coke.

"Hungry?" I ask sarcastically.

"Ravenous. And I want lunch for breakfast." She pops the top on her drink and starts downing it immediately. Under the edge of her shirtsleeve, I notice a glint of gold.

"Is that a new bracelet?"

She chokes on her sip and then tugs down on her shirt. "Sometimes-boyfriend is getting more serious." She smiles. "Next time I'm asking for diamonds."

"Hope he's worth it," I say, undoing the tie on the bread, deciding that lunch for breakfast actually sounds pretty perfect.

"He's not," she says automatically, and then brings over the meat, slapping it down next to me. "Okay, so Abe is out. What about this other guy? I'm intensely curious about who can make Abe Weston go primal with jealousy."

We start building our sandwiches, Lucy grabbing a steak knife to dig around in the jar of mayonnaise.

"He rides a motorcycle."

"And you're blushing already." She bumps her shoulder into mine. "He must be sexy."

"He's very cute."

"Elise," Lucy says. "Cute guys don't ride on motorcycles. Sexy guys do. Or old guys. I'm guessing he's sexy, though, right?"

"So sexy."

"Then I can't wait to meet him."

"You sort of have," I tell her, biting into my sandwich. "He's the one you almost ran over with your car the other day."

The morning slips away as I get ready to meet Harlin, butterflies in my stomach. It's too gloomy outside for a sundress, and I'm afraid a skirt will fly up if he takes me on his Harley. So I opt for soft jeans and a snug T-shirt. I twist my hair into a knot and dab on some of my sister's perfume.

Lucy's asleep when I pop my head in to ask if her car is fit to drive, so I snag her keys to try for myself. The Honda purrs to life as if it hadn't had any trouble the night before, and I start toward Santo's. I want to pick up my check before going out with Harlin.

The rain starts almost immediately, pelting the windshield with angry splashes. Lucy's wipers can barely keep up.

When I pull into Santo's, there are only a few cars in the

parking lot. But no motorcycle. My heart dips until I see Harlin standing under the awning near the front door. I drive up to him, stopping as I roll down the passenger window.

"Why in the world are you waiting out here?" I call, my voice barely carrying over the rain.

His mouth stretches into a smile when he ducks down to see it's me. "I'm not. I just got here. I didn't want to ride my bike in the rain, so I hitchhiked. Interesting town you have here."

"I bet it was an adventure."

He points over his shoulder. "Should we grab some lunch first?"

"At Santo's?" I cringe at the thought. Other than the fact that I'm entirely sick of Mexican food, Abe might be in there. And he might accidentally-on-purpose drop a plate of enchiladas into Harlin's lap if we're together.

"Bad idea?" Harlin asks.

"Think so." We're quiet for a second, and then I shrug. "We can go back to my house. I can make sandwiches."

Harlin seems to think about it, as if he's not sure it's a good idea. But then he glances at the sky—at the rain—and climbs inside the car.

CHAPTER 17

Lucy?" I call when I open the front door. The house is quiet in response, and I glance back at Harlin. "No idea where my sister is," I say.

"Nice place," Harlin says as he walks in. "It's big."

"Really? It's only three bedrooms." Our house in Colorado had four, plus an office. But once my mother was gone, it always seemed too big without her in it. I swallow down the memory.

"You should see the apartment I live in," Harlin says, examining a picture of me from middle school hanging on the wall. "Two bedrooms, three guys. It's a disaster."

I try to picture where Harlin comes from. I wonder what his bedroom is like, if he has paintings hanging on his wall.

156

Portraits of girls he met in restaurants.

Harlin slips off his leather jacket, laying it over the arm of the sofa. He's wearing a black T-shirt, the muscles of his arms filling out the sleeves. "I live with my older brothers," he explains. "They're slobs."

I smile, thinking it's sweet that he lives with his brothers. I'm curious about his parents, but it seems rude to ask. So instead I motion toward the kitchen. "Drink?"

He agrees and follows me, taking it all in as if truly curious about every aspect of my life. When I hand him a soda, our fingers touching once again, the smile that makes me melt returns to his lips. "So," Harlin says, leaning against the tiled counter. "Where do you want to do it?"

Kitchen scissors are probably not the best choice for cutting hair, but they're all I can find. I set up a chair in the middle of the room and wrap a striped towel over Harlin's shoulders. I read once that it's best to cut dry hair, so I stand behind him and use my comb to smooth a section. I hold it between my fingers and then trim off the ends without incident. Okay, so far so good.

I move to his side, my hip brushing his arm as I try to level the hair above his ear, but decide that's too short and opt to keep it longer.

"How you doing up there?" Harlin asks, sounding amused. "You're awfully quiet."

"Shh, I'm trying to concentrate."

He laughs and I run the scissors over his sideburns, my fingers grazing his cheek. His eyes flutter closed and it sends a rush over me, that I can affect him like that. My breathing starts to deepen; my hands shake.

I round the front of him, brushing back his hair with my fingers and admiring how handsome his face is. He keeps his eyes shut, his lips slightly parted like he's enjoying every touch.

I nudge his knee aside, sliding my thigh in between his as I lean over him, gently combing through his hair. His hands reach to hold either side of my hip. It's barely a touch, but it sends vibrations over my entire body.

I want him.

I'm cutting, sort of, when his fingers graze the bare skin above my jeans, just under my T-shirt. I make a soft sound, willing him to do more.

Harlin tilts his face up toward mine, his eyes still closed as he pulls our bodies together. He licks his bottom lip and I lean down, ready to finally press my mouth to his. At the last second, he looks at me—a mix of emotions in his eyes.

"Whoa. I'm sorry."

I jump at the sound of my sister's voice and turn quickly, the scissors falling from my hand to the tile floor. Lucy is standing in the doorway of the kitchen, barely concealing her smile.

"I am *so* sorry, Elise," she says again. "I didn't know you, um, had company." I can only imagine how I look—the flush still on my skin. I can't even bring myself to glance back at Harlin, not when I'd so nearly kissed him. Again.

"This . . ." My voice is raspy and I clear my throat. "This is Harlin," I tell Lucy. "Harlin, this is my sister."

Lucy holds out her hand in a stop motion. "Don't get up," she says. "In fact, pretend I'm not even here." She glances over her shoulder as she walks out of the room. "It was very nice to meet you, Harlin."

Harlin watches Lucy go, his brow creased with concern as he sits silently. When I touch his shoulder he snaps out of it, apologizing quickly. "Sorry, yes, it was nice to meet you too," he calls after her.

There's no answer, and I turn to Harlin, my cheeks still warm. "Why were you so quiet?" I ask.

Harlin meets my eyes and smiles. "My mind was on other things."

I laugh, thinking about his fingers on my skin, his face turned up toward mine. "Oh, yes," I say. "I noticed."

Harlin chuckles and shakes his head. "My hair is messed up now, huh?"

"No," I say, like that's a ridiculous statement. I lean to grab the scissors from the floor and walk behind him. "But I should even it up."

His hair is, in fact, *really* messed up, one side longer than the other. I end up having to cut it shorter than I planned, but at the same time, it shows off more of his face—which I happen to find gorgeous anyway.

As I'm finishing, Harlin's laugh breaks the silence in the room. I stop, loving the sound of it. "What?" I ask.

"Oh, nothing," he says innocently. "Except to note that you are now my all-time favorite hairstylist."

"Maybe I should open my own salon," I say, grinning ear to ear.

"Pencil me in for every day at three."

I slap his shoulder, telling him to shut up, and soon the moment begins to settle into something normal. Something peaceful. When I'm done, I comb the front of Harlin's hair to the side with my fingers, brushing all the loose hair from his temples. He's silent, his eyes never leaving mine.

Then I drop my arm, stepping back to admire my work. "So," I say to him finally. "Want to stay for dinner?"

"You have a motorcycle?" my father asks Harlin from the head of the dinner table. We don't normally use the dining room, but when my father came home to discover a guy here, he suddenly became very formal. Well, besides the pizza box in the middle of the table.

"I do," Harlin says, wiping his hands on a napkin. "It's a Harley-Davidson, very safe. And I never ride it when it's raining. Which seems to be every day around here."

My father nods. "Wettest summer on record."

I bite my thumbnail, watching nervously as my father continues to interrogate Harlin. Next to me Lucy picks the pepperoni off her slice, keeping her head lowered. During a lull in the conversation, Harlin asks me to pass him the Coke. When I do, he winks, as if letting me know I shouldn't be nervous.

"And you're from Portland?" my dad continues. "I was just there to help set up a mission downtown. Beautiful city."

"It is gorgeous. I'm originally from California, but my family moved to the Northwest a few years back. I was traveling there when I ended up taking a detour through Thistle. Decided to stay awhile."

"It's not a bad place to stop," my father says. "What do your parents do?"

"Dad," I warn, not liking the game of twenty questions that he's playing. I'd think Lucy would make a joke, but she hasn't said a word. I'm guessing she's tired from staying up all night, which is the only rational explanation for her not admiring Harlin right now.

Harlin takes a sip from his drink before glancing sideways at my father. "I don't really talk to my mother anymore," he says quietly. "I live with my older brothers."

My father immediately shoots me a look and then folds his hands in front of him, as if fascinated. "What about your father?"

Something in my chest suddenly aches, and I reach under the table to put my palm on Harlin's knee. He doesn't flinch, but instead presses his lips into a sad smile. "My father was a police officer, killed on duty," he says. "Gone three years now."

Lucy looks up as my father's expression falters. Yet somehow it's almost as if I knew what Harlin was going to say. Confused, I pull my hand back into my lap, but Harlin reaches to gently run his fingers over mine, intertwining them. It gives me comfort, and it's clear it does the same for him.

"I'm so sorry to hear about your father," my dad murmurs sincerely. "I work closely with the police department here. Very honorable folks."

"Thanks," Harlin responds. Tears gather in his eyes before he blinks them away. "My father was a solid guy," he says. "It's been a really difficult time, especially since they hadn't caught the perp. But last year . . ." He pauses, fighting back the emotion in his voice. "Last year they found him, brought him to trial, and sentenced him. Everyone said it was a miracle."

"I'm glad you finally found justice," I say. "Your family needed that."

When the dinner conversation picks up again, my father asking Lucy about her upcoming semester, Harlin leans his arm against mine, his voice just a whisper in my ear. "I think you're amazing," he says. And then, without waiting for a response, he goes back to his pizza.

CHAPTER 13

After dinner I tell my father I'll be back later and drive Harlin to his motel. It's a run-down place off Route 5 with a light out in their vacancy sign. I wonder how long he's been living here.

When I park in front of his room, there is a tug of sadness. I don't want this day to end. I don't want Harlin to go. As if sensing my mood, he turns to me and smiles.

"Did you want to come in?" he asks. My heart kicks up its beats.

"Well," I say. "You've already seen my place."

He waits as I turn off the car and climb out. I almost reach for his hand but stop myself—surprised by how comfortable I am with him.

The room is small, but immaculate. There are two beds, although one has a sleeping bag on top of it. In the corner is a small desk, and I notice the sketch pad lying there.

"You're very neat," I say, walking toward the desk. "Were you a well-behaved child?"

Harlin grins. "No."

I touch the edge of the sketch pad and look over my shoulder at him. "Can I?" I ask.

He hesitates, but then nods before going to sit on the bed. I open to the first page: a landscape of a beach, the ocean at low tide.

"That's where I grew up," Harlin says quietly from behind me. "Near Oceanside, California."

"It's pretty," I say, turning to the next picture. It's another landscape, this time a bridge in the background. "Portland?" I ask. He agrees, and I continue turning the pages until the images start to change altogether. There's a sinking feeling when I get to the pictures of a girl. Something about her is familiar.

Harlin stands and looks over my shoulder. He's so close that I no longer care about this other girl. I feel the warmth from his body as he reaches to take the pad from me. "Let me show you something," he says, flipping to the back. I realize then that the entire book is filled with pictures of this other girl as he skips past them.

I turn sideways, my face close to his as he concentrates. I want him to notice me the way he obviously noticed her. Her every curve. Her every feature.

"Here," he says, setting the book down and tapping the

page. "I did this after that first day at Santo's. It's not great, but I was drafting from memory."

I look down, startled to see a picture of me. The edges are blurred where he rubbed off the pencil several times, but the likeness is there, and it's flattering. He reaches to turn the page. "I thought about you a lot," he says quietly.

There's another picture of me, laughing. I'm struck with an emotion I've never had before, or at least, not like this. I'm completely and totally in love with Harlin—even though I hardly know much about him at all.

He reaches for the book, but I turn to him, putting my hand on his chest. He tenses before slowly lowering his gaze to mine. By his expression, I think we've gone well past mutual attraction. And I don't think I can wait anymore.

I lean up to put my lips to his, testing his reaction. He doesn't move at first—as if he's scared to touch me. I kiss his top lip. His bottom lip. I slide my hands until they wrap behind his neck, pulling myself closer to him.

There's the slightest touch of his tongue and I make a soft sound, renewing my kisses. He's so gentle, so careful—but all I want is for him to grab me, hold me. "Harlin," I murmur between his lips. "Kiss me."

He moves his hands to my waist, drawing me tighter against him. But he turns to rest his cheek against mine. "You are so beautiful," he whispers, his breath hot on my ear. My eyelids flutter closed. "But I can't," he adds.

"I want you to," I say, my fingers threading through his hair.

"I know." He leans his forehead against mine, looking into my eyes. "Please believe me when I say it's taking every ounce of my willpower to do this: But I think you should leave."

I'm frozen at first, but when I realize he's serious, I back out of his arms—humiliated. I feel utterly rejected and it stings, especially since he's the first guy I've ever tried to kiss. He winces when he sees the hurt on my face.

"It's not what you think, Elise," he says quickly, reaching for me. But I push his hand away.

"And what do I think?"

"This has nothing to do with you."

"Oh, well. That makes me feel so much better, Harlin. Thanks for the explanation." I walk quickly around the bed, mortified and shaking. I can't believe this is happening. I can't believe I could have misread him completely.

I open the motel room door, the first bit of tears stinging my eyes. Harlin steps in front of me, backing me against the wall. He stares until I look at him. When I do, I'm surprised to see the tears gathered in his eyes. "I'm in love with someone else," he says. "But she's gone. And I—"

I push him then, nearly slapping him. If he's in love with someone, then why did he come to my house? Why talk with my *dad*?

I move past Harlin, walking through the door, when he takes my elbow to stop me. "Elise, please—"

"Don't," I say, pulling my arm from his. "Just . . . don't."

With fresh hurt on his face, Harlin nods and steps away.

* * *

My dad is asleep when I arrive home, and the day's dishes are still in the sink. I didn't let myself cry on the way back, refusing to let a guy—one I just met—so thoroughly wreck my self-esteem. And as I start in on the bowls and plates with soapy water, I keep myself calm, even though I'm devastated. What's most troubling is that beyond embarrassment, it shouldn't be this painful. How can someone I just met hurt me so much?

I'm nearly done when my father comes out of his room, his blue eyes concerned when he finds me in the kitchen. "You're cleaning?" he asks. "Is it that bad?" He comes to kiss the top of my head, spurring on my sudden urge to cry, but I fight it back.

"I wish you'd buy a dishwasher," I say instead, turning off the water. I grab the red towel to dry my hands and stare out into the dark night.

"Why would I need a dishwasher when I have you?" my father replies, going to the fridge to pull out a foil-covered plate.

"That joke never gets old, does it?"

"Not to me."

I sit at the kitchen table, and my father sets the plate of chocolate cake in front of me, leaving a fork at my side. When he sits next to me, I take a bite of cake, slowly chewing as the silence drags on. I'm not sure if I have the guts to tell him what happened tonight. It occurs to me that I've been lying a lot—and I hate the thought of it.

"Harlin's not interested in me," I say quietly, setting down the fork. Embarrassed, I feel prickles of heat break over my face and neck.

"What?" my father asks. "I don't believe that. He looked completely smitten."

"Yeah, well. He just told me he's in love with someone else. So he's apparently not smitten with me."

"Oh, kid," my father says, putting his arm over my shoulders. "I'm not convinced this is true, but I'm sorry. He seemed like a very genuine person at dinner. Maybe he's confused. I'm glad he was honest with you, though."

I scoff. "He could have been honest before having dinner with us. Before agreeing to come to church with me. I feel ridiculous."

"He agreed to come to a service?" my father asks, sounding impressed.

"Yeah. But he's a heathen, so who cares."

He chuckles. "There is that possibility, but I don't think you should write Harlin off just yet. I have a feeling we'll be seeing him around."

I push the plate away, unwilling to have another bite of cake when I'm too depressed to enjoy it. Just then Lucy walks in, wearing her pajamas—something I haven't seen her wear in a while. They're polka-dotted and long-sleeved, and all at once I think that she appears younger. Well, except for the heavy foundation that seems too tan for her skin.

"You're still home?" I ask. "It's not even curfew."

"Thought I'd grace you all with my presence." She pauses to smile. "I can occasionally be the responsible child, especially when my little sister is off riding around with a strange guy. And besides," she says, pushing my shoulder, "I've missed you."

I'm slightly taken aback by Lucy's words, but at the same time, I want to hug her. I haven't seen her this vulnerable since . . . well, since our mother died. My father must notice too, because he comes to put his arms around both of us, resting his chin on the top of Lucy's head.

"I love you girls," he says. "You make me proud every day." Lucy and I start to groan, ready to tell him to stop being so sappy, when he laughs. "And I'm most proud when you're home by curfew without any boys around."

Lucy pulls back and rolls her eyes. "If you ever tire of being a pastor, I think you have a real chance at stand-up comedy." She reaches past me for my fork, scooping up a bite of cake before popping it into her mouth. "And yes," she says to my father. "We love you too."

Lucy and I stare at the TV in the dim living room after she finishes the cake. She rests her head on my shoulder as the sink runs in the kitchen, my father rinsing off the plate.

"Elise," my sister says in a low voice, barely audible over the movie. "Do you remember when Mom died?"

I tear my eyes from the television to look down at her, her face hidden from view. "Yeah?"

Lucy starts playing with a loose string in the couch blanket, twisting it around her finger. "There was that night," she says. "The night before she died, when we laid in bed while Dad was at the hospital. Praying."

A lump forms in my throat. "They wouldn't let us in anymore," I add. "It was against their policy." It hurts to think about it, my mom in that hospital bed, unconscious. During her last week, she stopped waking up, drugs coursing through her system. They said it was better that way, but I've always wondered. What would she have said to us in those moments? Had we robbed her of them?

"That night," Lucy continues, "when we were curled up and you were crying, I told you that I had a secret. Do you remember that?"

It's a little foggy at first, but I do vaguely recall the conversation. I pull back then, looking at my sister as tears glisten in her eyes. "Lucy, what's wrong?"

"How come you never asked?" she whispers, her voice cracking. "How come you never asked what my secret was?"

The question is so loaded with accusation and pain, I wrap my arms around my sister and pull her to me. "I don't know," I say. "I guess I thought you'd tell me when you were ready."

Lucy sniffles, brushing at the back of my hair with her fingers, shuddering once as she holds back her cry. Then she straightens, touching my cheek lovingly. Like it's the last time she'll ever see me.

"What was it?" I ask, seeing the desperation in her eyes. "What was your secret?"

Lucy smiles sadly, tilting her head as if apologizing. "It doesn't matter now," she whispers. "I guess nothing ever really did." Then she stands and goes to her bedroom, closing the door behind her.

CHAPTER 19

ucy's comment haunts me as I lie in bed. I only vaguely remember the conversation from when we were kids, but my sister has always hidden things. Or at least, hidden her feelings. She's told me about her boyfriends, about her friends. But our talks were always under a veil of jokes. I wonder what could be going on with Lucy. I'm scared to ask. I'm scared for her.

I fall into a restless sleep, determined to fix my life, fix my sister's life. And I know the only person who has answers is Marceline. So after work tomorrow, I'm going to her house. And this time I won't let a guy distract me.

When I wake up, I feel exhausted but anxious to get started. I'm working the morning shift for our after-church rush and opt out of going to my father's service, telling him I picked up an extra shift to keep my mind off of Harlin. But that's not true. This is my opportunity to see Marceline.

My father drops me off at Santo's on his way to church, and when I hug him good-bye, he tells me again that he doesn't think I should give up on Harlin. I can't believe he's actually hoping I get a boyfriend, and by the expression on his face, I don't think he can believe it either. But in the end, my father just wants me to be happy. So I appreciate him going against all of his fatherly instincts for me.

The OPEN sign buzzes to life in the Santo's window as I walk inside. I'm punching my card in the time clock when Abe clears his throat from behind me. He's leaning in the doorway, sipping from a cup of coffee.

"Morning," he says, smiling. It's the first time we've spoken since he brought donuts the other night.

"You're in a good mood," I say, stopping to tie my apron around my waist. I follow Abe into the kitchen, where he pours me a cup of coffee. I thank him as I take it, even if he does make it too strong.

"Missed you last night," he says, watching me carefully.

I pause midsip, uncomfortable at where this conversation might lead. "Did you work?" I ask, hoping to guide him to safer topics.

"I did. And it was boring and miserable. I didn't have anyone to entertain me." He leans close in a mock whisper. "Santo doesn't flirt back *at all*."

I laugh, remembering why I find Abe so entertaining. "Well, I'm here now," I say. "And I plan to make at least a million dollars over the next two hours. You?"

"Million five." Abe drains the rest of his drink. "What do you say we go out to lunch later? After all, we will be millionaires."

My stomach flips. "Uh . . . I can't." I don't dare tell him about Marceline. He'll realize there's something wrong with me—or at least strongly suspect I've lost my mind.

"Going out with your new boyfriend?" he asks, his expression curious.

I don't respond at first, focusing my attention on the wall clock, the hand-washing sign. Anywhere but Abe. I'm too humiliated to tell him that I liked Harlin, but he didn't feel the same way.

"You don't have to answer that," Abe offers. "I guess the nice thing to say is that I'm happy for you."

I look back at him, relieved to avoid the conversation. "Thank you," I tell him. I start toward the dining room when Abe reaches out to take my wrist.

"Then again," he murmurs, "I can be quite a bastard."

"Abe?" I say, my heart skipping a beat. "Let go."

He looks at my arm, as if surprised he'd touched me, and shrugs sheepishly. "Sorry." He takes his hand off, holding it up in apology. "What can I say? You bring out the devil in me."

"That's not a comforting thing to tell a pastor's daughter," I joke, trying to lighten the mood. I have no idea how I'm going to continue working with Abe. This is incredibly awkward.

"I don't know how we'll keep working together either," he says, as if he read my thoughts. "I tried to be different with you. And now, well, now you've gone and ruined everything."

"What are—"

Abe tears his dark gaze away and stalks toward the back room. Anxiety immediately begins to twist my stomach, the worry that Abe will never talk to me again. Whether it's true or not, I feel like I've been cruel. I'm not sure I can leave without at least trying to work things out. Maybe salvage some sort of friendship.

I look for Abe, but he's not at the time clock or the walk-in cooler. On the other side of the room, I notice the back door propped open with a bucket and go to peek outside. I find him there, leaning against the wall.

"Hey," I say cautiously, sliding out the door. Abe glances over, his apron balled up in his hand.

"What?" he answers evenly.

"I was hoping you weren't mad at me." I take a spot next to him on the wall.

"Then that's your fault for being stupid."

Ouch. This is exactly the reason why I didn't want to kiss him that night after camping. He hates me.

"Please don't be mean," I say quietly, looking down at my feet. He scoffs.

"You have no idea how *mean* I can be." Abe drops his apron and grabs me by the upper arms, swinging to pin me against the wall. I gasp.

"Why are you even out here?" he murmurs, as if he doesn't quite trust what my answer will be.

"I was worried," I say. "I never wanted to hurt you."

"No? You may want to rethink that." One hand slides into my hair, pulling my face closer to his.

"Abe, stop." I try to work my arms between us to push him away, but his expression changes to something sad. Crushingly lonely. I stop fighting, his sadness seeming to spread to me.

Abe moves his palm onto my shoulder, looking like he might cry. Against me his chest rises and falls, his pure desperation filling my heart. Then he leans in and kisses me.

Cold winds through my mouth, and I flinch, turning my face away from his. My lips are numb.

"Don't—" I start to say, but Abe takes my chin and tries to kiss me again. I push him back as hard as I can, only succeeding in breaking our kiss. I'm still pinned. "Stop," I whisper fiercely.

Abe puts a hand on either side of me against the wall. "This is getting really old, Elise," he says. "You're really starting to piss me off."

"Abe. I—"

He puts his palm over my mouth to stop me. The darkness in his eyes is no longer inviting. It's angry and sinister, and all at once I am very, very afraid of him.

"Look at that," he says, almost to himself. "I finally got your heart racing."

Although I've seen small glimpses of his anger before, it was never like this. This is cold, and dark, and void. Abe tilts his head as if thinking, lowering his palm from my mouth. My body trembles and I consider screaming for help.

Abe smiles. "No one will hear you."

My eyes widen, and I try to push him, try to get away, but he grabs me hard and slams me back into the wall. The force of it stuns me and I cry out in pain.

Abe leans forward, resting his cheek on mine like we're in an intimate hug. "I tried to play nice with you, Elise," he whispers. "But . . ." He pulls back just enough to peer down at me. "Since you won't remember this anyway."

He crushes his mouth against mine, his hand knotting painfully in my hair. I struggle, but he's unmovable—strong. Inhumanly strong. I'm trying to scream for help, but I can't get free of his mouth. He pushes up my shirt, his hands rough and careless on my skin. My body begins to shiver, splinters of ice tearing me apart from the inside. I bite down on his lip and he jumps away, cursing under his breath.

Abe touches the back of his hand to his mouth, checking the blood there. He shakes his head at me, smiling like he's impressed I fought back.

Completely weak, I slide down the wall as tears stream over my cheeks. My mouth aches, my body. Why did he do that? What's wrong with him?

"Didn't know you liked it so rough, Elise." He wipes his mouth again, and soon the blood is gone and his lip is normal, undamaged. "The things I can do with you."

My body convulses with the cold, and when I look down,

my skin is grayer. I begin to whimper, wanting Abe to go away.

He stands over me and exhales, like he's exhausted. "Just give in," he says. "If you want, I'll be sweet, treat you like a queen. Will that make it easier, *querida?*" He reaches toward me and I flinch, my teeth chattering. He gently runs his finger over my temple. "I don't know why you're different," he says. "And I don't care. You're the closest I can ever get to the light, the brightest thing I've ever seen. Just come with me and I'll never hurt you again. I promise."

His whispers are tender, the only sound in my ears. They wrap around me, covering me in fog. In shadows. My eyelids flutter, and the entire scene slips out of focus.

They've forgotten me. Mercy, Sarah—everyone. My destiny is unavoidable. My life is over. It's horrifying, and yet . . . I've lost the will to fight. I just want it all to be over. Because now I know that I never existed. That there is no such thing as me.

I open my eyes, completely disoriented. The memory still holds me with its sorrow, but I push it away when I realize I'm around the back of Santo's, sitting on the gravel against the outside wall.

How did I get here? The last thing I remember was searching for Abe. And then I woke up, filled with a memory that leaves me feeling helpless.

I hear my name and turn to see Abe rushing over, his eyebrows pulled together in worry as he kneels next to me. "Elise," he says, checking the back of my head for blood. "Are you okay? What happened?"

I touch my mouth. It's sore, like I've been punched in the face. My shirt is untucked, and my head feels like I smacked it on something.

"I must have fainted," I say, not sure I believe it.

"We should get you some water." Abe looks like he's so worried he can barely stand it. He takes my hand and helps me up. "You have to be more careful, Elise," he says. "I can't always be here to save you."

"What can I say?" I ask, still shaking. "You're my savior."

He pulls me into a gentle hug as he kisses the top of my head. "Close enough."

When we get inside, I know that I have to leave and find Marceline. The memories are getting more intense, the lines of reality blurring completely. I tell Santo that I'm sick—possibly with the flu—and that I have to take off. He reluctantly agrees. Abe makes me promise to call him when I get home. I don't mention that I'm not going there, or that I don't even have a car. But I'm glad that Abe and I are still friends. I think he might be the only one I've got.

CHAPTER 20

I walk to Marceline's, which luckily isn't too far. I'm halfway up her walkway when I hear a motorcycle pull up at the curb behind me. My stomach drops, and I have to force myself to turn around. There's no reason not to be civil. Just because Harlin hurt my feelings doesn't give me the right to treat him poorly. Look at Abe. I hurt him, and he's still a gentleman.

Harlin notices me, pausing a long moment before climbing off his bike. He seems miserable as he slips his hands into the pockets of his jeans and approaches me, head down.

"Hi, Harlin," I say evenly.

He lifts his gaze to mine before shifting it away. "Elise, I—"

I turn, walking toward the house before he can offer another excuse. Or worse, try to explain in more detail. Being this close to him and not being able to touch him is torture, a reminder of how much I like him. A reminder that he rejected me. I don't know why he's even here, especially when he knew I'd probably come back.

When I ring Marceline's bell, Harlin stands next to me with his arms crossed over his chest. Of course we'd get to the house at the same time. Hopefully he doesn't plan on staying long. I have a lot to talk to Marceline about.

The door swings open. Marceline is wearing a flowered housecoat, her white hair wild without the knit cap to tame it. She looks between Harlin and me, grinning.

"I figured you'd show up together," she says in her broken voice.

Harlin and I exchange a look, not mentioning the fact that we're not really on speaking terms at the moment. It also doesn't help that Marceline just rubbed some salt in my rejection wound.

"We're, um . . ." This is so humiliating. "We didn't come here together," I tell her. "We just happened to show up at the same time. A coincidence."

Marceline laughs, holding open the door as she waves us in, her bracelets jangling. "Child," she says, "there's no such thing."

Marceline's house is comforting in its clutter, in its oddness. I make my way to the couch, wondering if she's going to talk to me in front of Harlin. I'm scared. I don't want him to know the things she's said to me. Will he believe them? Or will he think I'm an idiot for sitting through her ramblings?

As Marceline shuffles in, Harlin stands in the doorway watching us.

"Harlin," the old woman calls as she takes her spot in the rocking chair. "Don't sulk around like some wounded puppy. Have a seat."

My eyes widen. Oh no. She's going to tell him that I'm a Forgotten. I start to panic, even think about leaving. Marceline pushes her bowl of mints toward me.

"I think I'd rather be lucid for this," I murmur.

"We'll see," she says, taking a piece and popping it into her mouth. I wonder how many of those she's had already today.

Harlin comes to sit next to me, my heart rate spiking the minute he does. His smell is so familiar, the heat from his body radiating toward mine as our shoulders brush against each other. I close my eyes, nearly overwhelmed by the sense of loss I feel.

"I'm going to be candid," Marceline says. I look to find her staring in my direction. "He should know what you are."

What I am. The phrase slaps me, breaks me apart. I think of the memory and the feeling that I was dying. That I'd given up trying to save myself. But I'll never give up.

"I know what she is," Harlin says. I turn to him suddenly, stunned by his admission. How does he fit into this?

"Do you know *who* she is?" Marceline asks gently.

Harlin's eyes narrow as he tries to find meaning in the old woman's words. The two of them stay like that, but my

181

stomach is twisting in knots.

"What are you talking about?" I demand. "Who . . . what am I? And how does Harlin know any of this?"

Marceline focuses her attention on me. "He's a Seer, child. He helps the Forgotten—leads them to their destiny." She gives him a sharp look. "Or at least he's supposed to."

"Seer," I repeat. I think back on the stories of the Forgotten. Harlin knows all about this. He's part of this.

"More importantly," Marceline says, crunching down on her mint, "he's in love with you. Again."

I'm about to ask Marceline what she's talking about, but I shoot a look at Harlin. He stares past her then, not seeming to react to her words. His mouth parts as he takes in a shuddered breath. His eyes well up, tears flowing freely down his cheeks. All without a word.

"I'm so sorry, honey," Marceline says to him. "I didn't know at first."

"What's going on?" I ask. Seeing Harlin this destroyed is killing me. He already told me he loved someone else. Marceline is talking in riddles again.

She gives me a weary glance, but it's clear she's worried about Harlin, who still hasn't moved or said a word. "Fine," I say, sick of constantly being left out of the loop. I stand up, ready to take off. "I'm leaving—"

"Wait," Harlin whispers, reaching to take my hand. Startled, I turn to him. He studies me with what can only be described as absolute pain. I nearly reach for him, but he lets my hand drop.

Harlin leans to put his elbows on his knees, his face in his palms. Marceline slides the bowl of mints toward him, but he doesn't lift his head.

The wrinkles in Marceline's skin seem to deepen. When her eyes meet mine, she shrugs apologetically. "You're the reincarnation of his girlfriend. A Forgotten."

I stumble back a step. "I'm *what*?"

"Your name was Charlotte Cassidy. Beautiful soul—very loving. In the end, you—"

Harlin jumps up then, rushing past us. He doesn't say a word, and when the front door closes, I know he's gone. Tears begin to gather in my eyes.

"He's never learned to handle his grief," Marceline explains. "He'll find you when he's ready. He always does."

I'm not sure how to process what's happened. Instead, I reach to take a peppermint. As I suck on it, my body begins to shake with the realization. "I had another life?" I ask. "It's all real?"

Marceline nods. "Take heart in the fact that you sacrificed yourself for the good of the world. That's admirable. And now they've sent you back to do it again."

I'm light-headed, and I'm not sure if I'm prepared to hear any more. "This isn't possible," I murmur. "None of this is possible."

"I assure you, there are many things in this world that you can't understand, child. But it doesn't mean they're impossible. In fact, like coincidences, there is a reason for everything. Even the things we can't explain."

I meet the old woman's eyes. "How do you know all this?"

"I'm a Seer, like Harlin. Only, my vision is keener—mostly because it's mixed with my psychic abilities. I thought I was retired, but it seems you've brought back my sight." She leans forward in her chair, the wood creaking. "You're special. And not because you're Forgotten. But because you've come back. And that's never been done before. There is a purpose in this, even if we can't see it just yet."

"So all that stuff—the skin turning gold, the people forgetting, that's going to happen to me?"

"Eventually. But you're still very new, and you seem to handle the Needs better. Maybe it's because you've done it before; maybe not. Either way, these things take time."

I sway with grief, but then something she said the first time we met occurs to me.

"Shadows," I say. "You told me once to watch out for them. But I don't know what a Shadow is." The mint has worked to calm me, not creating the same confusing sensation as last time. Now it's more like a warm blanket has been wrapped around me. I lean back into the sofa cushion and Marceline begins rocking again.

"The Shadows were like you once," she begins quietly. "They had the Need, gave people hope. They found them at just the right time, and said just the right thing. But instead of filling their destinies, they turned away from the light, binding themselves to Earth for selfish wants. And when you turn away from the light, all that's left are the Shadows. Those Forgotten didn't find the freedom they'd hoped for. Their existence is dark and cold. Lonely. They are compelled once again, but this time, it's with Want—the overwhelming desire to find someone and change their lives for the worse. They fulfill their Wants to stay powerful. If they don't, they'll wither, but never die. Being a Shadow is a fate far worse than death."

Suddenly my memories and hazy dreams click together. "There's a woman," I say. "I've seen her life. She . . ." It takes me a minute to recall, but when I do, I'm terrified. "She became a Shadow," I say. "I saw her become a Shadow."

Marceline straightens, and I think she knows exactly who I'm talking about. "Yes," she says. "Onika is like you in a way. Different from the rest of her kind. Stronger. That poor child is filled with hate and horror. She's the embodiment of misery."

"I'm having memories—of who I used to be, I guess. Does—"

"Oh, you're still Charlotte," Marceline interrupts. "The soul is the same, just a different body. But see, you've learned things, child. Things other Forgotten won't know until they cross. This will help you. This knowledge is what makes you strong."

"I don't feel very strong."

"You're here," she offers. "You didn't run to the doctors, who could never understand. Or run to your father, who is a wonderful man, I must say. You came to me on your own, and that is brave. Do you know what you're capable of now?"

"No."

"Control. You can control the light you spread. The visions. I saw it inside you that day in the parking lot. Child, you're just as powerful as the Shadows, maybe more so. I ask you to think—think of your soul. Do you know why you're here?"

"No," I murmur.

She nods, looking slightly disappointed. "Well, whatever the reason, your beauty is astounding. It's why the Shadows want you. They crave the light. And although most only want to tempt it away—are in fact compelled to—some want to keep it for themselves. Like Abraham."

At the mention of Abe's name my muscles tense, a sinking sensation in my gut. "He's a Shadow?"

She nods. "Oh, yes. He used to be my Forgotten, but I couldn't save him." Her expression softens as if I've struck a deep sorrow within her. She takes another piece of mint, and I wish I could help her somehow.

Suddenly, there's a tingling in my fingers. I blink quickly and look down at them. As the sensation spreads up my arm, I know it's the Need. And that I've willed it to start.

"Marceline," I say cautiously. Light begins to brighten behind her form, blotting out the small cluttered room beyond us. When she hears me, she straightens, but doesn't look pleased. Then I'm filled with ninety years of her memories.

She's a child on the streets of New York City, poor, but not unhappy. Her mother is clairvoyant and makes a living as a fortune-teller. Marceline's father died, along with her brother and two sisters. It's just her and her mother now. And from her mother she learns how to control her abilities. The memories go on; Marceline watches me curiously as she relives them all. She thinks then that she's never realized how old she really is. And I smile, sharing her thoughts.

But before we get even halfway through her life, my sight begins to change—speeding past all of her memories to now. I meet her eyes with an alarmed stare.

"Marceline," I say, a strong voice inside my head with a warning. "You're—

"I'm old," she interrupts me. "Don't you go worrying about my mortality. I'm tougher than I look." Marceline leans forward, a soft smile on her lips. "When it's truly my time, you can't help me. Not even with the Need. Now get out of my head." And then it's gone, the light, the visions. Marceline's rocker stills, the light filtering in the window illuminating dust in the air, dust that doesn't move. I sway back into the sofa as a memory pours inside my mind.

Harlin is in front of me, smiling confidently. "Where were you running to, Miss Cassidy?" he asks in a low, raspy voice.

I step up to him, looking deeply into his eyes. Thinking he's the most beautiful creature I've ever seen. "Here."

His smile falters just a bit, overcome with something else. And then as if he can't help himself, he puts his palm on my cheek and pulls me into a kiss.

"Harlin," I whisper, his name on my lips as I come back to the moment. He did love Charlotte. *Me.* The thought is both painful and comforting at the same time.

Marceline is now standing by the window, staring out

toward the street. "You still have so much to learn, and not nearly enough time." She sounds regretful.

I go to stand by her, struck with how odd it is that we're together now, so soon after she attacked me in a parking lot. Now I can see her for exactly what she is, an old woman— brave and smart. I put my arms around her fragile frame and hug her.

"I'll be fine," she says, patting my arm. "And don't start thinking you're all alone. You have your sister and your father. And of course there's Harlin."

"Harlin won't even talk to me," I say.

She chuckles at this. "I'm psychic, child. I've told you he'll be back. But there is something bigger at stake here. The universe is supposed to be balanced, both with good and evil. Onika is destroying that balance, corrupting things that were never meant to be corrupted. You need to stop her, for all of our sakes."

"How?"

"The answer's in here." She taps my temple gently. "You only have to look for it."

At her urging, I close my eyes and am immersed in another memory.

Onika is on the bridge, circling Monroe as she runs her gloved finger across his chest. His shoulder. "He really is still handsome," *she says to me as I watch them from the railing. "You have no idea how much he and I loved each other." She traces her finger across his lips. He stares through her, at me.*

"Why don't you let him see you?" I ask Onika.

"Why should he?" she growls, turning back to me. "He wanted me gone. He doesn't deserve to see me."

"Charlotte," Monroe calls, looking through her. "Don't talk to her. Don't listen to her. Please, honey. You have to go before it's too late."

I snap back, my body still shivering from the cold air on the bridge. "Monroe," I murmur. Marceline smiles to herself.

"Ah," she says. "Monroe Swift. I should have known. He contacted me about Harlin. Wanted me to explain to him some of the rules of being a Seer. Monroe will help you," she says, sounding confident. "Now, go on and get out of here. I have another appointment. I've told you all I can."

"But—"

"Hush, child," she says, turning away from me. "Do as I say. And you'd better steer clear of Abraham. He still believes you don't know what he is. It's best to keep it that way as long as you can. You won't like his real face."

"But I don't know what to do," I say. "How do I find Monroe? What do I ask him? I'm scared, Marceline."

She nods. "That's good. It's good to know when to be afraid."

CHAPTER 21

I'm no longer doubtful of Marceline's explanations, her predictions. As I rush toward the front door of her house, I worry that Abe will be waiting outside like he was last time. But the street is empty except for a few cars passing. When I'm halfway down the walkway, I look back at the window, but Marceline is no longer there. I swallow hard and take out my phone.

I call Lucy and ask her to pick me up at a coffee shop on the corner of Mission. My sister doesn't ask why, but she sounds distracted. Right now I can't worry about her. I just found out I've lived another life, another life with Harlin. That means I wasn't always here. In fact, I wasn't here even a year ago. My memories of my childhood . . . they're not real. Or at least, they were created rather than experienced. I'm not sure what's true anymore. Are anyone's memories real?

As I stand outside the coffee shop, I think about Abe. Marceline said he used to be a Forgotten, just like me. But now he's a Shadow, forced to do terrible things. I suddenly think back on Marissa at the campsite. I could have sworn I heard the words "jump off the cliff." Had he really said them? Is Marissa dead? Fear streaks through me and I start to wonder what else I don't know.

I cover my face, wanting to cry, but holding back the tears. I can't tell my dad or Lucy about the Forgotten—they'll have me committed. That leaves only Harlin. He understands. But the way he raced out of there . . .

A new feeling comes over me: anger. First Harlin kicked me out of his motel room, broke my heart. Then when he found out who I used to be—the very person he swore he loved—he ran away. I don't know if I can trust him not to hurt me again. Marceline is wrong. I am completely alone.

I wonder what else is locked inside my head. I wish I could break it open and know everything. Maybe in another life I sacrificed myself, but I'm different now. I have so much to live for. And if Onika is as horrible as Marceline says, there's no way I want to fight her.

Lucy's car pulls up, the music loud as it filters out of the half-open passenger window. When I climb in, she's chewing hard on a piece of gum, reminding me of our father. She stares straight ahead, pulling back out into the street.

"Aren't you going to ask why I'm here?"

"Nope," she says.

I wait, watching her. Lucy's makeup is heavy, her clothes dark and uncomfortable looking. "What's wrong with you?" I ask.

Lucy glances over suddenly and then goes back to the road. "Just been thinking." Her voice is low. "Things with my sometimes-boyfriend didn't exactly work out. Think it's time I see someone new."

"This is about a guy? Lucy, when have you ever let a guy mess with your head? Dad would be shocked and awed to hear this."

"Then don't tell him," she says. "That's the last thing I need. I'd rather forget everything. I'd rather just give up."

My eyes are wide as I stare at my sister, her entire personality different than I've ever seen her. "Hey," I say, reaching out to take her hand. It's warm. "Don't you ever give up. Don't you dare."

Lucy turns to me, her blue eyes gathering tears. "But I'm tired," she murmurs. "I'm so tired."

I tell her to pull over, and the minute she does, I wrap her in a hug. "What happened?" I ask. "Did he do something to you?"

Lucy sniffles, and then nods her head. "Yeah," she says into my shoulder. "He gave me hope when there wasn't any."

"He led you on?" I exhale. "The same thing just happened to me. What is it with us Landon girls? Maybe we're just too much for mere mortal men." I smile, and feel relieved when she returns it. I can't believe I didn't see the number this guy was doing on my sister. I'll knee him if I ever find him.

After a minute, Lucy seems better and shifts the car into gear, driving us home again. "Never give up," I tell her, taking her hand. She turns to me, squeezing my fingers.

"Never."

Lucy and I are sitting on the couch watching TV while my father works on his sermon at the kitchen table. The night has been eerily quiet, eerily normal. My phone rang only once. When I saw Abe's number, my entire body went rigid. So I hit ignore, not sure I could pull off pretending to not know what he is.

But just like always, once I'm back in my regular life, all the talk about Forgotten and Shadows seems surreal. I start enjoying the latest episode of *True Blood* before there's a soft knock at the door. Oh no.

Lucy looks at me. "You expecting anybody?"

I'm sure it's Abe, coming to find me. I nearly call out to my dad, but then I wonder if Abe would hurt him. Marceline didn't say what Shadows would do to a normal person who wasn't one of their Wants. "No," I tell my sister quickly. "But I'll get it."

At the door I pause, willing myself to act normally. I can't let him see.

I open the door and freeze. Harlin stands there, his leather jacket covered in dried blood, one sleeve tattered and torn open. His left eye is slightly swollen with a bruise underneath, his cheek scratched. He's dirty, mud caking his jeans.

I rush toward him, closing the door behind us. "What happened to you?" I ask, reaching for him. I stop myself. I'm not sure how to act around him anymore.

Harlin stares at me, his face drawn and desperate. "I told myself it'd be stupid to fall in love with you, knowing what you are," he says. "Knowing that you'll leave me."

I swallow hard. I can't believe he's standing here, bleeding, to tell me this.

"And I'd be stupid to let you love me back," he continues. "Especially with the choice you'll eventually have to make." He looks at me helplessly. "But Elise, the first day I met you, I couldn't get you out of my head. And when I saw you at Marceline's, I figured out why. I had no idea about your past— or if you can even remember." He pauses, seeming miserable at the thought.

"What are you doing?" I ask, not sure what he wants. "You need a doctor and—"

"I'm sorry for sending you away," he says. "But I'm more sorry for the fact that I can't help loving you. And I need you to love me, too."

Stunned, I'm not sure how to answer. I look over his injuries, his black eye. I think about how alone I felt earlier today and how he walked out of Marceline's without a word. He abandoned me.

"I'm mad at you," I whisper.

"I know," Harlin says, limping closer to me. "But please tell me there's more than that."

"There is . . . but I don't know if I can—"

Harlin puts a hand on my shoulder as he leans closer. He holds his other arm against him as if it's broken and closes his eyes tightly. "Please."

His face is pained with more than road rash. My heart aches for him. "I guess I'm stupid too," I murmur.

Harlin exhales, stepping into me to lay his forehead on my collarbone, as if overcome. I put my hand in his hair. "I'm still really mad," I say.

"And I'm still really sorry," he whispers, pulling me closer. We stay like that for a long moment, admitting our feelings for each other but neither knowing what to do about it. Just then the front door opens, flooding the porch with light and startling us. "What—" My father stops when he sees Harlin leaning against me. After a quick flash of fatherly protectiveness, he notices his condition.

"Harlin," my dad says. "Are you all right? What happened?"

"I was in an accident," Harlin says. "On my way over tonight I spun out. Wrecked my bike. Wrecked my face a little too."

"Your face will heal," my father reassures him. "But I should have a look at that arm. Have you been to the hospital?"

Harlin shakes his head no, and my father sucks at his teeth

disapprovingly. He opens the door and ushers Harlin inside just as my sister comes to check what's going on. She straightens when she sees Harlin, her expression tightening. He meets her stare, but then lowers his eyes as my father tells Lucy to go get the first-aid kit from the bathroom.

In the middle of the tidy living room, Harlin appears even worse. I want to hug him, but he's holding his arm close to his side, protecting it.

My father rolls up the sleeves of his shirt like he's getting ready to perform surgery. I touch Harlin's elbow.

"Let me take your jacket," I say, moving to unzip it, careful not to bump his arm. "I'll clean the mud off." I take my time pulling his arm through. He winces once, but bites it back. When I finally get his coat off, I can see why it was so difficult: His entire arm from wrist to elbow is covered in dried blood, probably from the gash in his forearm. As far as I can tell, it's not broken. I feel physically ill from seeing him this hurt. This vulnerable.

"Elise," my father says softly, noticing how upset I am. "Help him to the kitchen table, sweetheart."

"Were the roads slick?" he asks when I get Harlin settled in a chair.

"No," Harlin says, careful not to put his bloodied arm on the table. "Something happened with my bike. Locked up on me the minute I got onto the main road." Harlin shoots me a weary look, but I'm not sure what he means by it.

My father walks to the sink and runs a clean towel under

the water. When he comes back he begins to clean Harlin's arm, and Lucy enters with the first-aid kit.

"Do you want a couple of aspirin?" I ask, feeling helpless that I'm not doing anything.

"No, I don't mind the pain," Harlin says, and then flinches when my father gets to the cut.

"Get him the ibuprofen," my father says. "I think you could have probably used a stitch or two," he tells Harlin. "But a bandage might work now."

I go to the cupboard and pull out the medicine, Lucy standing against the counter watching silently. My fingers are shaking as I undo the cap, and then I pour a glass of water, bringing both over to Harlin.

"Thank you," he says in that tender way of his. I take a seat next to him as I clean the dirt and blood off his jacket with a damp paper towel.

"Is there anyone I should call?" my father asks him, beginning to wrap his arm in white gauze. "Where are you staying?"

"I'm out here alone," he says. "I was at the Sunset Motel on Route Five, but I had to use the money I had left to take my bike to the shop. I'll wait until morning and get my brother to wire me some funds."

My father pauses to look up. "How did you get here tonight? Did you hitchhike?"

Harlin nods and then swallows the pills I gave him, maybe wanting them more than he admitted. When my father's done, Harlin twists his arm to check his bandage and then thanks my father.

"Elise," my father says after washing his hands. "Can I speak with you in the living room for a minute?" He doesn't wait for an answer as he leaves.

"Uh . . . sure," I call after my dad. Harlin mouths *Sorry*, as if he did something wrong, and I put my hand on his shoulder as I pass him. When I get into the living room, I find my father pacing in front of the sofa.

"What am I supposed to do?" he whispers the minute I'm close.

"Excuse me?"

"He doesn't have a place to stay, Elise. It's dark outside and he's *hitchhiking*. Even if I paid for it, I'm not sure letting him stay in a rundown motel is the best option here."

"Dad, I have no idea what you're getting at."

"You're not going to ask me if he can stay the night?" My father crosses his arms over his chest.

"I wasn't. But now that you mention it . . ."

"You hadn't even thought of it until I brought it up, did you?"

"Nope, but it is a fantastic idea. And very Christian of you."

My father rubs his face before glancing around the living room, then toward the bedrooms. "I'm assuming from the porch that the two of you made up?"

"Mostly," I say with a smile.

"Harlin can stay on the couch," he says. "And I'd better not wake up and find him in your room, Elise. Or his motorcycle accident will look mild in comparison. I'm not running a dating service."

"Gross."

"Be quiet. Now find him some clean clothes, and I'll show him where the bathroom is so he can take a shower. After that get some extra blankets out of the linen closet." He pauses, looking me over. "I trust you," he says.

"Thanks, Dad." I give him a quick hug, closing my eyes as I think about how I've been lying to him. And I hope that someday things can go back to the way they were. Or at least, how I remember them.

CHAPTER 22

Harlin glances at the sofa and then back at me. He's been scrubbed clean and rebandaged, his hair wet and brushed to the side, making him look incredibly sexy. He's wearing his own T-shirt and a pair of basketball shorts that Lucy found in her room. We didn't ask who they'd once belonged to.

"Are you sure this is okay?" he asks. "I mean, did your dad really invite the handsome stranger who's dating his daughter to sleep on the couch?"

"I like how you added in the 'handsome.'"

"Thanks."

"And yes. My dad is cool like that, plus he thinks you're a lost soul in need of saving. He's not really that far off there." Harlin nods as if he agrees and I drop the blankets onto the arm of the sofa.

My father turns on the light in the hallway, keeping the living room extra bright before closing his door halfway. Lucy has gone to her room, leaving Harlin and me alone.

I take his cleaned jacket from the chair when he asks to see it. He holds it up, inspecting the rips and tears, cursing under his breath. He quickly apologizes, setting it on the back of the couch, and asks me to join him.

I do, but the minute I'm next to him, my heart speeds up. We have so much to talk about; I'm not even sure where to start. So I begin with the obvious.

"Why did you run away at Marceline's?"

Harlin lowers his head. "Because it hurt. Hearing about Charlotte—about you—hurt me. But I shouldn't have left. I'm sorry."

"We had a life together," I say, as if it's a fact of our past and not something I long for.

Harlin pauses. "Yeah."

"Were we happy?"

He looks over at me. "When you weren't hiding things from me? Deliriously happy."

The old memory I had of us fighting on the phone comes back to me. I'd hurt him then, kept the Need from him. I lied to him. "So maybe we do it differently this time," I offer. "We should tell each other everything. Always."

Harlin checks his bandage. "Okay," he says. After a moment he puts his good arm over the back of the sofa, turning toward me. "What else can I tell you?"

"Tell me about Monroe Swift."

201

"Monroe was your Seer. More than that, really. You'd known him most of your life; he knew your family. He helped you toward the end, even if I didn't approve of his methods."

"Meaning?"

"Lies. Secrets." Harlin swallows hard. "I understand more now, but at the time I was angry. Now I know that Seers aren't allowed to talk about their Forgotten. We're not allowed to tell *anyone*. It's our pact—our way to keep the light safe from the Shadows. We lead the Forgotten to their destiny and then remember their path." There is sorrow in Harlin's voice. "It's not an easy life, Elise. It's very lonely."

"You were there," I say, drawing his gaze to mine. "I had a memory, and you were there with me when I went off that bridge. You told me you'd remember everything."

"I do remember everything," he says. "I remember every minute of our lives together. And other than Monroe, I guess I'm the only one who does."

Sadness spreads through my chest. "I'm sorry I'm someone else."

"I didn't mean it like that," he says. "I love you. I'll love you no matter who you are." His fingers find mine, intertwining. "I just want us to be together. I want you to stop leaving."

"Believe me. I don't plan on going anywhere."

"I won't let you this time," Harlin says. "I'll fight for you." I can feel his resolve, his absolute belief in his promise. I look over his bandage, upset when I think about his injuries.

"How did you get in that accident?" I ask. "You strike me as an experienced rider."

"I'm a perfect rider," Harlin says, straightening and clenching his jaw. "Someone tampered with my bike, and to be honest, I'm seriously pissed about it."

I widen my eyes. "Didn't notice."

Harlin chuckles. "God I've missed you," he says. "Where have you been for the last nine months? Where were you hiding?"

"Colorado."

"I should have driven through Colorado, then."

"Maybe you should have."

He rests his head against the back of the couch as he watches me. "Have you . . ." His voice is unsure, worried. "Have you dated anyone?"

I laugh, partly embarrassed. "Unless you count one misguided date with a coworker, I've never gone out with anyone."

"Abe?"

My heart skips a beat. "You know about Abe?"

"I've never met a Shadow before," he says. "But I could see exactly what he was the day he came up to you in front of Marceline's, see the darkness surrounding him. Most Shadows hide from Seers, but he wanted me to know what he was."

Despite what I've learned, there's a part of me that is still crushed about Abe. "He was my friend," I say quietly. "I thought he was."

"Shadows can make you believe almost anything."

"So what do I do now?" I ask. "How do I see Abe, knowing what he is?"

"You don't. You stay far away from him. He's dangerous."

I agree, but avoiding Abe is going to be harder than Harlin thinks. I know his persistence. Closing my eyes, I force the thought away. Right now, I want at least a second of normal. So when Harlin wraps his arm around me, I lean into him.

We watch *The Daily Show*, and soon Harlin's breathing is deep and I think that he may be asleep. When the show ends, I yawn, and Harlin stirs.

"I'm sorry," I say, lifting my head.

"Don't be," he answers, and rubs his eyes. "Can't believe I would sleep through snuggling. Maybe I have a concussion."

"I would accept that as a valid excuse."

"Here," Harlin says, opening his arms. "Let's try it again." I hesitate before leaning against his chest, my entire body relaxing the minute I do.

Harlin's hand touches my hair, his fingers running down the length of it past my shoulder. "I can't believe I found you," he murmurs. "I've needed you so much." The emotion in his voice brings tears to my eyes. I wonder what Harlin's been through, and how much he's lost.

"You have me now," I say. Harlin sighs, holding me close. When he starts to drift off again, I sit up. "I should go to bed," I say. "Oh, here." I grab the blankets. "These are for you."

Harlin takes them and stretches out on the couch, extending his arms over his head as he groans, showing off a small sliver of skin between his shorts and his T-shirt. I help cover him with a sheet, since he has limited use of his arm, and when I'm standing over him, he turns his face toward me with the most sinfully innocent expression I've ever seen.

"A kiss good night?" he asks, barely above a whisper.

I nearly swoon with the thought of it, with the temptation of it, but then Harlin turns his cheek, touching a spot just above his beard. My heart thuds as I lean down, and in the second before I touch him, he closes his eyes.

I press my lips to his cheek, his skin warm—hot, even. I run my finger gently over the bruise under his eye and then kiss him there, too. He lets me do this all without ever touching me, ever speaking. And when I straighten up, Harlin's eyes open, glassy with tears.

"Don't ever leave me again," he murmurs.

I process his words, not sure if I can promise that after what Marceline told me. "I never want to leave you," I say, and go to my room, turning off the light on the way.

There's a rumble of thunder outside, and the world around my bedroom shifts and fades. When the new scene comes into focus, I'm on the high-rise rooftop again, wind whipping my hair painfully across my face as the city lights dot the streets below. There's another clap of thunder, making me start, and then the rain pours around me. The fat drops soak my hair and pajamas as I search for a way down.

The metal door in the corner of the building bursts open, banging into the wall behind it as a man walks out. He's tall, with dark hair and black pants, and I recognize him as the one who turned Onika into a Shadow. The rain doesn't touch him. He crosses the roofline to stand at the edge, staring out over the city.

The door opens again and Onika stalks through this time. She's beautiful, her straight blond hair flowing over her black jacket as her boots click on the cement floor. Her posture is menacing, and I feel myself shrink back even though I'm sure she can't see me.

"I've been looking for you, Rodney," she calls. "I believe we have unfinished business."

The guy laughs, turning to her. He meets her before she can reach him and puts his hand on her cheek, almost mockingly. "I can't change your outcome, my beauty, if that's what you're here for again."

The expression on Onika's face is absolute agony. But soon it turns to something else. I watch her skin start to change, cracking and graying, ripping open. She growls under her breath, less like an animal and more like a demon.

"You lied to me!" Onika snarls. "You ruined my chance at happiness."

"Don't be a fool," he says. "What were you going to do instead, burst into light?"

"I wouldn't be a monster!" She holds up her arm and pushes back the sleeve of her jacket, her exposed skin sickly in the rooftop lights. She digs her nails into the gray flesh there, pulling it away. But there is only more gray underneath. "Rotted straight through," she tells him. "I'd rather be dead."

Rodney starts to laugh, but Onika pushes him hard, making

him stumble back. His expression falters, as if he's surprised by how strong she is. Onika begins to slowly circle him.

"I've searched the world for an end," she says, narrowing her eyes as she crosses behind Rodney. "But as the saying goes, there is no easy way out."

Rodney whips his head around, trying to keep his focus on Onika as she continues to circle, stalking him like prey.

"But you know what I discovered?" Onika asks, her eyes wild. "That I am not only a Shadow. I am pure misery. Pure hopelessness." She chuckles then, a sad, sick laugh. "I cannot be destroyed by anything on this earth, not even if I wish it. How did I get like this?" she asks him. "How did I let you trick me into losing every shred of my humanity?"

Rodney doesn't answer, his fear rendering him silent. His smooth skin begins to crack, turning gray and rotten.

Onika continues on. "Was it when my mother sold me to the men in my Russian town? Perhaps it was later, when the man I loved told me I was going to disappear forever. Or maybe, lover," she whispers, "it was when you forced yourself on me, tempted me with your words until I didn't know better."

Onika comes to stand directly in front of him, her boots making a final *clack* on the concrete. "I'm capable of so much now. The Shadows pulse through me relentlessly, tearing me apart and then filling me up. I am tortured, darling. But"— she pauses—"there is one silver lining to my existence."

Rodney pulls himself up to his full height, his shoulders

still tense. "And what would that be, my beauty?"

She smiles like a mad child. "That I can finally kill you." She lunges forward, burying her hand deep inside his chest, her fist breaking through his rotted skin. Rodney screams in agony and falls to his knees in front of her, unable to fight even after Onika rips her hand from him. Black shadows seep from the hole left behind. Onika laughs, something low and filled with hatred as Rodney cries out, his flesh withering before flaking away. Onika watches, a smile on her lips as her skin smoothes like porcelain, gleaming against the dark night sky.

"Please," Rodney murmurs as he lifts his arm to touch her. Before he can, his arm falls away; his entire body falls away, into ash—scattering on the floor of the building's roof.

I scream, tripping over my own feet as I try to back away from the scene. Onika slowly turns. Her blue eyes widen, the skin around them cracking. And my heart stops.

"You," she says, pointing directly at me. "What the hell are you doing back?"

CHAPTER 23

I sit up, sweat cooling on my skin. My chest heaves as I gasp for air. The eyes—Onika's eyes—are still with me. I scramble out of bed, desperate to get away from the vision. It's dim in the hallway, the only light coming from the television on in the living room.

What the hell are you doing back? Onika's words are like a whisper in my ear. Fear surges through me and I move quickly toward the couch where Harlin is asleep. When I reach him, he wakes with a start.

"Elise?" He looks around. "Are you okay?" Harlin sits up, wincing when he puts too much weight on his arm.

"Can I stay here with you?" I blurt out. I'm trembling so badly that I'm not even sure I can stand anymore. Onika saw me in a vision. How is that possible? I wasn't really there.

Harlin takes an uneasy glance toward my father's room. "Wouldn't you be more comfortable in your own—"

"Please? I'm scared."

He reaches for me right then and pulls me to him. "You're shaking." His voice is low, concerned.

"I had a nightmare," I say, knowing it sounds childish.

Harlin picks up the blanket that fell to the floor and lays it over my shoulders. Slowly the images of cracking skin and the feel of cold rain start to fade, replaced with something calmer. Replaced with Harlin.

"Come here," he says, curling my body to his as he lies down. His hand slides over the bare skin of my arm, his breath in my hair. "Is this okay?" he asks.

I close my eyes. "Yes, it's perfect."

"What were you dreaming about?" he asks after a moment.

"Onika," I say. "A horrible woman with a shattered face."

Harlin holds me tighter, and when he speaks his voice is strained. "I know who she is. Monroe told me about her. And I know she's evil."

Sleep creeps over me, trying to steal my thoughts. It's so late, and the vision has left me drained. I snuggle into Harlin, blocking out the images that are haunting me. "Onika wants to kill me," I murmur. "And I have to find Monroe to learn how to stop her."

And when Harlin promises he'll help me, I drift away.

* * *

"Hi," Lucy calls from the kitchen doorway.

I jump, my forehead connecting with something hard, and yelp. Underneath me, Harlin clutches his chin, moaning in a half-sleep stupor. I quickly realize that it's morning and roll off the couch, banging my elbow on the coffee table when I do.

"Ow," I mumble, rubbing my funny bone.

"I'm sorry," my sister says. "I thought I should wake you before Dad sees you out here." She hitches up her eyebrow. "On top of each other."

Harlin slowly pulls himself into a sitting position, blinking as if trying to clear his vision. The clock on the wall reads 6 a.m. I turn to Lucy from my spot on the floor and see that she's wearing her coat. She must have snuck out again. "Are you just getting home?" I ask. She shoots Harlin an uneasy glance.

"Crazy night," she offers as if this can explain everything. The dark circles under her eyes are caked over in makeup, her hands barely poking out from her sleeves.

Harlin straightens. "Lucy, you shouldn't—"

"I don't recall asking your opinion, Harlin," she says.

Just then the door to the master bedroom squeaks open, and my father shuffles out. He's tying his striped robe when he sees us and pauses. "Is there a party going on?" he asks.

Lucy ducks her head and starts down the hall, patting our father's arm as she passes him. I'm surprised at her behavior toward Harlin, but he doesn't mention it. Instead Harlin starts folding the blanket as if he was planning to get up this insanely early all along.

"Sorry," I say to my father. "Hope we didn't wake you. After last night, I wanted to check on Harlin's arm."

He tilts his head like he is absolutely sure I'm lying. "And how is his arm, Elise?" he asks.

"Uh . . . better?"

My father stands motionless for a second, and then he shakes his head and walks into the kitchen. I hear the clink of cups, and then the running of water for the coffeepot.

"That was a nice save," Harlin says, sounding amused. "So detailed. Like a nurse."

"Shut up, Harlin," I say, trying not to smile. "I didn't hear you offer anything better."

"You sure you didn't want to tell him we were *playing doctor*? That might have sounded more believable."

I turn quickly and swat at him. He laughs, dodging my swing, and catches my hand. "I would tackle you right here," he says, leaning close. "Pin you and kiss you. But with the luck we have in your house, someone will walk in. And then what will you tell them?" he whispers. "That you were giving me CPR?"

"Stop!" I slap his shoulder again.

"Elise," my father calls from the kitchen.

"Yes?" I respond, ignoring the smirk on Harlin's lips.

"Maybe you can come in here and let Harlin get dressed." He pauses. "Alone."

Harlin and I exchange a look, and laugh. Then he heads down the hallway toward the bathroom.

When I walk into the kitchen, my father is pouring two cups of coffee. "So," he says now that Harlin is safely away. "Is he your boyfriend?"

I smile into my coffee cup as we sit at the table. "Wow, you said the word! I'm proud. And, sorry, I'm not going to discuss this with you."

My dad slips off his glasses and sets them on the kitchen table. "You and your sister used to talk to me about everything," he says. "I don't know when that changed." There's a hint of sadness in his voice.

"Is this really about Harlin?" I ask.

He exhales. "No, not entirely. It's your sister. I can tell that something is going on with her, but she won't talk to me about it. I worry that I've been too tough on her." He lowers his eyes. "On both of you."

"Oh, Dad." He looks so forlorn that I move to hug him from behind as he sags in the chair. "We know you love us," I tell him. "Lucy's going through a phase—a bad breakup. It's not your fault."

"All I want is for you girls to be happy."

"We are happy." I smile, giving him one more squeeze. "Especially when you let cute boys spend the night."

"Har, har, Elise," he says, seemingly at ease. "Can you take Harlin to get his bike after breakfast?" my father asks. "I have to be at church. Have a good time at work."

My stomach drops when he says it, dread coming over me in a strong wave. I'd forgotten all about Santo's. And Abe.

* * *

As my father goes to leave, Lucy emerges from her room and asks him for a ride to a café where she's meeting friends. At "friends" I give her a questioning look and she shrugs, as if to say that the sometimes-boyfriend is out of her life for good. I'm glad.

When Harlin comes back into the living room, his phone is in his hand and he's wearing his freshly washed clothes with his hair brushed smooth. We have the place all to ourselves. But when he sits next to me on the couch, I'm alarmed by his serious expression.

"What?" I ask.

"I talked with Monroe."

My heart rate spikes. "And?"

"I didn't want to tell him too much over the phone. I'm not sure he'd believe me about your past without seeing you for himself. So I told him that I needed his help with a Forgotten. That it had to do with Onika."

At the sound of her name, my stomach twists. She knows about me now, saw me in her vision. I'm terrified. "Is he coming to Arizona?" I ask.

"First flight out. He wants us to meet him. I told him we'd be at Diner 51 at seven." Harlin leans forward on the couch, his elbows on his knees. "Monroe's going to try to make you cross into the light," he says quietly. "Just like he did last time. But I can't watch it again. I think it'll kill me."

"Harlin," I whisper, resting my hand on his arm. I

understand the impossible position he's in—leading people to the end of their human form, even if he's helpless to stop it. I can't imagine how difficult it is, the burden he has to carry. The grief.

"After you jumped off the bridge," he says, studying my face, "I had to live without you, among everyone who had forgotten. Everyone but me and Monroe. He tried to help. He eventually sent me to Marceline, the oldest living Seer he could locate, when he found out he was—" Harlin stops himself. "Bottom line, I'm drawn to the Forgotten. Whether I want to be or not," he says. "And I've been so alone, Elise. Until now." His hazel eyes meet mine. "Until you."

Butterflies flutter in my stomach as I hold his gaze.

"I can never love anyone else," Harlin continues. "Not ever. What do you think about that?"

"I think that's a bit dramatic." I smile at the way he's watching me.

Harlin leans in, and my heart races as he puts his palm on my cheek. "What if all I want is for us to grow old together?" he asks.

"I'd say you should have bigger goals." I let the rest of the world fall away. Everything but Harlin.

"What if you could remember loving me?" he whispers, bringing his mouth close, his lips grazing mine.

His words make me ache, make me yearn. "I've already loved you twice," I murmur.

Harlin's eyes slide shut and he finally kisses me. His mouth is warm, spicy like cinnamon. I let him lay me back on the couch, my body humming with electricity as the tension builds.

I've never been with anyone, not like this. I pull his shirt over his head, breaking our kiss for only a second before he's there once again, his skin burning hot against mine.

"I've missed you so much," I whisper as he kisses my neck. "Even when I didn't know you, my soul still missed you."

CHAPTER 24

My phone vibrates on the coffee table, interrupting us. I pull back from Harlin to answer it and he groans, collapsing next to me on the couch. "By all means," he mumbles, lying facedown in the cushions. I laugh, but when I check the caller ID, my body stills.

Harlin sits up when he notices my silence. "Who is it?" he asks.

"It's Abe," I say, staring at the screen. "He's probably wondering when I'm coming in to work."

"You're not going back there," Harlin says.

"But if I don't, he'll know."

"If you do, he'll know. What are you going to say if he asks where you've been? You're not a gifted liar, Elise. Stay away from him. I'm pretty sure he's the one who tampered with my bike."

It makes sense. I'm not entirely sure what Shadows are capable of, and Abe can be very possessive. The phone stops vibrating and I relax slightly. "I should call in to work," I say, climbing up from the couch. "And I should probably do it before Abe gets there."

Harlin nods, bending to grab his shirt from the floor. I walk back to my bedroom to call off my shift at Santo's. Margie seems irritated, seeing as I've called in twice already this week, but I tell her I still have the flu. She seems to buy it. When I return to the living room, Harlin is at the front door, holding his jacket.

"Garage called," he says. "My bike's ready. I phoned a cab since I have to go into Ward, but I'll be back to take us to Diner 51."

"I can drive you to the garage," I say.

"I know. But I need some time to think."

There's a turn in my stomach. Does Harlin regret kissing me? Regret coming here last night? "I guess I'll see you later, then," I say, not even trying to disguise the hurt in my voice.

Harlin smiles softly and steps up, wrapping his arms around me as he brings his lips to my ear. I close my eyes. "I hate every second I'm away from you," he says. "Don't ever doubt that." And then he kisses me.

* * *

After Harlin's gone, I wait through the afternoon, alternating between snacking and calling my sister to see when she's coming home. Lucy never answers. When I talk to my father, he tells me he'll be stuck at work until late tonight. I don't mention that I called in to Santo's. Right now, the less he knows the better.

It's close to six thirty when I hear the engine of a motorcycle in front of my house. I check my reflection once more, still tingling from our kiss.

Harlin waits at the curb on his Harley, leaning back with his hands in his lap as he stares down the road, wearing his dark sunglasses even though the sky is overcast.

As if he knows I'm watching him, Harlin smiles and then slowly turns. "Hey, you," he says.

"Hi." I'm exhilarated, shy, and nervous all at once.

Harlin takes off his glasses and tucks them into the collar of his T-shirt. He's not wearing his leather jacket, which makes him appear more casual, less dangerous. I certainly don't mind noticing his arms.

"I can't believe I'm going to get on that right now." I motion toward the bike. "You got in an accident *yesterday*."

"That wasn't my fault." He frowns at this, looking down. I can see from here the large scrapes in the chrome, but otherwise the Harley appears to be in working order.

I walk over and he helps me climb on the back. When my body is against his, I rest my chin on his shoulder. "If you get me killed," I whisper, "I'm going to be so mad."

Harlin chuckles and then kicks the bike to life.

***

Harlin drives us across town to Diner 51. It's a small building with aluminum siding and a bright pink door. It's kitschy in a fifties, alien sort of way. As we walk inside, there's an Elvis song playing, a few customers at the counter. I check the time on my phone and see that we're early.

Harlin takes my hand and pulls me toward a table in the back. Since we're here, I order a milkshake. Then nervousness begins to twist my stomach. What will Monroe tell me about Onika when he gets here? What will he tell me about myself?

I'm only three sips into my chocolate shake when the diner door opens. I recognize Monroe Swift immediately. He's handsome—in his early forties, with blond hair slightly graying at his temples and bright blue eyes. He's definitely thinner than I've seen him, his features exaggerated by the sharp angles.

He nods to Harlin as he approaches, his expression unreadable. When he pauses at the end of the table, Monroe holds out his hand to me. "Now who do we have here?" he asks in a British accent.

"Elise Landon," I answer, sliding my palm into his cool one.

"It's a pleasure to meet you." He squints as if studying me, and then moves to take a seat.

"This is the one I told you about," Harlin says to him. "She needs your help."

"Help that you can't provide as her Seer?" Monroe asks.

Harlin shifts next to me, and Monroe straightens, looking between us. "Wait, is she even your Forgotten?"

"Not exactly," Harlin says.

"What are you doing?" Monroe whispers harshly. "Why did you drag me out here? Who is this girl, and what does she have to do with Onika?"

I make a sound when he mentions Onika. Monroe turns, his hands balled into fists on the table. And just then, another memory appears, blocking out the world around me.

I'm in the passenger seat as Monroe drives down a busy Portland street. "Yes," he says. "You are my last Forgotten, but it doesn't mean this is easy for me. You have no idea what I'm going through."

"What you're going through?" I snap. "What about what I'm going through?" I've lost everything. Lost Harlin. Lost my face. And soon, I'll lose my life.

I start, the diner scene filtering in once again. I wait a beat as the fear fades, the feeling of hopelessness. I don't want that to happen to me. I refuse to disappear. A new streak of bravery rushes in at the thought of losing everything.

"I'm a Forgotten," I tell Monroe, almost confused at the sudden affection I have for him. "But I'm not like the others—not exactly. You used to be my Seer," I say. "You used to be my friend."

Monroe swallows hard, his expression softening as a slow realization comes over him. He glances at Harlin, who's still smiling. "Is she—" He stops. "How is that possible?"

"As Marceline told me," I say, "there is no such thing as impossible."

"Marceline?" Monroe's mouth quirks up. "Is that old psychic a part of this?"

"She's my Seer. She's also *actually* psychic. Marceline told me who I used to be. She told me about Charlotte." At that, Harlin lowers his head, as if there's still pain at the sound of the name. Across from me, Monroe's blue eyes fill with tears, but he blinks them away.

"I see," he says. "Well, sweetheart. You have been missed. You've been missed dearly."

I smile at the thought of this, the thought that I hadn't been completely forgotten. "I don't remember everything," I say. "But little bits and pieces have come back. And then, of course, there are the visions." I pause. "Of Onika."

Any joy on Monroe's face quickly fades. "The beast has come for you."

I'm taken aback by his choice of words. Even though I remember Monroe calling Onika a monster, I also know that he once loved her. Could his feelings truly have changed so drastically?

"She hasn't come for me," I say. "At least not yet."

"I'm sure she will," Monroe responds. His knuckles are white as he keeps his clenched fists on the table. "She won't rest until she finds you. She knows how I cared for you. That alone is enough reason for her to destroy you." Monroe exhales and runs his fingers through his thinning hair. It's then that

I notice the dark circles beneath his eyes. The veins visible under his skin. I've seen that look before.

"You're sick," I murmur.

Monroe lifts his gaze to mine. Harlin clears his throat as he turns away, and I think that he already knew.

"Cancer?" I ask. When Monroe nods, it's like I've been punched in the gut. "Are you dying?"

"Yes."

Tears sting my eyes, but I'm not sure if they're for Monroe or for the grief I still have about my mother's death. Either way, I'm heartbroken. I tell him so.

"I've been sick a long while now," Monroe says gently. "Even finished all the stages of grief. But leading you to the light was my greatest gift. I'm so proud of you."

"I wouldn't exactly call it a gift," Harlin says. "It was a god-damn tragedy."

Monroe turns to him, compassion softening his features. "I know you see it that way," he tells him as if they've had this conversation before. "But there was no other choice. You know that."

Harlin shakes his head. "Well, the universe can find someone else, because I won't lose her again." His voice rises, drawing the stares of the other customers.

"Harlin," I say, touching his arm to calm him, but his gaze is fixed on Monroe.

"I'm not ready to go anywhere," I say to both of them. "I have a life. A family. Marceline said that I could control the Need, bring it on to get stronger. But I'm not going to let myself disappear. Not even for the light."

Monroe furrows his brow. "What else did Marceline tell you?"

"That I'm here to restore balance, to stop Onika. And I think you might be the only person who knows how to help me."

"I assure you I don't. But, sweetheart"—he looks concerned—"Onika's a very powerful Shadow. I'm not sure there is a way to stop her. Perhaps you should focus on your destiny, on being a Forgotten—"

"She *is* my destiny," I say. "But I don't even know where to start. I have to find a way."

Monroe covers his mouth with his hand, lost in thought. I wonder about the guilt Monroe feels. He's been helping the Forgotten, and yet the one person he obviously loved the most turned to the Shadows. It still haunts him after all of these years.

My phone vibrates in my pocket. I slide it out cautiously, afraid it's Abe again, but I'm relieved to see my father's number. I stand and wander to the corner of the diner for privacy.

"Hey, old man," I say. "Everything okay?"

"Hi, kid. Sorry to bug you, but it's the strangest thing. I'm here filling out insurance paperwork for the upcoming school year, and I can't for the life of me remember your sister's middle name. Do you know it?"

"Dad." I start to laugh, but then I stop cold. A sense of

dread slips over me. "It's Constance," I whisper with a catch in my voice. "Dad, she's named after Mom."

"How did I ever forget that?" he asks, sounding bewildered.

"I guess you're getting old," I offer, but shoot a look back at Harlin. When I do, his shoulders tense as if he knows something's wrong. He stands.

"I have to go, Dad," I say quietly. "I'll see you soon." I hang up and push the phone back into my pocket. As I approach the table, a fresh fear pulls at my heart.

"My sister," I say, glancing between Harlin and Monroe. "She hasn't been feeling well. And just now, my father forgot her middle name. Lucy's been sneaking out, wearing a lot of makeup. She . . . she told me she had a secret." I stop then, not sure I can go on.

Harlin reaches to take my hand. "Lucy's a Forgotten too," he murmurs. "I'm sorry, Elise. I wanted to tell you, but—"

I yank my fingers from his. "You knew?" I shout, my voice echoing in the small diner. Harlin lowers his head.

"I'm her Seer."

I stumble back a step, feeling completely betrayed. Harlin said he loved me, agreed that we'd tell each other everything. How could he keep something like this from me? "Take me home," I say coldly. "Take me home now."

"Elise," Monroe says. "As a Seer, Harlin isn't allowed to tell—"

"She's my sister!" At the words, I break. Lucy is like me,

and that means she has a terrible choice to make. I think then about the Shadows, wondering if they've been tempting her too. Oh no. What if they've gotten to Lucy?

I don't wait any longer as I rush toward the exit, hearing the heavy sound of boots behind me. Just as I make it outside, Harlin is next to me, trying to take my arm.

"I'm so sorry," he says again. "If you'd let me—"

I push him back. "Don't," I growl. "Just get me to Lucy."

Harlin's expression is absolute regret, but I can't worry about him right now. I have to find my sister.

CHAPTER 25

I keep my head on Harlin's back as he races through the streets toward my house. I can't believe I didn't see what was wrong with Lucy. How could I not know? Tears stream down my face, my heart pounding in my chest. I tried to call her before we took off, but there was no answer.

I need my sister. I need to find my sister.

The night has darkened around us as Harlin pulls into my driveway and cuts the engine. He scrambles to help me but I push him away and climb off by myself, nearly falling.

"Elise, wait," he calls as I hurry toward the front door. I don't respond, but then he speaks again in a quiet voice. "Lucy doesn't want to go to the light."

I take in a startled breath and then slowly turn, looking

back over my shoulder. "Are you saying my sister is a Shadow now?"

"No, I'm just saying it's possible." He holds up his hands, as if offering a truce. "And if she is, you understand that she won't be the same, right?"

"She'll still be my sister," I murmur. "She'll always be my sister." I turn and start toward the house once again.

The blinds are drawn, the interior dim as I push open the unlocked front door. The house is silent as I click on the lights, the living room empty. Worry starts to cloud my senses. It's like I can feel that something is off. Harlin walks in just as I move down the hallway toward the bedrooms, moving boxes still piled there.

When I get to Lucy's room, I'm startled by what I find. Her posters have been torn down, along with all the pictures of her friends in Colorado. I see them piled in the trash next to her vanity, her clothes ripped and strewn about.

Harlin enters, his hands in his pockets as he takes in the scene. He makes his way over to sit on Lucy's unmade bed. "Your sister's angry," he says. "Has been for a while. She probably tossed out the photos when her image began disappearing from them. Trashed the rest in a rage." Harlin leans to put his elbows on his knees, his interlaced fingers under his chin. "I'm no longer drawn to her, Elise." He meets my eyes. "I think she's made the choice to stay."

I almost can't digest his words. I spin around the room, searching for something. Anything that can give me hope that it's not true. I'm the one who told Lucy not to give up. I hadn't realized what she was. I would never have let her stay—not like this. Not like Onika.

"What does this mean?" I ask.

"She's lost, Elise. If she's a Shadow, she's lost. Consumed with hatred and temptation. Want. Your sister's gone." He whispers the last part, and I have to lower myself to the floor, not sure I can stand anymore.

"How did you let this happen?" I ask, even though I know I can't fully blame him. But maybe if he would have told me, I could have done something more.

This isn't happening. None of this is happening. I'm going to wake up in my bed, and my sister will be next to me, whispering secrets, and our father will be making pancakes in the kitchen.

"The first time I met Lucy was a few weeks ago," Harlin begins in a low voice. "I found her sitting near the office of my motel, crying. She'd been there fulfilling a Need, although she calls it being a Good Samaritan." He smiles sadly. "I hadn't told her my name, just that I understood what she was going through. She was so glad. She was so alone."

Harlin brings his fist to his mouth as he holds back his emotion. "We met a few more times after that. I told her about the destiny she had to fulfill, and it devastated her. She asked then about the Shadows. Said one had been coming to her, telling her that she didn't have to go. I explained what the Shadows were, but I could feel her slipping further and further away."

Harlin looks up. "And then I met you."

I almost can't hold his gaze, the desperate way he watches me now.

"At first," he says, "I didn't know you were a Forgotten. When I realized, I still couldn't stay away, even though I tried. Shadows were after you; I saw them myself. I wanted to protect you."

"And my sister?" I ask.

"I didn't know she was your sister until the day I came here. When she saw me with you, Lucy was furious. She was afraid I'd tell you what she was, begged me not to. It's my duty. I keep her secrets, Elise. She was my Forgotten."

"I could have helped."

"Are you sure?" he asks. "Are you sure you could have sent your sister into the light? Could you have really let her go?"

I don't know the answer. Instead sickness washes over me, the devastation of the situation settling in, twisting my insides. My life—*my* life—is falling away. My sister may be gone forever, or really, something much worse. My poor father, who has dedicated his life to helping others, to loving us, will lose his entire family. It's too much for me to bear. It's all just too much.

When I'm calmer, I get to my feet and walk about my sister's room again. In the trash, I see a picture. It's when I pick it up that I know. I smile sadly at the photo of me and Lucy from last summer. We were up in Colorado Springs—hiking to a waterfall. My father had snapped the picture. We stand there dressed in tank tops and baseball caps, grinning madly with our arms over each other's shoulders. Her image isn't the least bit faded. She's a Shadow.

No one will forget her now, but she probably doesn't know the consequences. Know that she'll have to spread evil in return.

I tuck the picture into my back pocket. I turn to Harlin, feeling a mixture of anger and love for him. I hate to see him so broken, but at the same time I'm not sure I can forget that he kept this from me.

"We were supposed to be honest with each other," I say. "We were going to tell each other everything."

"I understand if you can't forgive me," Harlin murmurs. "But I don't think I can survive you not loving me anymore."

I nearly sway with the grief in his words. But I won't make him feel better right now. I need to wait for my sister—I need her to know that I'll be here for her no matter what she's become. "Get out of my house," I say.

There is a hint of memory wanting to come out, but I don't let it. Instead it fills me with knowledge. I suddenly know that Harlin has always bottled everything up—the pain from his father's death, from my leap from the bridge. He never lets anyone see what's breaking inside, but I always could. There was a time when all I wanted was to take away his pain. But in front of me now is the remains of a guy who gave up—only to find a reason to go on again. Me. But I can't save him. I never could.

I walk out of the room then, forcing away my feelings. All I let myself think about is Lucy—and how I'll fix this somehow. I don't care what my destiny is. There has to be a way.

When I open the front door and wait, Harlin emerges from Lucy's room, his face blotchy, drawn. I think that it's dangerous for him to ride his motorcycle, but then decide that he's an adult. He can take care of himself.

"I'm staying with Monroe at the Sunset Motel," he says quietly as he pauses in front of me, unable to meet my eyes. "If you need me—"

I step back, not acknowledging that I do need him, but won't have him. I think that maybe we love each other too much. That it causes us to be reckless and stupid. That in the end, maybe we're just not meant to be.

"Good-bye, Harlin," I say. And when he walks out onto the porch, I slam the door behind him.

I wait on the couch for my sister. I don't call my father, unsure of what I'd even tell him. Now that Lucy's a Shadow, he'll remember everything about her. But what will he think when he sees her? What will she be like now?

The hours pass, and I glance at the clock. My father said he'd be working late, but I hope he stays out all night. I'm afraid of what will happen if he's here. When my eyes begin to slide shut, I go to my room.

I lean back into my pillows, trying to keep all of the misery out of my thoughts. But soon, I drift off to sleep. Unable to wait any longer.

* * *

I'm in the middle of Main Street. Santo's is to my right as a tumbleweed rushes past, bouncing out of my line of vision. My hair blows in the wind, and when I hear his voice, I look up to see Abe dressed in black—his hair slick—standing in front of me.

"I guess it didn't work, huh?" he asks.

"What didn't work?" I ask, taking a step back from him. I used to be grateful to see Abe, but his perfection frightens me now. Especially since I know what he is.

"Killing your boyfriend," he says. "He must be pretty good on that Harley."

"You caused his accident? Why?"

He scoffs. "Isn't it obvious? I called dibs."

I move farther back, the cement ice-cold under my bare feet. "You can't claim me."

"See"—he puts his hands casually in his pockets—"that's where you're wrong, *querida*. You're mine. Just because he's a Seer doesn't mean he can have you. You're not his Forgotten."

I'm dreaming, I know I am. "I thought we were friends, Abe."

His eyes soften. "Elise," he says, shaking his head. "I'm in love with you. I want us to be together—for all time. You're mine," he pleads.

"I'm not."

The temperature around us is quickly dropping, goose bumps rising on my skin. Abe's expression hardens, as if my

233

refusal has snapped him back into his twisted reality. "Come here," he says, spreading his arms wide.

"Stay away from me," I shout, continuing to back up.

He laughs. "No."

"Please," I say, but my voice cracks. Abe reads the fear there, and for a second, he almost looks sorry. He stops in front of me, his dark eyes searching mine as he reaches to run the backs of his fingers over my jaw.

"If you don't give in," he murmurs softly, watching the trail of his fingers, "it'll get so much worse." He meets my eyes. "I'll kill them all."

The fear surrounding me is thick, suffocating. Abe slips his arm around my waist to pull me against him. "No more crying," he whispers in my ear. "I'll take care of you. And I'm sorry that I have to kill your boyfriend. But he'll never go away otherwise."

"Just leave him alone," I say.

He pulls back to look me over. "No."

"That'll do." A sharp voice cuts through the air. Suddenly the wind stops dead and Abe stands motionless, frozen in time. I break free of him, but when I spin around, a scream catches in my throat. Onika stands behind us, her blond hair cascading over her black jacket, her smile cracking the skin around her mouth—skin that's gray and dead.

"I've looked everywhere for you," she says, walking slowly toward me. "Or rather, I guess you were looking for me. Very rude to invade someone's dreams, darling."

234

"I have to stop you," I say, surprised by my own bravery when I'm so terrified. She laughs.

"I believe we've had this conversation before. And like I told you then, you're not nearly strong enough. Nothing is."

Her flesh begins to wither, curling up and flaking off her face. But under my skin, I feel heat, growing and pulsating. For the first time in a while, I feel powerful.

"We'll see," I say, and force myself awake.

I wake with a start, my room pitch-black around me. I hear murmurs from another room, the voice hushed. Haunting. Fear streaks through me as I slowly rise. I think that my sister has finally come home. And I don't know what to expect.

I ease open my bedroom door and peer out, the hallway too dim to see very far. A sliver of light escapes from Lucy's room, the moon shining in her window. I was right. She must have just gotten home.

My entire body shakes as I move toward her room. When I'm just outside her door, I pause.

"Come in, Elise," Lucy calls as if she knew I was standing there. I swallow hard and step inside the doorway.

"Why are you creeping around?" she asks from her bed. "Are you trying to give me a heart attack?" Lucy is lying under the covers, her pale skin reflecting the moonlight. She's my sister, but . . . different.

"Sorry," I say, trying to sound normal. I'm suddenly very afraid of her. "I thought you might need help sneaking in."

She tilts her head, studying me. Lucy climbs out of bed, walking slowly in my direction.

"Oh, I don't need that kind of help anymore." She smiles. "Plus I'm turning over a new leaf," she says. "I think Dad will be pleased." I tense at the mention of our father.

I don't respond at first, but when my sister pauses in front of me, I'm overwhelmed with grief. "I love you, Lucy," I say softly, meeting her eyes, which are now a darker shade of blue. Her mouth twitches before she reaches out to hug me suddenly. I sag against her, but then I feel it—a slow, aching coldness. A shadow over my heart. I pull back.

"I think I'm going to take a shower," I say. "I feel gross after working today."

"You went to work?" she asks, her eyes narrowing slightly. Oh no. Does she know I'm lying?

I nod weakly, backing away. Lucy watches me, leaning her hip against the doorframe as she taps her finger on her bottom lip, as if thinking. I hurry down the hall, shutting the bathroom door tightly behind me.

Inside the locked bathroom, I'm not sure what to do. How to talk to her when she's like this. When she's so cold. Abe seems reasonable most of the time. But Lucy reminds me of Onika, and the idea is unimaginable.

I rest my hands on either side of the sink as I stare into the mirror. I take in my dark hair, my blue eyes. I think about the Needs I've had, about the things I've seen. I think about losing Harlin yet again. I can see now that there wasn't much he could have done for Lucy. The Forgotten have an impossible choice. Even Marceline couldn't save Abe.

Marceline told me to look inside my memories for a way to stop Onika. I found Monroe, but maybe there's more. Maybe I need to remember who *I* was. Filled with terror, I stare at my reflection, willing it to change. I stare at the image until my vision begins to blur, my fingers tingle. The reflection falls away and I see blond hair, a light dusting of freckles. I see . . . me.

I see Charlotte.

Shocked, I step back, nearly falling into the bathtub. I steady myself against the tile wall with my hand, my heart pounding in my chest. The mirror regains its focus—but it doesn't erase the knowledge flowing in—the unstoppable force growing inside me.

I'm Elise Landon now, but I wasn't always. I was Charlotte Cassidy. And as a Forgotten I saved people. I helped them.

Tears begin to stream down my cheeks as I'm struck with an acute sense of loss. The heaviness breaks through my chest, and I collapse onto the floor as the emotions crush me.

I remember Mercy, my adoptive mother, and how she found me all alone as a little girl. She raised me as her own, loved me as her own. But then—like everyone else—she forgot me. "Oh, Ma," I whisper, wishing for just another minute with her. Wishing I could have told her how much I loved her.

The other pieces flow back: my time with Sarah, with

Alex. The way they stared at me as if they'd never known me. I remember Monroe picking me up after all of my skin had worn away, and how he helped me hide it.

And of course there was Harlin. There is always Harlin.

I remember standing on the railing of the Rose City Bridge, looking behind me to the choppy water, terrified of what would happen if I jumped. But more afraid of what would happen if I stayed. And so when it was time to let go, I did just that. I gave myself to the light. I gave up everything.

My body shakes with sobs and I cover my face with my hands, bringing my knees toward my chest as I curl up on the bathroom floor. I'm ragged and broken, and barely able to breathe.

Because, worst of all, I remember every second of what it was like to lose my life.

CHAPTER 26

I'm not sure how long I lay there, but when I hear footsteps in the hallway I know I have to leave. It's like I have two histories—that of Charlotte and that of Elise. But I am Elise. Even though the universe allowed for my existence, bending and creating this body and my past, it doesn't make my life any less real. It's all me.

I don't know what happened when I jumped off the Rose City Bridge nine months ago, but I know I left—left for what feels like forever. Now I'm compelled forward to find Onika. But first I need Monroe. I have an idea.

When I ease open the bathroom door, the hallway is deserted, the moving boxes still where my father left them a month ago. There's a pang of sadness when I think that I wasn't really always with him, although it feels that way to all of us.

The house is quiet, but little pinpricks break over my skin. A tingling of fear. I swallow hard and slip into my bedroom to grab a coat just in case. I'm not sure when I'll get back here. I'm not sure of what's going to happen now.

I rush back out into the hallway and stagger to a stop. Lucy stands, blocking my way, wearing a long black dress. Her skin is like porcelain with a dusting of blush high on her cheeks. I'd call her beautiful, but I know what she is now.

"You're running out in the middle of the night? That is so unlike you," she says with a small smile.

"I'm meeting Harlin," I reply, trying to sound natural so she'll let me leave.

There's the click of the front door opening and I'm suddenly terrified of what will happen when Lucy sees my father. But she just chuckles, looking back over her shoulder. And then I see why.

Abe's shiny black shoes tap on the tile as he approaches, handsome as ever. A wry grin settles on his lips as he walks up behind my sister, placing his hands possessively on her shoulders.

My expression falters, although I try to stay calm. Every inch of me is petrified of him.

"You're not happy to see me," Abe teases, moving past my sister as he approaches me. "No hug?"

I take a step back and he halts, his eyes narrowing. "Leave," he murmurs to Lucy. My sister nods. With the Need gone, her personality has shifted into something much darker. Knowing my past, I can understand that she's angry about having to give everything up. But it would have been better than becoming the damned.

"You lovebirds have fun," she calls. "I'll lock the door on my way out."

When I hear the dead bolt, my body begins to tremble. I hold Abe's gaze, refusing to become his possession.

"Who are you?" he asks then, irritation in his voice.

"Elise Landon."

"Let me rephrase," he says. "What are you?"

"Just a girl—"

Abe growls and reaches out to grab me by the upper arms, his nails digging in and making me wince. As he touches me, though, a slow realization slides over his face. "That's why you're so bright," he says. "But how? Souls can't return."

As a Shadow, Abe can infect others with just a whisper, a touch. But I won't let him trick me into trusting him this time.

"Well, I guess I'm special or something," I say. And before he can respond, I bring my knee up hard, nailing him in the thigh. He yells out and I push him enough to move sideways, slipping inside my bedroom before slamming the door. My fingers are shaking so badly it takes three tries to turn the lock.

Silence.

Unlike Onika on the bridge, Abe isn't trying to tempt me away from the light; he can't. Instead he wants to keep me as a prisoner, bending me to his will for as long as he can. I know he won't stop until he has me.

I take a steadying breath, pulling myself together. I glance toward my window, wondering if I should try to escape. I'm not sure I'll even make it across the lawn before he catches me.

Tap. Tap. Tap.

I freeze at the sound of an impatient finger on the door. "Elise," he says. "You know I can just come in, right? That your lock won't work?"

"Please don't," I say. "Just leave me alone."

I hear him exhale. "I wish I could. You should have come to me willingly."

"Please . . ."

The door opens smoothly, like it was never locked in the first place. Abe stands there, still dressed in black, but now his face is different. It's no longer handsome. It's dead and gray, fine cracks in it like the dried desert floor.

He seems almost offended as I recoil. "I tried to charm you first, *querida*. It's your own fault that you have to see me like this. The others never fight."

"Why are you doing this?" I ask. I think of Onika and how she never let others see her—only me. But Abe hasn't hidden himself. He's still acting out his old existence.

"I'm not done," he says simply. "My life was taken from me, as was yours. As was Lucy's. As were all of the Forgotten's. I made the choice to stay, and Elise—" He steps closer. "I plan to do just that. Stay. Take what I want. And what I want . . . is you."

"I can't help you now," I say. "I can't guide you or bring you into the light."

"I know that," he shoots back. "But you're filled with more light than any Forgotten I've ever met. You can handle the Shadow, you can stay bright, even next to me. You make me feel warm. When the time comes, I won't let you cross. You'll learn to love me back, and then we can spend the rest of time here. It will all be ours."

I stare at him, amazed that he believes this. Light and Shadows can't mix, but he obviously missed that memo. His eyes are earnest, as if having me by his side will make up for all the horrible things he's done, things he will do. He's a Shadow—by definition he spreads misery.

"No," I say. "I don't want you anywhere near me."

That seems to wound him. "I was kind to you," he snaps. "I made it as easy as possible. I was *careful*." The cracks in his skin widen as his anger grows. And before I realize what's happening, a vision from Abe's mind slides in.

It's late at night in the desert, the remains of a campfire glowing red, the tents silent around it. I see Abe approach one of them, his shoes quiet on the sandy ground. He pauses, as if waiting for someone. Just then, Marissa stumbles out. She looks as if she's been crying.

"You came back," she says.

"I always come back. You know that."

She nods and crosses over to him, putting her arms around his waist and hugging him. Abe brushes his fingers through her hair.

"You love me so much," he whispers. "You love me so much that it makes you sick."

At that moment, Marissa turns away, retching and convulsing.

243

Abe smiles. "Remember that time," he begins, "when you told me that I didn't have a chance with someone like you? When was it? A year, two years ago?" She slowly lifts her head to meet his gaze. "Then you started dreaming about me," he continues. "You tried to run. But I got you back. Next thing you knew, you were calling me, following me. You were completely crazy for me. You let me do whatever I wanted to you."

Tears run down Marissa's cheeks. "And what do you want now?" she asks.

Abe shrugs. "You've outgrown your uses, Riss. And now I just want you to jump off that cliff. It's so much easier, don't you think?"

"No," Marissa murmurs, tears wet on her cheeks. "Please, no."

"Shh . . ." Abe hooks his finger under her chin as he beckons her up. When she's standing, he kisses her softly, almost sweetly. When he pulls back, her eyes are glazed over, almost dreamlike. "You were a fun toy," Abe says affectionately. "But you're broken. I need something new, and I won't have you ruin that for me. Now"—he opens his arms wide and steps back—"go on and jump."

My eyes flutter open and I gasp, horrified by what I've seen. "You killed her," I say, fresh fear pulling at my chest. "You killed Marissa."

"I had no choice," Abe says. "As Marceline would say, she was my Want. I was compelled—had been for a while. If anything, she should have been grateful. She'd been meaning to kill herself for months."

"You're a monster."

"Not completely. But I will take you by force, if I have to."

Abe reaches out and grabs my wrist, wrenching me

painfully closer. He stares down into my eyes, the lines in his chin smoothing until he's handsome once again. "I can make you believe anything I want," he whispers. "But I know you hate being manipulated. So this once . . . I won't. Just so long as you don't fight."

And then he leans forward to kiss me.

I'm wearing a winter jacket but still shaking uncontrollably as I get into Lucy's car. It's nearly three in the morning and my father never came home. I'm hoping he fell asleep on the couch in his office. I don't want him anywhere near our house right now. My fingers almost can't turn on the ignition, but when they do, I back out of my driveway—lucky my sister left her car behind at all.

Abe took just one kiss from me, one that seemed to rob me of all the warmth I had left. Shadows and light can't be close. So when he touches me, touches me as himself and not as the vision he projects—it hurts. It rips me open, cutting through my soul. If he wanted, he could whisper to take away the pain, but he didn't this time. This time he let me writhe as his darkness fed on me.

And then he left me crying on the bedroom floor.

I'm incredibly weak when I pull into the lot of the Sunset Motel. Harlin's motorcycle is parked in front of his room—room 126. With considerable effort, I turn off the car, nearly dropping the keys as I climb out. I stumble to his door and put my hand against it, fingers spread to rest for a second.

I knock softly.

When the door opens, Harlin is there in just his boxers, his hair messy from sleep. He looks stunned to see me.

"Elise, what's wrong?" He brings me in quickly, locking the door behind us. His room isn't nearly as neat as it was the first time I came to his motel. Pages from his sketch pad are scattered on the bed, crumples of paper on the floor.

Although my teeth chatter, warmth is slowly returning, the light never truly abandoning me. Even now it pulses under my skin with energy.

Harlin watches, filled with concern, and I remember everything about us. How he cried for me on the bridge, how he kissed me just yesterday. Harlin found me. Harlin will always find me.

There's too much between us, secrets and lies, but beyond that is unconditional love and the belief that we're meant only for each other. No matter how short that time is.

I step forward and wrap my arms around Harlin, resting my head against his chest. He staggers a step at first, but then he hugs me back tightly, like he'll never let me go again.

"I remember," I whisper into his skin. "I remember everything."

Harlin lays his cheek on the top of my head, but doesn't respond. Instead he holds me close, strong and protective. I close my eyes, sad about what I have to say next.

"I saw Lucy," I tell him.

There's a long silence. "And?" he asks.

"She's a Shadow." I choke on the words. Despite what Lucy has become, she's still my sister. Only now she's left to rot, having been convinced to turn her back on hope. "Abe turned her," I say. "And then he came for me. He kissed me."

Harlin's entire body tenses, his muscles rigid. "I'm going to kick his ass for touching you," he growls. "And for wrecking my bike."

"I'm glad I came first in that sentence."

"Baby, you always come first. And I don't care what Abe is—I'm going to kill him."

"You could never kill anything," I say.

"Oh, I'll make an exception just this once."

Harlin's homicidal urges slowly start to fade, and he gets me a cup of water and has me sip from it, noting that the color is returning to my skin. We sit on the bed, quiet until there's a sharp knock at the adjoining door. The clock reads four a.m.

"I can't even begin to handle Monroe Swift right now," Harlin says, rubbing his face. "But I'm guessing you're here to talk to him too."

"The thought crossed my mind."

Harlin stands, shooting me a helpless glance before opening the door.

Monroe is there, buttoning his blue collared shirt. "Thank you," he says, not looking up. "Now, I know it's early, but I thought I should—" He lifts his head and stops when he sees me sitting on the edge of the mattress.

Monroe Swift has taken care of me—Charlotte—since I was seven years old. A family friend, a father figure, a Seer—he's known me longer and better than anyone. Monroe is not just family, not just friend. He remembers me. And other than

Harlin, he's the only person who knows Charlotte ever existed.

"She remembers," Harlin says before going to lean against the dresser. "She remembers everything, which I'm sure includes how obnoxious you can be."

"Ah, well, that's good," Monroe says. "That way we can skip the formalities." He eases down next to me on the bed and exhales heavily. Harlin and I exchange worried looks.

"How are you, sweetheart?" Monroe asks me once he's settled. I reach out impulsively and hug him, feeling how frail he's become. The idea of Monroe dying terrifies me, as if I'll somehow be alone without him. We stay like that for a long minute before he straightens, looking embarrassed that I'd fuss over him.

"It's fascinating, really," he says, running his gaze over me. "That you're a different person and yet still so lovely."

I close my eyes against the tears welling up. "I need your help, Monroe," I tell him. "I have two Shadows after me, one who wants to kill me, another who wants to keep me. And I want to get rid of them both." Monroe looks as if he's about to argue, but I hold up my hand to stop him. "I know you hate Onika, but you didn't always. I saw that. I had an idea earlier—that maybe if you could remember what it was like to love her, you can see how to stop her."

His expression tightens. "What do you suggest?"

And it starts, as if my body knew what to do before I even thought it all through. My fingers tingle, my skin vibrating all over. I give in to the Need, and let it pull me into Monroe's past.

Monroe and Onika are sitting on the steps of a large

248

building, a college where they're students together. Onika is wearing a summer dress, her blond hair curled at the ends. She's laughing, and moves to rest her hand on Monroe's knee. Monroe glances down at her fingers, his smile slipping. As if realizing the shift in his mood, Onika leans to kiss him. It's the first day they met.

I open my eyes now and find Monroe next to me, his lids brimming with tears. "And then?" he asks softly, reliving the moments with me.

Onika is walking just ahead of Monroe, sneaking glances back at him with a devious smile. She's wandering down a dimly lit hallway, occasionally crooking her finger to tell Monroe to hurry up. I can feel Monroe's desire for her, his want to steal her away from her mother. To protect her. To marry her.

When they get to the doorway of her apartment, he pushes her against the wall and they kiss, murmuring words I can't hear, but I can feel. They are in love.

The memories speed by as they talk of their future, of Onika's past and how it tortures her. But the night she tells him about her compulsions, everything changes. Monroe listens as she sobs, his body chilling. He knows what it means and what he's supposed to do. And when she finishes talking, he can only smile sadly. "You need to jump, darling," he says softly. "It's the only choice."

Onika stormed out after screaming at him, but she doesn't know how he cried, curled up on the floor of his living room. How he stayed up night after night, feeding on painkillers as he searched for a way to save her. And when he discovered that the collagen could keep Onika's skin on a little longer, he rejoiced in her happiness. All she wanted was to fight her compulsion. And he swore to help her. In his heart, it was the only thing left to live for.

"I betrayed her," Monroe says, breaking me from the thoughts. "I promised I'd fight, but when I saw what it was doing to her, I had to stop." Tears roll down his cheeks, but he doesn't wipe them away. "And the day she disappeared, long after she'd turned to the Shadows, was the worst day of my life. Physically she was gone, but she haunted my dreams for years—all the way up until you left. And then I thought I lost her for good."

"She still loves you," I say. "Her feelings for you are the only shred of humanity she has left, a part she thought she lost. Maybe if you talk to her, you can—"

"I haven't seen Onika in years," he says. "She won't appear to me, even when I beg. Besides, I doubt she'll want me to see her how she is. And I don't think I do either."

In his eyes I see the truth. "You want to save her," I murmur. "You don't want me to extinguish her."

"I want her to have peace," he says solemnly. "I wish only for her to have peace, but she can't find that. No Shadow can when they can't die."

My heart leaps with an answer. "Onika killed a Shadow before," I say quickly. "The man who turned her, she reached inside of his chest and . . ." I pause, trying to think of the right words. "She reached in and ripped out his soul."

Harlin makes a noise from across the room as if he just now realized how truly dangerous Onika is. "Elise," he starts, but Monroe cuts him off.

"Can you do that?" Monroe asks me. "You're full of light, more light than any Forgotten—what can you do?"

"I can bring on the Need."

Monroe smiles then, something small and private. He stands with effort, steadying himself on the table as he passes. "I have to go see Marceline. I think I have a plan." He pauses to look back at me. "But, sweetheart," he says sadly, "this always ends the same way. You know that, right?"

My lips part with the start of an argument, but I say nothing. Not now. Not after everything I've seen. The Shadows are awful, and if I can stop them, won't it be worth it?

"What does that mean?" Harlin asks, coming to sit next to me. "I know you're not suggesting she sacrifice herself again, because that's not going to happen."

"Harlin, friend," Monroe says. "She's not of this earth. She can't stay, not when she isn't meant to."

"Maybe that's why she's back," he challenges. "She not like the other Forgotten. You don't know what her destiny is."

I stare down into my lap, grief enveloping me. I don't want to give up my life, but I'm not sure there's another way. Harlin begins to argue with Monroe. His harsh tone becomes raspy with the strain of his words. He threatens to leave—to take me with him.

When I finally lift my head, Monroe gazes over at me with a pleading expression. "Talk to him," he murmurs, standing at the door. "Get some rest and call me when you wake. I believe Onika will be waiting for you." He turns. "It's nearly time."

CHAPTER 27

I watch Monroe cross the parking lot to his rental car. When I turn, Harlin is standing close by with his shoulders slumped. He's torn, probably debating whether or not to kidnap me and run far away. I wish we could.

I close the door, leaning against it as I throw the lock. I'm no longer weak from my run-in with Abe; instead a buzz hums under my skin, my memories strong and clear. I know who and what I am. And I know what it means for me and Harlin. No matter what, there was never a chance for us—the universe didn't allow it.

"This is probably our last day," I tell him. When he doesn't raise his head, I move to put my fingers on his bare chest. His heart beats wildly beneath them, and I know it's breaking. I can't say good-bye like this. "Tell me you love me," I whisper.

Harlin raises his head and slides his hand along my waist to pull me closer. His hazel eyes search my every feature. "I love you," he says in his low voice. "And I'll never lie to you again." Harlin runs his thumb over my lips. "Which is probably why I should tell you that I have no intention of letting you sacrifice yourself. Now kiss me."

I press my mouth to his, hot and desperate. I can't focus on anything but being with him, about the fire between us. We stumble back toward the bed as Harlin pulls at my clothes, murmuring that he loves me. That he'll die without me.

His hands are gentle on my skin as my fingers thread through his hair. Soon my words blur into whispered promises. I tell him that I love him, have always loved him.

And I promise that I'll never leave him again.

I stretch my arms over my head as I wake, a little sore, but otherwise okay. I hear the shower going in the bathroom and smile to myself, thinking about Harlin. I barely have time to sit up before my phone vibrates on the side table.

"Hey, kid," my father says when I answer. I immediately remember my sister, and there's a sinking in my gut. We'll never truly be a family again. How can we be? Lucy handed me over to Abe last night, an obvious sign of her darkening intentions. She might be dangerous to my father. At that thought, I brace myself.

"Dad," I say. "I need you to stay away from Lucy."

He chuckles. "Uh, well, that's kind of difficult seeing that she's here right now. She surprised me with breakfast this morning. Sorry about yesterday, not sure how I fell asleep at my desk." He pauses. "Hold on. Here's your sister right now." My breath catches in my throat.

"Hi, Elise," Lucy says brightly. "I went by the house and you weren't home. Where are you?"

Dread spreads through my body. "What are you doing?" I ask quietly.

"Spending time with our father. That's what matters now, right? Time."

"Are you going to hurt him?"

Lucy chokes out a laugh. "What? Why in the world would you think that? Elise . . . have you been drinking?"

"Drinking?" I hear my father say off-line, concern in his voice.

"Please don't harm him, Lucy," I whisper. "He doesn't—"

There's a loud *click* as the line goes dead. At that moment, the shower shuts off in the bathroom. My body trembles as I set the phone aside.

My sister has the power to tempt my father into doing anything. It doesn't mean my dad will, but sometimes those whispers blot out the sense of things. Sometimes the whispers become our thoughts, driving us to do things we wouldn't normally do.

Harlin walks out wrapped in a towel, drops of water still clinging to his skin. He smiles at me broadly, but soon his expression clears when he realizes that something is wrong.

I tell him we should find Monroe, and he quietly agrees before going to get dressed. I sit there a minute longer, looking out the slightly open curtain to the hazy parking lot. The Need hums under my skin, and my heart is full of love and regret. I don't know what's to come, but I'm glad I won't face it alone.

The sun is shrouded with clouds as we head to Marceline's to meet Monroe. We're riding down Main Street past Santo's when a sudden gust of wind blows by us. It's so unexpected that Harlin swerves after having overcorrected and we nearly spin out.

Harlin quickly lets off the gas and puts down his boots, skidding us to a stop. He curses, and then asks if I'm okay. I nod, my heart pounding in my chest as I start to climb off the bike.

I feel a cold prickle over my cheeks, the bridge of my nose—like someone is watching me. My body stills because I recognize the feeling.

Standing in the middle of Main Street is Abe, wearing a black suit, his hair slicked smooth. Smiling. The fear that strikes me is so acute, I'm not sure I can move.

Santo's Restaurant is on my right, the lights inside burning bright even though there doesn't appear to be anyone inside—the CLOSED sign illuminated in the widow. A tumbleweed rolls by me and travels down the road past Abe.

The motorcycle engine cuts out and then Harlin is next to me, his hand sliding into mine. When it does, I feel myself relax slightly, my bravery returning.

The street is quiet and I think Abe has sent everyone away, back to their homes, out to dinner. He's isolated this small space just for us.

Abe's face is calm and unreadable. "Wish you would have listened to me, Seer," he tosses in Harlin's direction. "You're meddling in things you shouldn't."

"You can't have her," Harlin says simply.

Abe's dark eyes flick to our hands and he shakes his head. "It was really that easy?" he asks me, his voice thick with contempt. "To fall in love with him even though I was right here?"

"You're not really my type, Abe," I say.

"I'm too handsome?" He grins.

"Too evil."

He nods, like he accepts that description. "You probably won't believe me if I say that I've changed. That I'll bring you flowers and chocolates if you just come over here right now. Hell, I won't even touch you."

"That's not going to happen," Harlin says.

"Fine." Abe throws his hands up. "Lucy?" he calls. "Come out here." My chest seizes and I hear the jingle of the front door of Santo's.

My sister walks out, the hoops gone from her lip and her eyebrow. Her hair is brushed back, and she's wearing the long black dress I'd seen her in earlier.

She watches me as she struts toward Abe. "Good to see you, Elise."

Tears sting my eyes, making me blink. Even though I

wasn't always here, as Elise, I still feel like Lucy is my real sister; I still have those memories as if I lived them. It kills me that she chose to become a Shadow. I'm not sure she realizes what she's done yet.

"Hello, Lucy," Harlin says. I look sideways at him, surprised to hear him call to her. He sounds compassionate. Caring. He sounds like a Seer.

"Always nice to see you, Harlin," my sister says, a wry smile on her lips.

"Thanks," he replies. "But you should have gone with the light. You should have fulfilled your destiny. Now you're stuck here forever."

"Forever's not that long," she says. "Not when you consider the alternative is never having existed."

Harlin concedes, but tilts his head. "What did the Shadow promise you?"

"This," Lucy says, motioning to herself. "A body. Life."

"You're not alive."

I push Harlin's shoulder, both in defense of my sister and because I'm wondering what he's trying to do. I'm not sure he should be ticking her off right now.

"Maybe not," she snaps. "But I can do all sorts of neat things now. Like this—"

Lucy flicks her hand, a movement I've seen Onika use before when she'd make the pain of the Need disappear. But when my sister does it, Harlin blinks quickly, staggering back a step.

"You okay?" I ask, reaching for his arm. But his face has

gone sickly pale, and he falls to his knees next to me. "Harlin," I say. And then to my absolute horror, he raises his eyes to the empty space in front of him.

"Dad?" he asks.

CHAPTER 23

My gaze flicks back to my sister, burning with anger. "Don't you dare!" I growl. "Make it go away, now, Lucy!"

But my sister isn't paying attention to me. She's watching Harlin, her lips moving soundlessly with whatever she's telling him. Just like when I was Charlotte, Onika showed me Mercy and Sarah on the Rose City Bridge to trick me into leaving with her, Lucy is showing Harlin his deceased father. And I might just kill her for it.

"Stop it!" I scream fiercely, the gold under my skin glowing stronger, burning my flesh.

My sister finally looks to me, but she's changing as she does. Lines begin to crack her skin, peeling away to the gray underneath. "Maybe it's what he wants. He's always wished he could see his father again. Maybe if Harlin dies, he will. It's poetic, really." She turns back to my boyfriend. "Harlin," she whispers. "It's okay to let go. It's okay to—"

"No!" I drop down next to Harlin, putting my hands on his face, turning it roughly toward me. "It's not real," I whisper, trying to get him to see me past his tear-filled eyes. "He's not here, Harlin. He's just an image cast by a Shadow. You know that."

Harlin's mouth is open, gasping in horrified breaths. "He's bleeding," he murmurs. "Elise, he's bleeding to death." Harlin looks back at the space where I assume he can see the image of his father dying—something he's never dealt with. Grief he's never let himself feel.

I blink, tears falling down my cheeks when I do. The light grows within me, and I take my arms from around Harlin and stand, facing Lucy. Facing Abe.

"Make her stop," I tell Abe, choking back the sorrow in my voice. "Make her stop before she kills him."

"Why would I do that, *querida*?" Abe asks, shaking his head. "It's inspired, actually. Who knew your boyfriend was so tenderhearted?"

"Abe," I plead. "Please."

Abe stares back at me, appearing almost hurt that I'd want to save Harlin. But soon the moment passes, and he reaches to pull at his bottom lip as if lost in a thought. "Leave him be," he says to Lucy, not looking at her.

My sister sighs, and directs her gaze on Harlin. Her hand flicks out and then Harlin moans, leaning forward to rest his forehead on the pavement, his body still shaking.

"You're a terrible Seer, Harlin," Lucy calls. "You know that, right?"

"I'm aware," he says weakly, not lifting his head. "And if I ever question it, I'll think back on the great times we've shared."

"See, Elise," Abe calls. "I'm not all bad. I'll treat you well, especially when you're glowing so beautifully bright. I just want to hold you in my arms. Kiss you."

"I will kick your ass if you ever touch her again," Harlin says evenly, finally climbing to his knees as he tries to stand. "I will seriously beat you senseless."

"You're almost adorable," Abe says to him. "Not the smartest guy I've ever met, but your dogged devotion is an attractive quality—even to me. Of course, I'm going to kill you. But I won't make you suffer."

Harlin shrugs as if Shadows hit on and then threaten to kill him all the time. "I don't think that will happen, Abraham."

Abe seems to consider. "We'll see."

The clouds above us gather, blotting out the sky as they plunge us into a darkness, even though it's still morning. The streetlights click on, bathing the Shadows in a filtered yellow glow.

Lucy checks over her nails and then meets my eyes. "If you'll just listen to him"—she motions to Abe—"he'll make it better. You won't have to worry about the light, the Shadows. Hell, we can go back to being a family—at least for a while. Don't you want that?"

My face stings as if she slapped me. "Of course I want that," I say. "But, Lucy. You just almost killed my boyfriend! You're filled with evil impulses and Wants. I can't exactly sit down for lasagna with you now."

"You can forget." And for the first time since she's changed, I see a bit of hope on her face. "Maybe we'll even take Dad and run away."

"Not likely," Onika's voice rings out. "She's not going anywhere—not when I've only just found her."

The pressure that's been building finally explodes in my chest as I look past my sister to see Onika walking toward us down the road.

"How are you, Charlotte?" she asks.

"It's Elise," I tell her, trying to keep my face brave. She shrugs like she doesn't care.

"What's happening?" Harlin whispers, tilting his head near mine as his eyes sweep the area.

"Onika's here." Nothing has changed since the last time I saw her in person. She's still beautiful—or at least she projects herself that way. And she still doesn't let anyone see her other than those who were once Forgotten.

Being this close to her again, I feel the light under my skin react to her. Warming me up from the inside, my bones hot enough to tear through my skin. But I don't wince, or show any signs of the pain.

Abe turns to her, his features painted in anger. "She's mine," he growls.

"Abraham." Onika laughs dismissively. "Don't be a child. You can't handle her sort of light, can never change her or possess her. She should only be destroyed."

"Still mine."

"Listen," Onika says to Abe, hand on her hip. "You will not be the first Shadow I've had to extinguish, and believe me, I will enjoy doing it. Elise and I go back a while. This is meant to be, so to speak." She gazes at me almost adoringly. "Our shared destiny. Now come here, darling. Leave your boy there."

My first instinct is to grab something sharp and stab her, but I know it would hardly matter. She's immortal.

When I make no move she rolls her eyes. "Fine."

Onika reaches to grab my sister by the throat and spins her to face me. "How about now?" Onika asks calmly. "I can rip your sister open and turn her to ash. You've seen it. But I'm curious, Elise. Do you think I can do that to a Forgotten? I've never tried before, but I think it'll work."

"Let Lucy go," I call, shrugging off Harlin's hand, where he's gripped my arm. "And I'll come willingly."

"No," Harlin says. "I won't let you."

I turn suddenly, pressing my lips to his as I wrap my arms around him. He goes to move back, probably thinking I've lost my mind, when I murmur between my kisses to hide my words. "Get Monroe," I whisper, and kiss him again.

"This is lovely," Onika says, sounding impatient. "But if you two don't mind, there are more pressing issues than your desire for one another."

When I pull away, Harlin keeps his arms around me, his face still tense with worry. Even though there are no more words to hide, he kisses me again, deep and passionate.

I let my fingers run slowly through his when he pulls away, glancing back only once before going to his bike. Onika and Abe seem pleased that he's leaving.

When Harlin is a safe distance away, I turn my glare to Onika. "Do you think I'll turn to ash or to light when you rip out my soul?" I ask her defiantly.

"Don't care."

I take a few tentative steps toward her, not exactly sure what sort of plan Monroe has. But before I make another move forward, my vision starts to blur.

I am on the streets of Portland, my black hood up over my head as the rain mists down. He's just ahead of me, dodging through the crowd at the Saturday Market. His blond hair is longer than the last time I'd seen him on the roof, his walk more confident. I see he's doing just fine without me. My anger begins to coil around me, blotting out the sadness that had brought me here today.

"Get out of my mind!" Onika snarls. She pushes Lucy aside and brings her hands to her head as if she can protect her thoughts from my intrusion. I close my eyes, willing the Need to let me see.

I am Onika, following behind Monroe in the middle of the day, invisible to everyone. Refusing to let them see me. As Monroe pauses at a vendor, smiling at her the way he used to smile at me, I growl. He's replaced me so easily, so effortlessly. I

264

gave up my destiny to be with him.

As Monroe continues to talk, I snake around him, running my fingers over his shoulders, across his jaw. I get right up in his face, peering into his bright blue eyes, and feel my heart constrict. What I wouldn't do to have them looking back into mine now.

I lower my head, hugging myself to him as if he could feel it. As if he could hold me. And for a second, I think that he will as he raises his arm. But when I look, he's only paying the vendor as she hands him a brown paper bag. My heart sinks, and I move away, following behind him once again.

As long as Monroe Swift walks this earth, I will be here, watching him. I'll never let him get close to a woman; I'll never let him have children—the children that he should have had with me. I will never find peace—and will never let him have it either.

On the road in front of me, Onika laughs cruelly. Her face breaks open, peeling as she lets her facade fade away. "Do you think you have me figured out?" she asks, her mouth pulled into a sneer. "Perhaps you should see more." She closes her eyes and I'm shoved back into her visions, only this time I'm not on the streets of Portland.

I'm a child, in a filthy basement in Russia. And I'm not alone.

I don't last thirty seconds before I force myself out of her head, my body shivering. "No," I say, my voice cracking. "I can't take it."

Onika smiles sadly at this. "Neither could I. But that didn't much matter, now did it?" She pauses, as if contemplating her next move.

"If I destroy you," she says quietly, "destroy the light—there will be no hope. The misery I spread will be unstoppable, not by anything. And only then, Elise, might it let me go. Can you imagine if your every thought, your every impulse, was covered in thick smoke—a choking desire that's only relieved by the most dastardly of things. Those men from my past—" She stops, composing herself. "The Shadows create the horror of this world," she continues. "And humans cultivate it—putting it into action. I'm cursed, darling. And that curse is that I can't die. I will never have peace. And that's the cruelest fate of all."

"What if there's another way?" I ask.

"There's not," she says instantly. Then she raises one finger, beckoning me toward her. "I'll let him live," she whispers. "Your boy? I won't harm him, or let Abraham harm him. I think that would be a fair trade."

I shoot a glance at Abe, and he seems offended that Onika is speaking for him. At the same time, I see that he's calculating a move. I don't think Abe likes to lose. Lucy still sits on the ground, watching us with curiosity, a bit of fear.

"Harlin would rather die than see me give up so easily," I say, knowing it's true. If she's going to take me out, she'll have to take me out fighting.

"Oh, he's not enough?" she asks, as if I'm being petty. "Well, I've got more. You know better than to think that a boy is all I could take from you." She grins, her face filling in, becoming beautiful again. "I have your father."

From the corner of my eye, I see Abe turn to Onika. Lucy

sucks in a startled gasp, finding her way to her feet, and my heart feels like it might stop beating at any second.

Onika stands in front of Santo's, looking human. "Doug," she calls sweetly.

A moan escapes me when I see my father walk out from the door of the old antique shop two stores down from Santo's. His clothes are dirty, his glasses missing. I know that he's not a projection, not a trick. She truly has him.

"Oh, Daddy," I whimper, taking a step toward him. But I stop, not sure what to do. I need Monroe.

"Hey, kid," my father says, sounding a bit dreamy. I notice then that Onika's lips are moving in tandem with my father's. "You've been a naughty girl, playing with Shadows."

"Stop it," I say, glaring at Onika. "Leave him alone." I'm grateful that he's not dead, but her control over him is clear. Although Shadows can influence thoughts, they're not supposed to take people over. There's always supposed to be a choice.

"Yeah," she says, as if she's part of the conversation in my head. "But things are different now, Elise. What is free will, really?" Her attention snaps to Lucy. "Don't even think it," she sneers. "I don't mind killing my kind. In fact, you and Abraham are really starting to grate on my nerves."

Abe's expression is weak as he watches my father, as if it bothers him.

Onika continues to talk, but I stop listening. I close my eyes, reaching for the light, the warmth. I try to reach Abe with the

Need. For the first time I can see something inside him, a dull glow, a shred of humanity. I wind my way to it, drawing him out, finding the memory of when he was Forgotten.

I see Abe. He's a boy in Yuma living with his parents and his little brother. They don't have much, but the house is clean. Always enough to eat. His dad takes him four-wheeling every summer on the dunes while his brother watches, cheering every time they pass. They're so happy.

I open my eyes to see Abe staring at me, his eyes glassy as he experiences the memories at the same time I do. He doesn't want me to see what's next. He doesn't want to feel it again. But I press on anyway.

When Abe is sixteen, I watch as his parents are killed in an accident, a hit-and-run. His father lies on the road, his lungs slowly filling with blood as he tries to keep breathing long enough to make sure help arrives. He doesn't know that Maria is already dead not three feet away. Abe is still strapped in the backseat, unconscious.

The scene changes, and his brother, Richie, is on life support. Abe clings to his bed, begging him not to leave. Begging for his family. And as I watch, his baby brother slips away. Leaving him truly orphaned.

In front of me now, a tear streams from Abe's eye. But he doesn't blink or look away. He lets me have it all.

It's later that same year that the Needs start. He's living with his aunt, a decent woman who's never home. It's easy at first, doing the good deeds with Marceline's guidance.

But then Abe meets a man, a Shadow. He tells Abe he won't be Forgotten if he leaves with him, but it doesn't mean anything to Abe. His family is already dead. He doesn't care who remembers him.

And it's then that the Shadow figures out what Abe will stay for. He promises that nothing can ever be taken from him again. That he can have power over people, over situations. He promises to make him strong. And most of all, he tells him that he will never hurt again.

I start to cry, knowing that it isn't true. That even though he agreed, Abe still screams every night. Missing his family. Wanting to go home to them. But he's trapped, here, in the Shadows.

My heart swells and I'm overcome by his misery. His pain.

"I should have gone," Abe murmurs.

"I'm so sorry," I say, wishing my words could mean anything. But in the end they're just words. He made his choice.

"What is this?" Onika asks, looking between me and Abe. "Elise, I'm not going to play games this time. You come with me now, and *maybe* I won't make Daddy dearest go play in traffic." She hikes her thumb at my father.

I glance at my dad, knowing he's still in there somewhere. "I love you, old man," I say, wiping at my face. "I hope you know that."

He stares blankly at me.

I have to make things right—there are no other options. I have to save my father. I straighten, clenching my hands at my sides, letting the Need build up, the heat. The fire. I start walking toward Onika, ready to have it out, not even sure what that would entail.

"Elise," Abe says warningly. "Don't do that."

"This is it, Abe," I state, growing calmer. "This is what I'm here for." My shoes are soundless on the pavement as Onika opens her arms, welcoming me.

"No!" Abe shouts. I faintly hear the sound of running as I continue toward Onika, licking my lips and thinking how they taste of cinnamon. How they taste of love.

Onika bares her teeth, looking ready to pounce. I brace myself for her attack, but just then something hard knocks into me, pushing me aside. There is no silence before the screaming starts.

Abe is in front of Onika, her fist buried in his chest. He falls away from her, writhing in pain on the ground as the shadows slowly start to seep from the gaping hole in his chest. His skin is tearing off, ripping to shreds. I cover my mouth in horror, and Onika steps back. Not sorry, just stunned.

But Abe is slowly dying, and it looks painful—nothing like the quick death that Rodney got on the roof.

Abe stretches out his hand to me, and I lower myself to the ground, gripping it. He's moaning as his skin slowly burns, dissolving to ash. The horror is too much. No one should suffer like this. I begin to weep.

"Elise," Abe chokes out. His fingers dig into my forearm as agony consumes him, slowly breaking him apart.

"I'm sorry," I whisper. "I'm so sorry, Abe." When his dark eyes meet my gaze, he stills—even as his body continues to wither.

"You're so bright," he murmurs.

I look down at my arm and see the gold glowing bright under my skin, not tearing through but illuminating me in light. Abe is entranced by the beauty of it. He takes my golden palm, pressing it to his cheek before turning his face to kiss my skin. It's the closest he'll ever be to the light again. And it's all I can give him now.

Abe's body scatters then, falling as ash over my hand and onto my clothes. I choke back a cry, trying to gather the ash, trying to do something—but the wind catches it, washing him away.

CHAPTER 29

I sit motionless, staring down. Lucy moves quickly, grabbing my father from the ground and backing him out of Onika's reach. I think then that Lucy hasn't lost her humanity. At least not yet.

Next to me Onika makes a soft sound, and when I look up, she's staring at me. "He sacrificed himself for you," she says as if she can't believe it. "Why would he do something so stupid?"

I climb to my feet then, no longer afraid. I know what I'm here for—despite the love I have for my family, for Harlin, there are things bigger than me.

My body begins to heat, the glow becoming more intense. I feel so incredibly powerful, as if I could burst at any second and cover this place in light. Onika's eyes widen as she watches, the gold illuminating her face. She's in awe.

"Elise!"

I turn to see Harlin running up, stopping short when he sees me. A mix of admiration and devastation crosses his face. He knows what this means. He knows I have to do what's right.

"I wish it could be different," I say to him.

There's a sudden gasp, and I turn to Onika, but she's staring past me. I follow her line of vision. Monroe approaches in the distance, slow as he limps slightly with exhaustion. I let the Need take me into Monroe's mind. I see the plan that he and Marceline came up with, the plan at my expense. I know what I have to do, and how this will end.

Onika's skin begins to crack and tear as her emotions roll over her. Monroe was the last person to see her other than the Forgotten. She gave up everything for him, and he turned his back on her.

"The good doctor isn't looking so hot," Onika says coldly to me. "Perhaps he's lonely. Should I whisper him a love poem?"

"I'm sick," Monroe answers instead, his voice gentle, as if she'd been actually concerned. "I'm dying, Onika. I'm leaving soon."

Before she can even process his words, Onika stumbles back. She's stunned by the fact that he can see her. "How—" Tears fill her blue eyes.

"I'm letting him," I say. "I can control the visions too, remember."

"No," she says, covering her face with her hands. "I don't want him to—"

"Onika," Monroe breathes in the most tender voice I've ever heard him use. When she shifts her devastated gaze back to his, he smiles. "It's been too long, darling."

As I watch, the layers of bitterness wrapped around Onika fall away, revealing the vulnerable girl beneath, the girl who tried at twenty to save her life, forgoing the rest of the world.

Monroe begins to walk purposefully toward her, his gait weak from illness, but determined. As he approaches, Onika's face begins to slowly repair itself. She doesn't want him to see her as she is. Even now . . . all she cares about is Monroe. I slowly back away until I feel Harlin touch the small of my back.

I turn to let him wrap me in a hug, and he holds me tightly against him. My Harlin. I start to cry, the tears evaporating off my cheeks the minute they touch. The energy inside me is becoming almost too much to hold together.

"You promised you wouldn't leave me again," Harlin murmurs in my ear. "You promised, Elise."

"I'm sorry." I lay my head on Harlin's shoulder. His hand brushes my hair, a silent acceptance, as I watch Onika and Monroe. Marceline had told Monroe that if he could find the humanity in Onika, get her out of the Shadows for even a moment, then maybe I would be able to extinguish her. To do that, I'll need to burst into light. Of course, I still have a choice. But I know which one to make.

Monroe pauses in front of Onika, letting her look over his failing body. Then as he steps forward to put his hand on her cheek, Lucy comes into my line of vision.

"You're so bright," she says to me. "It's really beautiful."

"I wish I knew what to say right now," I tell her, untangling myself from Harlin as he moves back to give us privacy. Lucy won't harm me now. "I wish we could have been sisters forever," I say, and my voice breaks.

Lucy's lower lip trembles and she glances away. "Maybe this once I can love you enough to let go," she says.

"I don't want you to," I answer. "I don't want you to ever let go."

A thoughtful expression passes over Lucy's features, her blue eyes welling up. "Elise," she says. "Do you remember when we were little girls and I used to sit you at Mom's vanity, dressing you in pearls and makeup? I dragged you around everywhere with me. My own little baby doll." She stops. "That feels real to me."

I nod. "Me too."

"When it came time to choose," she says, "I didn't think I could give it up, that love I had for you. For Dad. For myself. Maybe I wasn't strong enough, or maybe this was my true destiny. I'm not sure.

"I'm not able to help my temptations." She lowers her voice. "I'm forced to do them, compelled, even, by something inside me. Something shadowing my heart. But there's one thing I want you to always know."

"What's that?" I ask.

"No matter what choice I made, all I ever wanted was to be remembered by my family. I wanted you to know that I loved you more than anything."

My composure shatters and I sway on my feet, beginning to sob. Harlin comes to steady my shoulders, and I reach into my back pocket, taking out the picture of Lucy and me by the waterfall. I hold it out to her.

"I'm sorry I couldn't save you," I murmur. "I'm so sorry, Lucy."

My sister takes the picture of us and lets her grief spill out as she looks it over. When she glances up again, she smiles sadly. "It was never your job to save me, Elise. You were only meant to love me."

She turns away then. I call her name, but she walks slowly down the middle of Main Street. My chest aches with cries as Harlin holds me up, holds me close. And we watch after Lucy as she leaves as a Shadow—compelled beyond her will to spread misery. We watch her until she disappears completely, leaving me behind.

Harlin doesn't speak. He keeps me pressed to him, his heart pounding against mine. He feels like warmth and love, and above all else—peace.

"Harlin," I say, lifting my head to look at him. When he meets my eyes, he doesn't respond, tears spilling down his cheeks.

I kiss him softly then, once. Twice. I bring my lips close to his ear. "In another life we are happy," I murmur, squeezing my eyes shut. "In another life we grow old together."

My light radiates, sending him this small bit of hope, love. It's not true, but I hope the thought of it can replace some of his pain. When I'm done, I back away as Harlin watches me, a soft smile on his lips, as if he believes my words with all of his heart.

I turn and walk to where Onika stands with Monroe, and it's like they're frozen in time. Monroe's hand is on the smooth surface of her cheek. Onika's eyes are glassy as they stare back at his.

"Do you despise me?" Onika asks in a small voice.

"No," Monroe says, studying her delicately, as if she's a butterfly that will fly away at any moment. "I shouldn't have let you stay," he says. "And I shouldn't have turned my back once you did."

Onika puts her hand over Monroe's. "No, lover. You tried to save me. I just didn't listen."

"Let me see you," Monroe whispers, his hand sliding along the waist of her black coat, drawing her closer.

It's then that I can see him—the Monroe who loved her. He is soft and gentle. He is vulnerable to her, for her. "Let me see what you are now," he says.

Slowly, Onika's skin begins to pale, the color draining away to the gray underneath. It begins to split and crack, gruesome and rotten. But Monroe keeps his hand on her cheek, his eyes never leaving hers. When she's done, she smiles bitterly.

"You were right," she says. "I'm a monster."

Monroe doesn't flinch from her words; instead his palm slides over her cheek, the skin flaking away under his touch. But it doesn't stop him as he brings his mouth to her dry lips and kisses her.

I glance back at Harlin, who looks horrified, and then I walk toward them once again. Monroe pulls back, staring at her as if he still sees the beautiful blonde she once was.

"I have always loved you," he says. "I always will."

Closing my eyes, I think that it's time. That Onika has regained her humanity, if only for a moment. This is my choice. I don't let myself look back at Harlin as I walk toward her, the Need twisting my insides as it heats, stronger and brighter than ever before.

Monroe coughs and then touches his lips, his fingers coming back with blood. I fight back the cry that wants to escape because I know he won't survive the day. But he's beyond my help. Instead, I pause in front of Onika, overwhelmed with love for her from the light inside of me. "You'll find your peace now," I say. "At last."

Onika trembles with the promise of it, the promise of relief from the darkness she's been submerged in. "But it'll end you, too," she says quietly, as if reminding me.

I nod. "I know. But you're my final Need. My purpose is to find a way to set you free. The Shadows have fed on you long enough."

Onika smiles then, almost childlike. Monroe lowers himself

278

to the pavement, unable to stand any longer. Across the road, Harlin watches. I bow my head to him once, saying good-bye—knowing that I'll never need anything as much as I need him.

And then I outstretch my arms, stepping forward as the light starts to burst through my form. Onika closes her eyes as her skin peels away. She reaches for me, reaches for her finale.

When we collide—everything stops. In that split second, I can see them all: Harlin with tears fresh on his cheeks, Monroe's solemn expression. My father has the first look of recognition on his face, as if he's about to call out to me.

And in front of me is Onika, her eyes still, her broken face serene in expression. All she ever wanted was to live, but then she found out there were worse things than death. But the light is merciful—and it sent me back to grant it.

So I close my eyes and do just that: I wrap Onika up in my light and extinguish her, sending her into oblivion.

AFTER

There is noise around me, the shuffling of feet and the jangling of bracelets. Murmurs are unfamiliar until the words begin to make sense. "Am I dead?" I manage to ask.

"Oh, heavens no," Marceline's ragged voice answers with a laugh. "Although I'm not sure you want to see what's left."

There's a sinking feeling in my gut, and I wonder if I'm stuck in some kind of purgatory with an old psychic as my only companion. My entire body hurts as if it's burned and blistered.

"Don't move, child," Marceline says. "You stay right there and rest a minute." As she talks, my skin begins to tingle, much like the Need. But I'm too weak to bring it on. This is something else. There's a touch as Marceline brushes back my hair, intertwining her fingers as she braids the ends.

"You really would have done it," she says. "Even with a new body, you'd still give up everything."

My eyelids flutter open, but I'm surrounded in a blinding glow. I bring up my palm to shade my eyes, but it doesn't help. I'm not sure where I am, but it's so . . . beautiful. "What's that light?" I ask, blinking against it.

"That's you, child," Marceline says, her image only a silhouette among the gold surrounding us. "But don't worry, we have time."

"Time for what?"

"Tell me," she continues, ignoring my question. "How many times would you do it, you think? How many times would you sacrifice yourself for good?"

"Every time," I answer automatically. I watch as Marceline pulls a long strip of fabric from her pocket, a ribbon, before tying it on the end of my braid. The movement is familiar, and I wonder what other secrets Marceline has kept about my past.

The light continues to grow, and Marceline leans closer, her face finally coming into focus. "You are hope," she murmurs. "You can restore balance, but it won't be easy."

"It never was," I say, struggling to sit up. I realize then that I'm filled with memories, both mine and Charlotte's. It's like I've lived one full life and not two separate ones.

"Not yet," Marceline says, gently pushing me down. She's quiet for a while, rubbing my arms, my hands. "Harlin needs you," she whispers. "He loves you too much."

I smile a little. "I know. But I like that about him."

"As a Seer, he has so much left to do," Marceline says. "Both of you do."

I pause then, digesting her words. "Again?" I ask. Sadness spikes through me. I'm not sure my boyfriend can take much more loss. "Harlin will have to watch me leave again? It'll kill him."

"No," Marceline responds, as if I should know better. "Your time for crossing is over. Now you must help Harlin find the Forgotten and lead them to their destinies. And, of course, extinguish the Shadows where you can."

"My sister?"

"Lucy, too." She pauses. "Unless you find another way."

"I will."

She smiles. "You really are such a brave soul. Your father will be happy to see you again." Her bracelets clink together as she moves away. "Well then, Elise," Marceline says, using my name for the first time since I've known her. "I guess it's time for you to wake up."

There is still so much I want to know, want to ask. But before I can say anything else, the world stops. There's silence around me.

I wait a beat, and when I finally sit up, I find Harlin waiting for me—ready to start again.

ACKNOWLEDGMENTS

This book is in large part due to the brilliance of my editor, Donna Bray. Thank you to the team at Balzer + Bray and HarperCollins. Thank you to my brave and fearless agent, Jim McCarthy, who has to put up with so much more from me than any human should. Thanks to Michael Bourret, Alice Pope, and SCBWI.

I want to acknowledge my dear friends and support system: Michael (Andy) Strother, Amanda Morgan, Bethany Griffin, Heather Hansen, Trish Doller, Kari Olson, Sara Gundell, Lisa Schroeder, Kimberly Derting, Daisy Whitney, Vania Stoyanova, Amber Morris, Nova Ren Suma, and my muser besties. There are countless others to thank, but I'm trying to keep this short. And failing.

Thanks to my mother, Connie. My sisters, Natalie and Alex, and my brothers, David and Jason, plus all of my cousins and other family members. Thank you to Portland, Oregon; Utica, New York; and the entire state of Arizona. And, most of all, thank you to my husband, Jesse, and my kids, Joseph and Sophia. You are all wicked awesome.

As always, this is for you, Gram!